Next of Kin
D. Emily Smith

This book is dedicated to the following people...

Daddy, there is no perfect father, but you were my first supporter. Thank you for the typewriter at Christmas. I love you.

Mary, Chelsea, Felicity, Rose, Wendy, Lynnette, Ginnie, Pam, Rachael, Jenna: I don't think you ladies will ever know just how much your encouragement spurred me on. God used you.

Zach, Josh, Abi, and Micah: You have an amazing earthly father, but I know he and I both pray daily that you can say God is your Heavenly Father. You are dearly loved by us, but also by Him.

Trigger Warning: This book contains brief descriptions of child abuse and violent content which may be distressing to some.

Copyright © 2023 by D. Emily Smith

All rights reserved.

No part of this publication may be reproduced, distributed, or transmitted in any form or by any means, including photocopying, recording, or other electronic or mechanical methods, without the prior written permission of the publisher, except as permitted by U.S. copyright law.

The story, all names, characters, and incidents portrayed in this production are fictitious. No identification with actual persons (living or deceased), places, buildings, and products is intended or should be inferred.

ISBN-979-8-218-31068-4

Book Cover by Kat Schmitz

1

Tom Benson closed his eyes and listened to the wind blowing the leaves on the trees. Fall had always been his favorite season. He had a perfect view of God's handiwork from his front porch. Vivid reds, oranges, and yellows bordered his property like a wall offering the seclusion and protection he cherished. Soon those leaves would be gone, and the trees would be left bare by winter. He'd be gone by then as well, but he was at peace with that knowledge. Many well-intentioned people suggested that he move into a facility close to medical care, but his home offered comfort and memories. Some of those memories were good and other memories were not so good. Nonetheless, Tom was where he needed to be. He was where Kate could find him if she ever chose to.

He had grown up in that house nestled in the quaint town of Deer Creek in upstate New York. The town was the typical old-fashioned, small town - a piece of Americana. Deer Creek was the type of place every parent wanted to raise a family. It was close enough to bigger cities to enjoy all that comes from being near a metropolis, but separated and rural enough to enjoy the solitude and the fortification Tom needed. Separation from the world was exactly why Tom relocated himself and his daughter back to his parents' home after his wife's death. Most days, Tom had very little contact with anyone other than his doctor, the home health nurse, the pastor, and the Tyler family who were his closest neighbors.

The sound of gravel crunching under the weight of car tires caused Tom to snap out of his reverie. He slowly rose from his chair and held to the wooden railing of his porch as a gray sedan approached. He frowned in uncertainty until he saw who sat at the wheel. The car came to a stop and a man similar in age to himself stepped out.

"You're late." Tom barked at his old partner gruffly, but a smile tugged at the corner of his mouth.

"GPS doesn't recognize your road as a real road. You weren't kidding when you said you were in the middle of nowhere." Peter McKinney stepped onto the porch steps and found a soft spot in the wood, almost putting his foot through the boards. "I bet these rotten boards are almost as old as you, Benson."

With a smirk, Tom held out his hand to steady his friend. "They're *older* than me. The neighbor boy is going to fix it next week. Just waiting on lumber."

"Glad you have someone looking out for you. Man, Tom ... you look horrible." Pete never was one for sugarcoating his words.

Tom laughed and slapped his friend on the back. "You don't look so hot either. Where's your hair, Old Man? Come on in. Watch your step."

The two entered the dimly lit house, maneuvering through clutter and power tools.

"Doing some repairs?"

"The neighbor put in a bathroom down here so I don't have to go up the stairs. This stuff is so he can fix the stairs next." Tom motioned to a pile of tools safely tucked away to the side.

"Sounds like a nice guy."

"Great kid. I sold him the house. Our arrangement is that he lets me live here until... you know." Tom's voice trailed off. "He's been fixing a lot of the dangerous things I can't do myself."

"You *sold* the house? Did you tell Katie you did that?"

"What do you think?" Tom bit out defensively before softening his tone. "She won't care anyway. The money she'll get from the sale is more practical for her than this old, dilapidated house."

Tom cleared his throat as familiar emotions threatened to creep in. "I assume she is why you insisted on meeting up?"

Peter nodded, "I have news."

"News you couldn't tell me over the phone?" Tom sighed as that thought sank in. "Can I get you anything to drink before we get down to it?"

"You have a beer?" Peter smiled mischievously, already knowing the answer.

Tom laughed. "Haven't had that stuff here for a couple of years. The hardest thing I have now is apple cider from the neighbor's orchard."

"I'm good. Why don't you have a seat, Tom?" Peter motioned Tom to his recliner and Peter took a seat across from him on the sofa.

Tom knew the news must be bad for Peter McKinney to make a special trip from Boston. Instinctively, he reached for his cigarettes and his lighter on the side table and lit one up.

"Should you be smoking?"

"What's it going to do? *Kill* me?" Tom laughed until his laughter dissolved into coughs that racked his body. He hated it when that happened. His friend stared at him with concern. Tom tried his best to stifle the remainder and motioned his friend to go on with his news.

"I'll just come out with it. I'm retiring. Next week is my last week and then Hannah and I are headed to Florida."

"Florida? Congrats." Tom managed to choke out.

"Well, it's time. It's been forty years on the force. I'll be sixty-three this year." Pete smiled, but it quickly disappeared as he got to the point of his visit. "I told you I would keep an eye out for Kate over the years and I have. She's grown into a beautiful young woman, Tom. You should be proud. She's still with the advertising firm. We had her over for dinner the other week and she seemed very established. She's recently started seeing a very nice young man who I think will take good care of her."

Tom grunted. "Did you bring pictures?"

"I did, but there's something you need to know."

"Don't tell me she's getting married to this guy!" The idea was like a knife in Tom's chest. It wouldn't surprise him if she married without telling him. She'd made it clear that she never wanted him to be a part of her life ever again.

"No, nothing like that. Mark's nice, but I don't think Kate is thinking that way yet." Peter opened a manila envelope that he had been carrying. "She's still living at your sister-in-law's house. She's excited because she'll be signing a lease on a condo in Boston next week."

"Still with Lilly? She has the patience for that old bat, but she can't find it in her heart to talk to me?" Tom was a Christian man now, but there were old sins that were hard to overcome, his loathing of Lilly being one of them.

"You know you've not exactly made it easy." Peter's brow furrowed as he handed a pile of snapshots and papers to

Tom. There were pictures of Kate with Peter's family on the Charles River on his boat, a picture of her in front of the Christmas tree, and a few candid shots he snapped while she was unaware - just living her life.

"Does she ever mention me?" Tom regretted asking the question almost immediately. He knew the answer.

"No. If I bring you up, she threatens to stop speaking to me." His friend sounded apologetic and the knife in Tom's chest twisted a little more.

"So, you came all this way to show me how happy she is without me?" The pictures in his hand landed with a thud on the side table.

"I came to tell you Kate is in danger." Peter reached into the envelope, pulled out a newspaper, and tossed it to the man in his chair.

The headlines looked rather dull. Large amounts of rain in the city. A few sports headlines. Nothing stood out to Tom right away. He looked up at his friend quizzically.

"Bottom left corner."

The words finally struck Tom. *McCullough Released from Prison After Fifteen Years.* His eyes scanned the small blurb in the paper. It said something about good behavior and how he had participated in a renowned rehabilitation program. Tom's eyes met Peter's and unspoken understanding registered. In seconds, Tom was transported back to Boston fifteen years in the past.

He had worked undercover for months to get in with a crime cell run by three brothers. They came from a prominent family and seemed to get away with just about everything. No matter how many times charges were brought up, they were dropped due to a legal technicality or missing evidence. The news media seemed to love reporting on the failed attempts to put them away without success, but Tom was determined to make sure they went to jail for a very long time.

Tom had earned the McCullough brothers' trust by doing things he would rather forget. When it came time to raid the building where they stored an arsenal of weapons one brother, James McCullough, was arrested. Another brother was shot and killed after he opened fire using an AK-47, killing two officers. The third brother, Tony, hadn't been in the building and managed to escape arrest.

Two nights later, Tom and his partner heard a call over the radio. Shots fired. The address given was Tom's own home. Speeding down streets with lights and sirens blaring, Tom pulled up to the scene to find his wife lying in a pool of blood at the bottom of their porch steps. Though the responding officers suggested it could've been a robbery gone wrong, Tom knew better.

One week after Rose's funeral, Tom was back to work. He knew he probably should've listened to those who urged him to take more time off, if for no other reason than to care for his little daughter. Yet, he couldn't sit around knowing Tony McCullough was still on the loose. It didn't take long for Tony to reappear.

Pete and Tom decided to grab dinner after a particularly hard day. When walking back to their respective cars someone called out to them. Tony was standing near a car parked in the shadows, his arms crossed at his chest.

"I'm sorry to hear about your wife, Benson. It's so sad when someone you love is taken from you, isn't it?" He called out. His speech was slurred and he reeked of alcohol. "She had the prettiest blonde hair."

Tom instinctively reached for his side arm.

"I saw your daughter today at school. She looks so much like her mother."

"Let me see your hands! McCullough, raise your hands slowly." Peter called, now at Tom's side, his gun drawn as well.

"I wonder if she will ever get to grow up and know what type of man her father was. Should I tell her about all the times you hurt and killed people, Benson?" Tony stumbled forward and fell back against a car before righting himself again.

"Tom, call it in. I've got Tony." Peter warned.

Tom nodded at his words, but when McCullough reached into his coat pocket, Tom didn't hold back. He pulled the trigger and the man who most certainly killed his wife fell to the ground. Blood started pooling beneath his head from the oozing hole in his forehead.

A scream pierced the night air. Inside the car that Tony had been standing in front of was a young boy, banging against the rear window in panic. Tom estimated his age to be ten, the same age as his Katie. Peter swore under his breath as he ran to the dead man, checking the coat pockets and finding nothing but a small bottle of whiskey. He looked back at Tom and shook his head. Peter then ran to the car and shouted orders for the sobbing boy to exit the car and sit on the curb away from the scene. Tom watched as Pete used his handkerchief to lift a gun that was lying on the driver's seat of the car and place it in Tony's lifeless hands.

"You keep quiet, Tom, and it will be okay. You killed a killer, that's all."

"He was unarmed," Tom muttered dazedly under his breath as the truth dawned.

"Shut up, Benson. You keep quiet," Peter warned.

"Daddy!" The young boy left his place on the curb and fell to his knees near his father's body. Tom looked at the young boy as if seeing him for the first time. "Daddy, don't die! Don't leave me, Daddy! You killed him! I hate you!"

"Tom!" Peter called out, snapping him from the horrific memory. Tom's hands trembled much as they had that night.

"James McCullough is out of prison. I got it," Tom spoke the words softly.

"Yes. But that's not the *whole* problem." Peter waited until Tom's eyes finally met his. "Tony Jr. has been on Kate's street. I did my nightly drive by and he was there. I don't think he saw me, but I recognized him right away. He looks just like his father. And guess who picked up Uncle James from the prison when he was released?"

Tom didn't need to answer. He saw the danger in what Peter was saying.

"You have to call her, Tom. It's time you two talk."

"She'll hang up. She won't listen to me. Maybe if it came from you… she listens to you…"

"You know I love Kate as if she were my own daughter, but she's *not* my daughter. She's *yours* and you need to take your role in her life back before it's too late." Peter got to his feet and looked back down at his old friend. "After next week, we'll be in Florida. Lilly's landline number and Katie's cell phone number are in the envelope. Call her."

Tom didn't get up when Peter left. In truth, he didn't even know *when* his friend left. He had sat in his chair deep in tortuous thoughts, trying to process the information he had been given. The daylight was disappearing as the sun set behind the tops of the trees. Memories of the young boy calling him a killer haunted his dreams for years after that night. Now they resurfaced to haunt him all over again.

He had to call Kate. Yet, the thought paralyzed him. Her last words to him were as torturous in that moment as they were the day she first uttered them. *"I'm done trying to win your love. I know I'll never have it and I can't stand to be here one minute longer. Don't bother calling. I won't answer."*

He deserved every ounce of her hatred and anger. Following their move to Deer Creek, he became a drunk and an angry shell of a man. He left raising his daughter to his mother. After she passed away, his neighbor Colleen Tyler stepped in as a type of mother figure. Would Kate even answer his call now? It had been seven years since she stormed out. He doubted himself as he lifted the phone and sought out the paper with the numbers scribbled on it that Peter supplied. Did he have a choice? It was time to man up. He had to let Kate know the possible danger she was in. He wanted to make things right before he went home to the Lord. He wanted her to know how God changed him.

A familiar pressure arose in his chest and he tried to pray it away. He had one last job to do. He pressed the numbers even as the coughs started. His sister-in-law's answering machine picked up as Tom gasped and clutched his chest. *Please, Lord. She needs to know. Protect my Katie.* The phone fell from Tom's hands and onto the floor as blood bubbled from his mouth and his body wracked against the spasms. He managed two weak words ... "Kate... Danger."

2

The candy apple red Audi coupe pulled in front of the dark row home she temporarily shared with her aunt. Kate Benson didn't make a move to leave the safety of her car. It was just a couple of days shy of October and houses were starting to decorate for Halloween, one of her least favorite holidays. It added an extra ominous feel to the already lonely house that awaited her. Aunt Lilly left that morning for her girls' trip, a Caribbean cruise. She had invited Kate to come along. However, sunbathing and flirting with the ship's crew along with Lilly and her friends didn't exactly appeal to Kate.

After the day she had, maybe the cruise would have been the better choice. Mark wasn't answering his cell even though he told her to call as soon as she got home. Her boss took credit for her ideas at work … *again*. Despite the fact she had been looking forward to a weekend of nothingness, now that it was here, she wished she had made plans. A group of colleagues normally spent Friday night at the lounge near the office, but Kate felt uncomfortable in that scene. They weren't real friends. In truth, she didn't know when the last time was that she had a true friend. That is why Mark was such a breath of fresh air. He came into her life just when she needed him the most. A smile tugged at her lips as she remembered the first day they'd met. He awkwardly asked to sit next to her at the coffee shop in the lobby of their shared office building.

Kate checked her cell phone one last time to see if he had tried to call, but nothing showed on her screen except the time. 7:30 PM. It was getting darker earlier these days. The threat of thunderstorms didn't help ease her angst.

"Well, I can't stay here all night." She finally propelled herself out of the sports car and pushed the button on her key fob several times to ensure it was locked up tight.

Aunt Lilly's Street was hardly crime-ridden and dangerous, but Kate thought the vampire mannequins and the ghosts swinging from the trees in the neighbors' yard made the night feel menacing. The breeze picked up lifting her blonde hair from the back of her neck, giving her a chill. Quickly she fumbled with the keys and let herself into the house. The radio on the kitchen counter played big band music softly in the darkness. This was not out of the ordinary, as Lilly left it on for her cat, Sassy. Lilly insisted that it kept the cat content during the day. She also left a small lamp on in the living room, even though she knew perfectly well that cats could see in the dark.

Kate shut the door behind her, locked the three different deadbolts, and leaned against the door with a sigh. A blinking red light flashed off and on from the table next to the couch. Kicking off her shoes, Kate strode to the archaic machine and pushed the play button. Why her aunt insisted on using the landline and a vintage answering machine was beyond her. The cell phone Kate bought her for Christmas remained in its box in the side table drawer, unopened.

The noise that filled the room was horrific. It was quite gruesome even for a prank caller, Kate thought. In the middle of hacking and gurgling, she heard her name. Her brow furrowed. She checked the caller ID on the phone and stared at the words *"unknown caller"*. Kate shuddered. Maybe she was mistaken. Maybe it just sounded like her name. No one she knew would be so immature as to resort to prank calling her. Then it hit her. Blake. The annoying kid down the street whom she yelled at for riding his bike too close to her car. It had to be him. *Stupid kid.* No, it couldn't be him. Lilly didn't give out her telephone number to just anyone, and definitely not to Blake or his family.

They were, according to Lilly, *riffraff*. Maybe it was the intern that she had written up for using office time to look up real estate. Kate shared her contact information with the new interns in case they had questions or needed to call out of work. But why? The interns were irritating, but not immature.

Grabbing her cell phone from her purse, she dialed Mark's number again and the call went straight to voicemail. She hung up rather than leaving a second message. Their relationship was still new and she didn't want to come across as needy. Yet, she didn't want to be alone either. She sighed, deleted the message from the machine, and decided to move on. She was a strong, independent, professional woman. Not a timid, scared, little girl.

Sassy sauntered into the room, casting a glance at her bowl near the kitchen entrance, and then turned her gaze to Kate.

"Are you hungry?" The words activated the cat into motion and the white Persian began rubbing up against Kate's legs and purring. "Hey, stop that. We talked about this, Sassy. We'll get along just fine if you don't put cat hair on me."

The cat looked up into Kate's face and blinked slowly.

"Fine. Let's see what we have to eat. You just keep your fur to yourself."

After Sassy was satisfied with her can of wet food, Kate searched the fridge and cabinets for her own dinner. Aunt Lilly had been sweet to make meals ahead of time and put them in containers in the freezer. Each one was labeled with the day of the week in case Kate needed help knowing what meal to eat on which night. She grabbed Friday's container. Meatloaf and some kind of squash. With a thud, Kate tossed it back into the freezer and turned to the pantry. If she remembered correctly, there should be a container of Oreos behind the wheat bran cereal. Yes, there it was. It felt like an Oreo and pizza delivery kind of night.

She had just ordered her pizza when her cell phone rang. A vaguely familiar area code popped up. An upstate New York area code. Reluctantly, she answered.

"Hello?"

"Katie? Katie Benson?" It had been years since anyone had called her *Katie*.

"This is Kate Benson. Who is this?"

"It's Dan Tyler. I know it's been a while."

Images of fishing at the river, chasing each other through the corn fields, and getting scolded together as kids flashed through her mind. It didn't take long for the sweet childhood memories to switch to memories of their first date, prom, and her first kiss to surface. The last time Kate saw Dan was the day she left Deer Creek. She watched him grow smaller in her rear-view mirror as she drove away. The memory caused her heart to ache. He had proposed marriage to her in hopes she would stay. They were just kids back then. She had just graduated high school. Clearly, it had been her father who had masterminded the gesture. He had tried everything to get her to stay where he could control her. Dan was just an unfortunate casualty in the war between the father and daughter. How it broke her heart to say no! It wasn't Dan that she wanted to hurt, but her father.

"Oh, my word! Dan Tyler! How did you get my number? Not that I'm unhappy you have my number… It's just been so long! It's great to hear from you!" Why did she sound so breathless and unstable? "How are you? How are your parents?"

There was a silent pause and Kate wondered if he was still bitter. Surely, he recognized they were too young to make such an adult decision like marriage right out of high school. They had tried to keep in touch, but it soon became evident things weren't going to be the same again. She went to college in Boston and he stayed in Deer Creek.

"We're good. Life is busy as usual." Dan cleared his throat before talking again. "Kate, there's something I need to tell you."

"Is Mike okay? Sean? Jen?" She ran through the list of his siblings that she once viewed as her own brothers and sister without really hearing his tone.

"Yeah ... We're all good," he repeated. This time she heard his frustration. She pictured him raking his hand through his hair like he always did when he wanted her to let him talk. "Look, Kate ... this is hard. It's about your father."

Kate remained silent.

"Are you still there? Kate?"

"Yes. I'm here." A steely cold ire rose up in Kate. "What happened? Did he finally get a DUI?"

"He's dying, Katie," Dan stated bluntly, a trait he'd always possessed. "I came by to deliver dinner from Mom and he didn't answer the door. When I let myself in, he was on the floor. He had your phone number on a piece of paper in his hand. The phone was on the floor next to him so I assume he was trying to call you himself when he... collapsed."

"I see." Kate blinked a few times as the news registered. A lump rose in her throat and she coughed to try to clear it away. An odd mix of emotions threatened to surface. She was past these feelings... or so she thought. The fact she felt *anything* at all about Tom Benson bothered her. She had to shut it down and fast. "Well, I'm sorry to hear that. I really am."

"You need to come home, Katie. He listed you as next of kin. The doctor needs you to make decisions for him. He didn't sign an advance directive or a DNR."

"I'm sorry... what?"

"DNR ... It means *Do Not Resuscitate.*"

Silence. Dan must have thought she still didn't comprehend because he continued, "It's to keep them from putting him on a ventilator in case..."

"Yes. I get it." Kate sat down on the arm of the couch as she collected her thoughts. "You have my permission to give the doctor my number and I will talk to him, but there is no way I can come to Deer Creek at this time."

"Kate, I know things weren't great between you two, but ..."

"You're right. Things *weren't* great. It was a nightmare, Dan," Kate spat out. "To be honest, he's been dead to me for years."

"Tom's different now. He got saved. I was there when he went to the pastor. He got baptized the next week, Kate." Dan's tone was pleading.

"That's great. Too bad he couldn't have done that when I was a kid."

Dan proceeded as if he ignored her last statement. "He's in ICU and calling out your name. He keeps saying you're in danger. He's delirious, but I don't think he will go peacefully until he sees you."

Kate glanced over at the answering machine. It had been her father that called! A chill ran down Kate's spine, but she refused to let the thought take root.

"That's unfortunate." She tried to keep her voice stoic. "I'm in the middle of quite a big ad campaign at work. There's just no way I can leave my team right now. They need me."

All lies. Guilt stabbed at Kate's conscience. Her father might have gotten close to God, but she admittedly had run away from Him. *Far* away.

"If there are papers that need to be signed I can text you my email. I can scan, sign, and send them to whoever needs them, but there's no way I can leave right now."

"Wow... Just wow. You've really made something of yourself, huh? You're so important that you can't tear yourself away for a couple of days to ease a dying man. Your *father*. Maybe I shouldn't be surprised, but I am. The Katie I knew wasn't this cold."

"Well, the *Katie* you knew was stupid and naive. The *Kate* that you are talking to now has moved on with her life. If that's all, I have company at the door."

Not a complete lie. The pizza man rang the doorbell with her dinner.

"Kate..."

"I'm sorry, Dan. Give your family my best. I have to go." With that, she hung up and threw her cell phone onto the couch in anger. She was angry at Dan for suggesting *she* was somehow wrong for how she felt towards her father. It was her *father* who abandoned *Kate* after her mother's death. He chose to get drunk. He chose to verbally, and sometimes physically, accost her and make her feel unseen, unloved, and stupid all at the same time for most of her childhood. She seethed as she paced the floor. Why should she care about Tom Benson? He never cared for her. Also angering her, Kate wondered why Dan Tyler's opinion of her still meant something.

The doorbell rang again and Kate hastily ran to the door, handed the money to the pizza man, and grabbed her box without saying more than a rushed *thank you*. This night needed to end! Not long ago, Kate had read an article on *self-care* and its importance. From that point on, she would make her night about caring for herself and try her best to block out the negative. Kate dressed in her coziest pajamas and buried herself under blankets and pillows on the couch. She mindlessly munched on pizza and Oreos while watching superfluous television shows. Yet, no matter how comfortable she made herself or what indulgence she allowed herself to partake in, she couldn't ease her mind.

Her cell phone chimed and she reached for it only to see Dan had texted.

"Do the right thing. He needs you." She wanted to throw the phone again but instead pressed the volume button on the TV remote to turn it up. Hopefully, the noise would drown her frenzied thoughts. One thing was for sure, Kate was *not* going back to Deer Creek.

*****

Tony Jr. moved from behind the tree and watched the woman leave her expensive red sports car and walk into her house. Crushing his cigarette onto the sidewalk, he grinned. He couldn't have planned things better himself if he tried. At first, he had panicked when the old lady left with suitcases that morning. He worried that Benson's brat daughter was going also. Not only was she staying back, but she was alone. The previous plan to kill the old lady

19

first had been simplified. She was out of the picture. Lucky for her.

His phone vibrated in his pocket, but he ignored the call. He assumed it was his uncle wanting intel on what he saw at Kate Benson's house. Everything in him wanted to act now, but he had to follow the plan, even if he thought it was going too slow. He had to prove to his uncle that he had it in him to carry this through. Maybe soon he could replace the idiot his uncle referred to as his *right-hand man.* After all, Tony Jr was family. That other guy ... well he was just in the way. It was *his* fault things were taking so long to carry out. *Now* was the time to act, but his uncle trusted the plan set in place by that idiot Eddie.

Tony shook with rage.

A priest once told him that anger and revenge would never lead to satisfaction and contentment, but Tony had to disagree. He found himself very satisfied and content at the prospect of making Tom Benson suffer for what he had done to him. Not one day went by that Tony did not see his father's face marred by a hole in his forehead, staring lifelessly ahead as blood trickled down. Every night he had nightmares and the only solace he had was knowing it would soon be over for Tom Benson. Every lying cop or accomplice who ruined his family's life would suffer like he had. The tide would change. Tom Benson would come out of hiding and he'd see his whole world end while Kate bled out.

3

The sun had been up for about two hours, but the thick rain clouds made the morning dreary and dark. It matched Kate's sullen mood. When she had gone to bed just six hours prior, she had no intention of leaving Boston. *None.* Yet, as she laid her head down on the pillow, Dan's words echoed through her mind, torturing her. Sleep wouldn't come. It was a lost cause. By two o'clock, Kate had a weekend bag packed and she had arranged for the neighbor to keep an eye on Sassy for the next few days. She didn't bother calling Mark again. She'd fill him in later. Kate drove through the heavy downpours, stopping only when she needed coffee and gas.

The plan was a simple one. She'd go directly to the hospital, talk to the doctor, walk by her father's room for one last look without stopping to talk, and head home. She'd grab a hotel in one of the surrounding towns. Deer Creek was near an Army base, which meant there would be plenty of lodging options without actually being *in* Deer Creek. The goal was to get in and get out without being noticed by anyone. This would be hard considering Deer Creek was not very large. However, Kate was determined to be back in Boston by Sunday evening, Monday afternoon at the latest.

She turned onto a road that ran parallel to the Black River. As she crossed a small bridge, she put her windows down and stopped her car. No one was behind her and she took in the smell of the water and the sound of the rushing rapids. A serene smile crossed her face. Her childhood wasn't *all* bad. That river and the surrounding lakes, hills, and mountains were a huge part of how she healed after her mother's death. Grandma Lydia and Grandpa Bob took her on hikes and berry picking excursions. There were summers at the beaches along Lake Ontario and exploring various waterfalls. Sometimes, she accompanied her grandmother on visits to extended family in Canada. The youth group at the church that she had participated in often went tubing or kayaking on the rapids. Deer Creek was an amazing place to grow up and Kate knew that despite her father, she was blessed in comparison to many.

A car appeared behind her so she was forced to move on and soon Kate was faced with a decision. She came to a fork in the road… literally. One road took her down a picturesque, curvy lane that would eventually take her to town and the hospital, but it also would take her past the Tyler's farm and her grandparents' home. Admittedly, she was curious about what the old house looked like now. The other road was a more direct route to the hospital, but less nostalgic. If she drove straight to the hospital as she had planned, there would be little to no risk of being seen by anyone.

The time was almost nine in the morning. Surely, everyone she feared seeing would be at work. If she drove by fast enough she'd have the safety of the trees to block the Tylers' view as she passed. Shaking her head at her sappy self, she turned down the road that led home. Almost immediately, the rain picked up and Kate had to increase the windshield wiper speed. From the passenger seat, her phone interrupted her car's amazing sound system to play her ringtone. Of course, she should have ignored it, but when she saw it was Mark she pushed the button on the steering wheel to accept the call.

"Mark?" she answered.

"Hey, Beautiful. Where are you? I just got to your house and your car is gone."

"It's a long story. Something came up and I need to take care of personal business out of town. I'll be back Sunday night hopefully."

"Sunday night? I was hoping we could go hang out with a few friends of mine today."

"I'm sorry. I would rather be with you, believe me."

"What is it you need to do? Why didn't you call me? Maybe I could've come with you."

"Mark, I tried to call you *three* times yesterday."

"I'm so sorry, Kate. I had to stay late at work and my phone ended up dying."

"It's okay. If you had answered I probably would've only made you miserable, too. It was a horrible night."

"Talk to me. What happened? Where are you?"

"I'm heading home. It's my father. He's not doing well and I guess I'm listed as next of kin. Lucky me."

There was silence on the other end and Kate wondered at first if the call had been dropped. After a few moments, Mark spoke again. "Oh, Babe. I'm sorry. Where are you? I'll come to you."

"I'm almost to his house now. I couldn't sleep so I figured, if I had to go I might as well make good time."

"Where does he live? If you had to drive that far, it can't be in Massachusetts."

The rain pounded harder and the winds caused leaves to blanket the street.

"Upstate New York. Dad's hometown. Listen, Mark. I better go. It's rainy and I'm still driving."

"Wait... I'll come and be with you while you go through this. You shouldn't be alone."

"No, really. I'd rather be alone. I don't plan on staying long. I just want to do what I need to do and get back to Boston."

There was a doozy of a curve up ahead.

"Don't shut me out, Kate. You need someone with you."
What I need is to pay attention to the road, she thought.

"Mark, you're so sweet to me. Let me give you a call in a bit. The weather is pretty bad. I have to go. I'll call you later."

Before he could protest, she ended the call and tapped on the brakes to slow her speed. Her speedometer clocked her at sixty-five, over thirty above the limit on that road. If she didn't slow down, she wouldn't get to take a look at her old house. She was getting closer. The Tyler family put up a huge wooden cross at the edge of their property and it came into view as she was about to take yet another curve.

As Kate rounded the tight corner, a familiar old raggedy dog sat in the middle of the road. She didn't have time to be amazed that the Tylers' dog was still alive.

"Move, Flossy!" Kate yelled out loud, but even if the dog had heard her, she most likely wouldn't have budged. "Stupid, Mutt! Move!"

Quickly, Kate swerved to avoid hitting the dog but skidded through the wet leaves and puddles. She scrunched her eyes shut and braced for the inevitable impact of crashing into the Tyler family's fences and hedges. The horrific noise of skidding brakes, cracking wooden fence, and ripping metal only ceased after Kate's car came to a stop under a precariously swaying sign that read, "Welcome to Tyler Family Farm". Funny, the things that pop into a person's head at odd moments. Kate could've sworn that sign wasn't there seven years ago. With a big whoosh, it fell backward.

Kate felt groggy all of a sudden but tried to stay alert to assess the damage to her car. From a distance, she heard a flurry of voices, predominately a female's voice that called out questions in rapid-fire succession.

"Who is it? Are they okay? Do we know them? Where's Mike?"

"I don't know, Colleen. I don't recognize the car." This came from a male voice. Kate recognized it as Mr. Tyler almost immediately. So much for passing through unnoticed.

As the voices drew closer, Kate shut her eyes even tighter. Her side door groaned and moaned as someone used their might to pull it open despite the fact its hinges were bent by damage.

"Are you hurt, Ma'am? Help is on the way. Just stay still." John Tyler's voice was etched with concern.

"I'm okay, Poppa T." Kate attempted to move but realized that she hurt worse than she thought. Mr. Tyler leaned farther into her car to see who addressed him with the name only a few were allowed to call him.

"Well... look who came home after all." His signature Tyler blue eyes smiled even though his mouth stayed in place. "You know, Dan will have a fit when he sees what you did to his fence."

Kate slid her eyes shut again. There was no way to avoid him now.

"I promise I'll pay for the damages. I need to get to the hospital to talk to the doctor." Even to her own ears, Kate sounded pathetic.

"Ha! I don't think that's going to happen, Katie Bug." The concern on his face belied the mirth in his voice. "Not unless you plan on going in an ambulance."

"Katie? Katie Benson? *Our* Katie?"

"Do you know another Katie that would make an appearance like this?" John took the umbrella from his wife's grasp and moved to let her through to their limp visitor.

"Oh, sweet girl. Are you okay? Don't move. Michael is on his way."

Michael? Why did it matter that he was coming?

"I'm fine really." Kate unbuckled her seat belt and tried to lift her leg out of the car. "How bad is the damage?"

"To your car or to the fence?" Mr. Tyler smirked.

"My car."

"It's not going anywhere without a tow truck."

Kate groaned. *This isn't happening! Not my new car!*

"Let's not worry about damage right now. Let's make sure you are okay first," Colleen soothed.

"Is Flossy okay? I swerved to miss her."

Both Colleen and John looked off to the side and saw the dog circling around repeatedly in a dry spot under a tree until she finally felt content to plop down in the leaves. Colleen sighed and reassured Kate. "Flossy is good. Don't you worry about her. She must've gotten out of her collar again. Here comes Mike. Let him look at you."

"What? Why?" Kate grew more insistent that she needed to get out of the car. Goofy Michael wasn't going to be able to do anything to help the situation. That is unless he knew how to fix cars in a hurry.

"Of course, it would be you crashing into the sign Dan just put up last week." Michael Tyler appeared at the door where Colleen had just been. She now was behind her son while he kneeled next to Kate's door. Colleen took over the task of holding the umbrella over his head.

"Mike?" Kate didn't know what she expected to see, but the grown man pressing on her temple and shining a light in her eye was not it. "*Mikey?*"

He smirked but kept his eyes on her forehead. "Does this hurt?"

"Ow! You Dork!" Kate swatted at Michael's hands, trying to block him from bothering her.

"Knock it off, Kate. I'm an EMT."

Kate stopped resisting as she let the information sink in. Little Mikey was an EMT? This was the same boy who put tadpoles in her thermos and chased her around the yard with a garter snake. Clearly, he matured a bit. He was the only Tyler child to inherit Colleen's chocolate brown eyes. His once scrawny arms were now seemingly muscular and strong. The rain made his dark brown hair cling to his forehead. Kate was glad he had grown into his huge head.

"I think you need to go to the ER and get checked. That's a nasty bump you have there."

"What? Where?" Kate made the effort to flip the mirror on her visor but regretted the action. It hurt to move.

"What hurts?" Kate did not appreciate how observant he was.

"Nothing. I'm just achy."

He pressed around her legs looking for a reaction and seemed satisfied when she didn't voice complaint. It was when he helped her move her legs from under the steering wheel to get her to sit sideways that Kate winced.

"Where do you hurt?" he asked again.

"Quit fussing. I'm fine."

He grunted in disapproval as he moved her arms out straight in front of her. "Squeeze my finger as tight as you can."

"I'm not going to fall for that. Is this like *a pull your finger* kind of thing?"

"Kate. Knock it off." His tone wasn't playful and she acquiesced. For spite, she used all her strength to squeeze his finger extra hard.

"Happy now, Dr. Mike?"

He ignored her and turned to his parents. "She seems okay, but I'd feel better if she went in for a full checkup."

"I am fine," Kate insisted. To prove her point she stood straight up. It was when she tried to take her first step that she got woozy, immediately falling into Michael's arms.

"Yeah, you're great."

"Let's at least get her inside and out of the rain," Colleen said as she came up to Kate's side with the umbrella.

Michael protested but took Kate's other side after his mother started leading Kate down the walkway to the old farmhouse.

"I need to get my car fixed," Kate said more to herself.

"I called O'Brien. He'll tow your car to his shop," Mr. Tyler said. He jumped ahead of them on the sidewalk so he could open the door to the house. "He's the best repair guy in town. If he can't fix it, no one can."

"But it's an Audi…" Kate's poor baby. She tried to turn her head to look back at her car but thought better of it. She could hear the radiator hissing even as she walked further away from it.

Nothing was going as planned and she suddenly felt like a fish out of water. So much for getting in and out without being noticed. Not only did everyone notice, but now Colleen was insisting she stay at their house while she took care of her father's affairs. Another rumble of thunder shook the ground. If she had any luck left, the next lightning strike would hit her and put her out of her misery.

4

The rain thudded softly on the window of the Tylers' bathroom. Katie sequestered herself inside the blue, gingham-clad room after Michael finished assessing and administering first aid to the cut on her forehead. She looked at her reflection in the mirror with disdain. He had done a great job applying the steri-strip bandage over the small gash, but nothing could hide the growing purple bump on her temple. She turned away in frustration, but the goose egg pulsated and throbbed as if to let her know that she couldn't ignore what had happened.

Why was this happening to her? She didn't deserve this. Kate had tried to do the right thing for her father despite the fact he was a horrible human being, and this was her reward. Why did she listen to Dan? Why did she let his opinion of her make her do this? *Look where it got me! What an idiot I am! I shouldn't have answered my phone. I should never have left the house.* A hot tear stung its way down her cheek and she angrily brushed it away, but then the tears began falling faster than she could swat them. Kate cursed at herself as the flood gate opened. She hated crying. She was not a weak person. She was strong.

Am I being punished, God? Is that what this is? Why would you let this happen to me? Kate seethed an internal prayer to a God that she wasn't even sure was real. Growing up, people told her "*God loves you*" and "*He has a plan for your life ... one to prosper you.*" Kate let out a scoffing laugh at the thought. Lies. Those were all lies. If there was a God, then He must be cruel to allow her to be stuck in the very place she fought so hard to escape.

A soft tap sounded on the door and Colleen's gentle voice followed.

"Katie? Are you okay? Do you need anything?"

"I'm fine. I'll be out in a minute."

Kate could tell Colleen didn't immediately move away. She could see the shadow under the door where Colleen stood. If she were honest, it was nice to have someone concerned for her. It had been a while since Kate felt a motherly influence. When she moved in with Aunt Lilly, Kate had hoped her aunt might fill some of the void. Lilly was always on the go and tried too hard to be Kate's pal. Grandma Lydia and Colleen were the closest Kate had ever come to feeling like she still belonged to someone. As a child, Colleen bandaged her knees and brushed out the tangles in her long hair. She made sure that she was bathed and clean for school and church. When she and Dan had dated, Kate dreamed of becoming a part of the Tyler family for real. Yet, when that option presented itself, all Kate wanted was to be far away from her father and their small town.

The window was open a crack and the curtains blew as the breeze picked up. Kate closed her eyes and inhaled the old familiar scent. Fresh air mingled with the nearby apple orchard's sweet smell brought peace to her heart. Memories of picking apples and driving on four wheelers through the trees made her smile. Then came the sound of a raised masculine voice and a door slamming.

"Will someone tell me what is going on?" Dan's voice boomed from the living room. "I got a call from Staci that someone crashed into the house."

"Well, that's a bit of an exaggeration. Our house is fine, as you can see." Colleen pointed out.

"But my fence… my sign…"

"I know, I know. You worked hard on it, but she promised to cover the damages." As Colleen reasoned with her oldest son, Kate slid out from the bathroom and down the short hall to where the voices came from. "At least no one was hurt, right?"

Silence. Kate peeked around the corner and instantly Dan's eyes met hers.

"Right, Dan?" Colleen prodded.

"Right." His eyes were still locked on hers as he mumbled the word, rather unconvincingly in Kate's opinion.

"Ah, speak of the devil." Michael smiled mischievously as Kate eased further into the room and he playfully nudged her arm. "You're wishing you had just let me take you to the ER now, aren't you."

Kate sent him a glare before clearing her throat. "Hi, Dan."

Dan didn't say anything right away. He stood staring at her awkwardly for a few moments before he nodded. "I see your driving hasn't improved."

"I'm so sorry about the mess. I promise I will pay for the repairs. The road was wet and I was trying not to hit Flossy…"

Dan grunted. "I'd rather you had hit Flossy."

"Dan Tyler." His mother's tone kicked him out of his perturbed mood.

"I'm glad you're okay," Dan said flatly. To Kate's ears, it reminded her of the times his mother had forced him to apologize when they were bickering as children.

"Hold off on that assessment." Michael piped up and directed his attention at Katie. "I was supposed to take her to the ER to get checked out before she went in to see her father. I assume you're ready now?"

Kate nodded and made a move to follow Michael until he stopped her. "I'll go get the truck. Wait here."

Michael walked out the door but not before smiling and punching Dan playfully on the arm. His brother did not seem as amused as he was. A familiar song rang through the room and Dan reached into his jacket pocket, pulling out Kate's cell phone.

"I guess this is yours?"

Kate nodded. "How'd you …"

"When I stopped to look at the damage it was ringing … so I picked it up. Someone's pretty desperate to reach you," he said as he handed Kate her phone.

Mark's name was on the screen, but she ignored the call and fidgeted uncomfortably until Michael reentered the house announcing that her chariot awaited. She started moving toward the door, but her balance was still off-kilter. Dan reached out to grab her arm and steady her. It was as if he finally noticed the second head she was growing out of her forehead.

"That's a nasty bump."

"It's fine. I'm fine," Kate mumbled as she allowed Michael to take her arm and lead her out to the car. Once they were out of earshot of the others Kate asked, "Do you think he'll forgive me?"

"For the fence or for leaving us?"

"Wow. Really, Mike? Don't hold back any punches."

Michael gave an apologetic sheepish look. "I'm sorry. It's not a joke, I know."

Once he got Kate up and situated in his truck, he looked at her and smiled warmly. "He'll forgive you. It's not the first time someone took the curve too fast and crashed into the yard."

"Well, he was a little ... *testy* ... with me on the phone last night. I'm sure this didn't help matters."

Michael laughed as he walked around the truck and took the driver's seat. "You sure do know how to make an entrance."

*****

Dan Tyler didn't know how to feel. Too many emotions and feelings were crowding in that he'd rather ignore altogether. He had been the one to call Katie to get her to come to her father's bedside. He should've felt relief that she actually showed. Yet, seeing her again caused his stomach to twist into a knot. The destruction of the fence was an annoyance at best. The uneasiness he felt stemmed from something else far more complicated. For over a decade of her life, Dan had a front row ticket to the dysfunctional relationship between Kate and Tom. Despite her anger and words to the contrary, he ultimately knew she would never abandon her father. Humanly speaking, she had every right to stick to her guns, move forward, and not look back. The fact that she came at all communicated that she still had a sense of what was right. So, what was eating at him?

"Hello ... Are you listening?" A voice from the passenger seat of his truck spoke up, pulling him back to the present. "Did you hear a word of what I was just saying?"

"Oh...sorry. You were saying your professor was being unfair." Dan hoped that was correct. Staci had been recounting the crazy syllabus for a class she just started that semester.

"He's being more than unfair! Nothing I do makes him happy. I spent hours researching ..."

And she was off again. For a few moments, Dan tried to track with his girlfriend's concerns. It didn't take long for him to go back in his mind to the very moment he saw Kate appear from the hallway at his parents' house. Pulling up on the car wreckage in his yard and seeing a Massachusetts license plate gave him a spoiler alert of what waited inside the house. Yet, when Dan actually saw her for the first time in *seven* years, he was stunned.

Kate had always been gorgeous. Even when she first moved into her grandparents' house and was an annoying shadow that insisted on doing everything he and his brothers did... even then she was the most beautiful girl in the world to him. The woman standing vulnerably in his parents' living room that day was disheveled and had a purple lump on her forehead. Yet, she was beautiful. Her eyes were still the bluest blue he had ever seen. She still wrung her hands when she felt unsure and it was still the cutest quirk to him. Even after all those years, Kate Benson still stopped him in his tracks and made him feel like an incoherent fool.

"Oh and get this .... Sabrina came home from her internship and blasted her music so loud despite the fact she knows I am sitting there studying. How insensitive is that?"

And then there was Staci. Dan looked over at her seeing she was expecting some type of response. Guilt stabbed at him and he searched for an appropriate answer. "Wow. That must've been ..."

"Frustrating! Exactly!" And she was off again, going on and on about her roommate's inconsiderate behavior.

Staci was a few years younger than the women he had dated over the last several years. Admittedly, there was a maturity that she lacked compared to the others, but this was a longer relationship at two months than some of his past relationships. She was finishing her final year of teaching and wanted to settle down. Somewhere along the way, Dan realized he'd like a family of his own. He had put everything into his family's farm, along with a side construction venture of his own. For so long after Kate and he lost touch, he just found contentment in work and in his faith. Then one day he realized he was lonely.

So Dan bought a house as a first step. Tom Benson approached him one day while he was helping fix a plumbing issue at the house. The two men struck up a plan to allow Tom to live out the remainder of his life there and Dan would be the deed holder, taking care of the property should a need arise. Tom had assured him that Kate would be told and that she would prefer to receive the monetary inheritance over the dilapidated house. The Benson property bordered his own family's land so it was ideal. Now all he needed was the Godly woman of his dreams. Until the time was right, he would continue living contentedly in the old farmhand's cabin located in what they used to call *no man's land* between Benson and Tyler properties.

"I tell you ... if it wasn't for the Holy Spirit I would've loved to tell her what I really thought..."

Dan's face must've given away his troubled thoughts because Staci shifted the conversation to something other than her schooling and roommate. "Are you still worried about the sign? Just be glad no one was hurt. Imagine if your mother was setting out the fall display today?"

"Of course, you're right." Dan smiled at Staci and directed his attention back to the road. *Please, Lord. You know how much I want this to work with Staci. Keep my thoughts away from distraction and focused on You.* Dan set his jaw and his mind. He would determine to avoid distraction, even if the distraction was named Kate Benson.

*****

Kate's sneakers squeaked on the waxed shiny floors of the ICU wing. The noise made her cringe. The unit was quiet except for occasional machines beeping and the low whispers of the nurses sitting behind desks at the nurses' station. Her squeaky approach seemed irreverent and unwelcome in that environment. A familiar emotion rose in her chest as she approached the nurses. It felt like a combination of uncertainty and the need to apologize for her presence. It was very much how she felt as a child walking to her father's room to tell him it was dinner time.

For a moment, she wished she had accepted Michael's offer to accompany her to her father's room. She had told him no after the doctor downstairs in the emergency room concluded that she had suffered a minor concussion and some bruised ribs. Nothing that would warrant extra attention. Now that she was near her father's room, she felt unstable. A nurse with kind eyes looked up and smiled at her, putting her somewhat at ease.

"May I help you?" she asked softly.

"Tom Benson's room, please?"

"Are you family?"

Kate nodded and choked on the word, "Daughter."

The nurse's eyes lit and she rose to her feet, walking to the other side of the desk to lead Kate personally to her father's bedside. "Dr. Buchanan was hoping you would come. I will let him know you are here. Follow me. Your father is in and out of consciousness. He's a stubborn man!"

Kate laughed sarcastically. "Yes, stubborn is a good word for it, I guess."

"When he has lucid moments, he asks for you. Don't be surprised if he doesn't make much sense. He's been saying odd things." The nurse stopped at the door and waited for Kate to enter.

"What kind of things has he been saying?" Kate couldn't bring herself to enter just yet and turned her full attention to the nurse. Out of the corner of her eye, she saw her father's legs under the blankets on his bed behind the half open door.

"It's not uncommon for patients this close to the end of their life to have delusions. He thinks you are in some sort of danger." The nurse smiled tenderly at Kate. "I'm sure seeing you will put him at ease."

Kate nodded and the nurse left to give her privacy, but she made no effort to move forward. Standing there at her father's doorway made her feel nine years old all over again. The same insecurities that plagued her all those years ago seized Kate and left her frozen. She was transported back in time to the first night after they moved in with her grandparents.

Kate woke up before the sun that first morning at her grandparents' home. Her new room had unopened boxes piled high, waiting to be unpacked. Kate's grandfather had put together a nice bed for her and her grandmother let her pick out one of her brightly colored quilts to sleep with. The room overlooked the front yard and a tire swing Grandpa Bob hung the day before she arrived. Kate lay awake listening to the mix of silence and occasional sobs coming from the room down the hall. She wanted to get up and go to her father because she knew it was he who was crying, but she was scared.

The darkness became a fearful thing even more so on the nights after her mother's funeral. Her imagination was full of bad guys and monsters waiting to kill her too. Grasping the arm of her stuffed bunny, she slid out from under the quilt. The floorboards squeaked under her and she paused. It sounded so loud against the pre-dawn nothingness. Slowly, she crept down the hallway to the door of her father's room. It was slightly ajar and she could see her father rocking back and forth, sitting up in his bed, in one hand was a bottle of something and the other hand was pressed tightly against his face. He was saying something repeatedly under his breath and she leaned in closer to hear the words, "I'm so sorry... I'm so sorry".

Her tiny hand pushed the door open further and she eased into the room.

"Daddy, it's okay. Please don't cry."

Instantly, her father's movement ceased and his head snapped up. "GET OUT! GET OUT!"

Kate's father was never an overly affectionate man to begin with, but he had never raised his voice to her before. When he wasn't working or on call, her father was more of a playmate of sorts. He had taught her how to wrestle and to get away from bad guys by kicking them in their shins. He had watched TV with her and laughed with her at the funny spots. This man with wide eyes full of rage scared the young girl. She didn't recognize him.

"I ... I'm sorry, Daddy. Please don't be mad. I heard you crying."

"I SAID GET OUT OF HERE!" Just then he hurled the bottle of vodka in his hands and it crashed against the wall

right next to Katie, sending the strong aroma of alcohol into the air.

Her grandmother and grandfather came up behind her, clearly startled awake by the sound of yelling.

"Come, Katie. The sun is just about up. Let's go make breakfast." Grandma Lydia put her arms around the shaking girl and turned her away from the sight of her father. Kate didn't miss the expressions exchanged between Lydia and Bob. Grandma Lydia nodded her husband into the room with Tom as she guided the frightened child downstairs.

Hot tears burned Kate's eyes and she clung to her grandmother's waist. She heard the stern voice of her grandfather and the loud bombastic anger of her father.

"He's angry at me."

"No, Love. He's not angry at you. You didn't do anything wrong."

Despite the soothing words from her grandma and the distraction of stirring pancake batter, Kate never shook the feeling that the father that she had known up to that point in her life was gone. In his place, was this new scary man ... a man that didn't love her anymore.

The sound of retching and hacking came from the room and Kate snapped out of her tortured thoughts. She backed away and started wringing her hands.

"Who's there?" A gruff masculine voice sounded from the room. Kate didn't answer. She didn't think she could find her voice in that moment. Instead of entering, she turned on her heels and walked briskly down the hall she had just come from, passing the quizzical nurses.

Once down in the lobby, she spotted Michael sitting in a chair looking at something on his cellphone.

"That was fast. Did you get to see him?" he asked.

Kate nodded but made no eye contact. Lying was easier than explaining what was going on in her head at that moment. "He was asleep."

"Oh. We can try again later if you want. Or maybe after church tomorrow?"

"Can we just go, please? I need to check on my car."

Michael's expression was soft and she tried not to look into his eyes or she would burst into tears. Why had she come? What was she expecting? Did she really think that she and her father could just forget all that happened... that they could somehow regain something before he died?

"I'll go get the truck."

As Kate watched her old friend walk towards the parking garage, a voice came from behind her. She turned to see the ICU nurse, breathless and running toward her. "Miss Benson? Miss Benson!"

"I'm sorry. You can have the doctor call me or I can meet with him tomorrow sometime."

"That's fine. I forgot to make sure you had this. Your father had asked one of the nurses to write this note for him when he first came in. He wanted to make sure you got it in case ... Well, anyway. Here it is."

Numbly, Kate took the folded sheet of paper with a nod.

"I know this is a tough time. I lost my father a couple of years ago. Please don't be scared to see him. I know he's not how you might remember him, but sitting with him for a bit would make the world of difference for the both of you.

He'll be able to relax knowing you're here and you can say what you need to before… he goes."

"I appreciate you coming to give this to me," Kate said weakly. "I have to go. I'll stop by tomorrow."

Once inside the truck, Kate opened the paper and looked at the first words. *Dear Katie.* She crumpled the paper and shoved it in the pocket of her jacket.

"What was that?"

"Nothing. Just a piece of paper." Kate turned her face to the window and watched the scenery blur as they drove back to the house. One pesky tear escaped and rolled down her cheek and she quickly brushed it away lest more follow. Even if she had to rent a car, she would leave as soon as she could.

Later that night, Kate lay in her bed in the guest bedroom staring at the shadows the curtains cast on the ceiling. She thought of the many ways that day had gone awry. When she came home from the hospital with Michael, the family was getting ready to sit down to a meal. Kate had excused herself to her room, insisting that she was too tired to eat. She imagined she was the topic at the table. Daniel barely looked at her when she entered. She assumed the woman sitting next to him was his current girlfriend. It was obvious due to the way she put a hand on his arm protectively as soon as Kate walked into the room.

What did it matter? Why should Kate care? She wouldn't be there long enough to concern herself with who Daniel Tyler was seeing. Her call to the garage where her car convalesced ended in more frustration and uncertainty. The garage did not have access to the parts her Audi needed. The closest Audi dealer was hours away. She could get a rental car, but not until Monday when the business office opened again. Kate tried to comfort herself, going over in her mind the revised plan of action. She would return to the hospital the next day, talk to her father's doctor, and leave as soon as the rental car company opened Monday morning. She just needed to get through Sunday.

A soft knock sounded. At first, Kate thought she had misheard, but a moment later the door opened slightly and Colleen poked her head in.

"Kate, will you be coming to church with us tomorrow morning?"

When was the last time Kate had gone to church? She guessed it had been at least six years.

"I appreciate the thought, Momma T, but I need to go to the hospital and meet with the doctor."

"I see. If you waited until after church, one of us could drive you up."

Kate thought in the silence. How would she get to the hospital with her car out of action? Thankfully, Colleen spoke up and offered Kate a solution.

"We can go in the truck tomorrow and I can leave you my car if that is helpful."

"Yes, thank you! That *would* be helpful."

"If you find that you are done at the hospital earlier than you expected, maybe you can meet us at the church. Church service starts at 10:30."

Kate thanked Colleen once more and sighed when the door shut behind her. A small familiar nagging feeling tugged at her conscience. Grandma Lydia was so devout in her faith and tried to instill the same faith in Kate. There was a time when Kate thought she felt God. Yet, if she were honest, she started resenting the feeling of His presence.

When Grandma prayed she referred to Him as *Father*. That name didn't come with a happy association for Kate anymore. As she closed her eyes to sleep, Kate concluded fathers were overrated and she was just fine without God or Tom Benson.

5

No one saw the black shadow dart across the street and into the narrow alley between the two houses in the predawn hours of Sunday morning. Tony slid in through the loosened basement window that he had visited several nights in a row to prepare for this very moment. However, in all of his imaginings of how the plan would transpire, he never expected Kate to disappear before they could act. His uncle was none too pleased with Eddie when he and Tony had pulled up to the house to grab her, only to find her car missing. While the setback was annoying, it secretly pleased Tony that his uncle was irate at his golden boy. Now was his time to show what he was capable of. His mission was to find something to tell them where Kate had gone. He was in a race against Eddie to come back to James with answers and a new course of action.

With a click of his Maglite, he worked his way through the boxes and random holiday décor to the steps that led into the main part of the house. He heard music which caused him to pause. It sounded like the radio. He reached into his jacket pocket and pulled out a hunting knife as he eased the basement door open. A white blob out of the corner of his eye drew his attention. A fat cat lying on the couch lifted its head, but apparently determined the intruder was no concern of his and went back to sleep. That was why he was a dog man, Tony concluded.

Only a dim lamp lit the living room, but, other than the cat, there were no other signs of life. Quietly, he moved up the steps to the bedrooms, trying to stay to the side of the steps so as not to cause a creak … just in case. It didn't take long to see that every bed was empty. All the doors were open and no one occupied any of the rooms. He began his search in the first bedroom he came to. Drawer after drawer was emptied onto the floor as he looked for anything that may have some clue. He moved to the closets and dumped the contents of the boxes onto the bed.

A picture caught his attention. It was a photo of a young family. The mother was a looker with her blonde hair and hourglass figure. If Tony didn't know any better, he would've thought it was Kate Benson. The man next to her was obvious. He saw that face in his nightmares. Tom Benson. The young girl around his legs was assumedly Kate Benson as a toddler. He flipped the picture and saw a Christmas greeting scrawled with the year 2000. He stuffed the picture in his pocket and moved to the next room.

The bed was unmade and on top was an empty suitcase. Clothes were strewn around like someone had been hastily packing. He started digging through drawers on the nightstand and found nothing useful. There were several moving boxes stacked against the wall and he sorted through them until he came to a box that had been labeled *"papers and stuff"* in black ink. He glanced through old bank statements and work-related papers until he hit the jackpot. There were old report cards and a diploma from a high school in a place called *Deer Creek*. Tony spotted a familiar name as he scanned a newspaper clipping announcing inductees into the honor society. He smiled when he saw the clipping contained the local paper's town name. Deer Creek, New York.

It would make sense that Tom would take her to some obscure place after he left Boston. What were the chances he still lived there? Tony made his way back downstairs and started going through closets. The sky was lightening and he knew he had to leave. However, he saw a piece of paper on the kitchen counter. It appeared to be a note signed by Kate and addressed to someone she had gotten to look after the cat. Nestled in the instructions was one line that made his early morning search worth the frustration. *"Please tell Lilly I am in New York. Dad needs me. I'll be back ASAP."*

Tony did not get much time to revel in his find as the sound of the side kitchen doorknob rattled as if someone was unlocking it. He moved to the pantry closet and hid himself just as a woman talking on a cell phone entered the kitchen. He watched her through the slats on the door as she waved her hands as she talked.

"Yeah, I hope she gets back soon. I think the cat is running out of food and I don't think I should have to buy it. They better reimburse me." The woman paused and glanced around the room as if she heard something, but determined it was nothing. She looked on the counter for the note, but it was still clenched in Tony's hand. "Where's the stupid note? It was right here last night. Ugh, I'm too tired for this."

The person paused again and looked around the room. Tony felt his pulse beating wildly in his neck. There was not much of an opening through the slats of the door, but he could see the woman enough to know she was coming towards his location. He glanced around him and cursed under his breath when he saw the bag of cat food on the shelf next to him. His hand slid into his pocket and his fingers wrapped around the hilt of his knife.

Meows came from the room and Tony saw the white fur ball walk up to the pantry door and scratch at it as if to show the neighbor where the food was kept.

"Yeah, I'll call you later. Let me feed this little guy and get going. Bye." The woman put her phone on the counter and bent over to call the cat to herself.

"Are you hungry, Sassy? Aww. Aren't you the sweetest?"

The neighbor moved closer and put her hand on the pantry door. Tony's heartbeat thudded loudly in his ears. He had to act fast.

Kill her. Kill her. Kill her. The words chanted in his head.

Pushing the door open, he jumped out and grabbed the woman quickly. He turned her so her back was to him as he clamped his hand over her mouth and slid his knife across her neck. Her body fell to the floor with a thud. Tony looked down at what he had just done. He had never killed anyone before. The woman's eyes were wide open, but their light was dimming. The growing pool of blood spread across the linoleum in a rather beautiful stream of crimson.

Sassy meowed and pawed at the pantry again as if nothing had happened. Tony reached into the closet, grabbed the cat food bag, and threw it on the floor so the cat could get to it. He looked once again at the woman, intrigued by the rush of emotions he felt.

Good job. I knew you could do it. Tony shook his head, trying to get the voice to stop. He felt his pocket to see if his bottle of pills were there, but he had forgotten them. Just then, the dead woman's phone buzzed alerting him to the fact he had to get out of there quickly.

The sun was almost fully up and soon someone would look for this woman. He wiped his knife on a dish towel, put it back in his pocket, and stepped over the woman. He took his gloves off and put them in the other pocket with the note and picture he discovered. Putting his hood up to obscure a clear view of his face, he slipped out the side door and casually walked down the street to where his car was parked. A rising feeling of power made his stride more confident. There was no going back now. Tom Benson and his precious daughter were next.

*****

Katie Benson stood at her father's door. She had wanted to see his doctor that morning, but the weekend nursing staff informed her that he wouldn't be back in the hospital to check on patients until Monday afternoon. The rising volcanic fire of her anger threatened to spew out onto the hospital staff. Kate started walking back down the hall to leave before she said something she'd regret. She would have kept going, but she heard a familiar voice calling out. She followed the voice until she stood at her father's door and listened. It was a mix of sobbing and praying.

"Please, God. Forgive me. I'm so sorry. I'm so sorry."

It reminded Kate of that night so long ago when she was little. His voice was weaker now and there wasn't a tinge of anger in the cries, but rather brokenness. She held her breath as she moved her head ever so slightly to look into the room. The television was on and it appeared to be a broadcast of a church service. His legs trembled under the blankets as he continued to cry out.

She moved ever so slightly to get a glimpse of his face. Something stabbed at her heart as she saw him. Tubes and wires were everywhere, obscuring much of his face. What she could see of the man was shocking. Where was his dark hair? His hair was white and so thin that she could see his scalp. His color was a sickening yellowish gray. She released her breath as silently as she could, but her father's head turned towards her. His eyes met hers and she tried to back away, but she was frozen in place.

"Kate?" Her name never sounded so pitiful. He tried to lift his hand, but he couldn't.

She didn't know what made her do it, but she took a few steps and entered his room. Her eyes couldn't look away from his face. He used to look so formidable and strong.

This man was frail. It wasn't the wrinkles and lines on his face that shocked her so, it was the sheer expression of sadness. Yet, in the blink of a moment, his look went from one of dejection to pure joy. At the sight of *her*!

"Hello, Dad." The words did not feel comfortable on her lips.

"You came! I didn't think you would." His voice was raspy and breathless with pauses between words. Something inside Kate ached for him and she hated it. Her jaw clenched as she tried to regain her composure.

Kate moved to a chair near the bed and sat down rigidly. "The Tylers called."

"Good people." Tom nodded and fell back against his pillow, his head still turned to see his long-lost daughter.

The silence was awkward and Kate fidgeted in her seat, contemplating whether to leave or not. The pastor on the television preached and she decided to comment on that.

"It's nice you can watch church from your room." *Well, that sounded dumb,* she thought to herself.

Tom nodded and his eyes started to fill up with tears. "Oh, Kate... I'm so sorry."

"Dad..." Kate searched for the right words to say. Did she say it was okay? No, because it *wasn't* okay. Did she tell him that she hated him for abandoning her? That seemed cruel considering the situation he was in. So, she said what she needed to get him to relax. "Please don't get yourself worked up. It's not worth it."

"Peter came. He told me to call you..." Tom wheezed.

"I see." Kate sat up straight. "Goodness knows you wouldn't have called if Uncle Peter *hadn't* told you to."

She wounded him. That was clear by the look in his eyes. Kate knew she was a time bomb waiting to go off on her father. She should just leave. As she got to her feet, he reached out again.

"Don't leave me." The words sounded painful to get out as he labored to breathe. "I know… I was a bad dad. You deserved so much… more."

"You don't need to say that."

"I do. It's… true." He tried to adjust on his pillow and the machines next to him started beeping as his heart rate grew erratic.

"Dad, just calm down. Rest."

"You need to know …."

The nurse came in and began pushing buttons to stop the machines from sounding off. She injected something into his intravenous line. "I'm sorry. This morphine will make him tired. I know you just came in to visit."

Kate nodded in relief, but jumped when her father yelled, "*NO!*"

"Now, Mr. Benson, please calm down. She can come back later."

"Danger! Kate…." His eyes grew heavy and he repeated these same words over and over until they were no more than a whisper. Then his words ceased altogether as he fell fast asleep.

"You can stay and be here for when he wakes up if you'd like. It's just that when he gets excited his breathing becomes labored and his heart…"

"No, that's fine. I have errands to run. I'll come back later."

Moments later, Kate sat numbly in the car she had borrowed from the Tylers. The clock on the dashboard read 12:30. Colleen had reiterated the invitation earlier that morning to meet them at the church if time allowed, but church was over by now. Kate reached into her coat pocket and found the crumpled letter that the nurse had handed her the day before. She smoothed out the wrinkles and read:

Dear Katie,

I don't expect you to forgive me, but please know I love you. I always have. I'm proud of you and I know your mom would be too. Talk to Peter. Go find Bunny. Very important.

Kate crumpled the letter all over again. What was that supposed to mean? *The ravings of a very sick man,* Kate concluded as she turned the ignition and headed back towards the main road. She knew she shouldn't try to make sense of the note. Her father was out of his mind clearly. Yet, he had been talking to Uncle Pete. Maybe he'd shed light on why he was fixated on her safety.

As she stopped at a light Kate called her father's old partner and listened to the constant ringing. It was Sunday morning. He most likely was out on the golf course. She left a message to call her and put her attention back onto the road. As she left the small town and headed back to the Tylers' property, Kate debated whether to stop in at her father's house for a look around.

As she approached the edge of her family's property line, Kate spotted the entrance to an old cemetery. No doubt it was where her father would be buried. It contained the graves of her grandparents, great-grandparents, and other ancestors who helped found the town. The cemetery always fascinated Kate. If one didn't know to look, they would drive right by it. It was up on a slight hill that bordered what used to be an old cornfield. In the summer and spring, the gate and entrance were covered with greenery and leaves. The only way one would know that the cemetery even existed was the old patch of mowed grass that led to the ivy-covered gates.

Various people who had relatives interred within took turns mowing it throughout the year. It was only in winter and late fall that the gates became visible at the top of the hill. In the bleak winters as a child, Kate knew to look to the top of the hill and she could spot the headstone her grandmother took her to often to put a wreath on during Christmas. It had been the headstone of Kathryn Benson, her great-grandmother and the woman she was named after.

Kate instinctively looked up and slowed the car. Somewhere behind the wall of trees and colorful leaves were her grandparents. Soon her father would be laid to rest there as well with her mother's urn with him. It was the only thing she knew for sure about her father's wishes. Kate assumed he would want her with him.

A tear surprised Kate as it trickled down her cheek and she continued to drive past the site. It started to hit her that these were her father's last days on earth. She had spent so many years being angry at him and pretending he was already gone. However, he wasn't gone yet and Kate had been made keenly aware of his existence once more. Just in time for her to ache over the loss of a relationship with him all over again.

6

Kate could smell Colleen's cooking from outside the house as she got out of the car. Earlier that morning, she had heard Colleen readying a roast in the crockpot before church. Judging by the number of cars in the driveway, the Tyler table would be quite occupied. Kate considered getting back in the car and finding lunch elsewhere when the door of the house opened and Colleen stepped onto the porch with a tender smile.

"You're just in time for lunch."

With a sigh, Kate nodded and entered the house with little opposition. The family had been more than gracious with her, all things considered. Kate knew she couldn't be rude. Colleen beamed at her and wrapped her arm around Kate's shoulder as she entered the living room. Good thing Colleen had a hold of her because when Kate caught sight of everyone sitting at the table staring at her, she wanted to bolt.

"Welcome back, Kate." A tall man with a warm smile rose to his feet and instantly Kate recognized the dimple on his cheek. It was Sean Tyler. He approached her and gave her a small hug. "Take my seat next to Jen."

"I'm not taking your seat." Kate tried to protest, but Sean had already grabbed the piano bench and forced Dan to scoot down further to accommodate him. Colleen already had another place setting waiting.

"Sit down, Katie, and we'll bless the food," Mr. Tyler instructed from his place at the head of the table. Kate complied, albeit reluctantly.

After the sincere and heartfelt prayer concluded, Kate didn't raise her head right away as she felt several pairs of eyes on her.

"Was your father awake this time? Did you get to talk?" This came from Michael who had already started passing the bowl of mashed potatoes to his mother.

"Yes. He was awake." Kate looked up and her eyes met Dan's and she quickly diverted her attention to the teenager sitting next to her. "Jen. Wow. You've shot up since I saw you last."

The young woman smiled and blushed.

"Are you a senior this year?" Kate continued her questioning to keep herself from being the focus of the conversation.

"Next year."

"That's exciting. Have you thought about what you'll do after?" Kate put a healthy serving of roast on her plate before handing the plate to Jen.

"She has time to think about that," Dan stated matter-of-factly and took a sip from his water glass. "There's no hurry."

"You're right. It's definitely wise to think it through." Kate bit a carrot awkwardly. She knew she should probably stay quiet, but the Benson stubborn streak urged her on. "Still ... There's nothing wrong with dreams and aspirations."

Dan grimaced and surprisingly Jen spoke up. "Actually, I want to be a nurse."

"Nursing? That's great! Very noble profession." The girl beamed under Kate's praise.

"What do you do, Kate?" Staci, who had had her hand resting on Dan's arm since Kate's arrival asked from her place at the table.

"I work for an advertising firm."

"An advertising firm? Sounds intriguing. Are you one of the people that come up with ideas?" Staci prodded. Her expression looked like she was trying to come across as sincere, but there was something off. Kate proceeded cautiously.

"I work with a team to put out various commercials, social media, and magazine ads." Kate smiled politely and hoped someone would change the topic.

"Anything we've seen?" Sean asked.

"I don't know. We just finished a campaign with Quasi Cosmetics."

"Really? They just had a commercial with Randi Lawson! I love her! Was that one of yours?" Jen asked, turning her full body in her chair to face Kate.

Kate warmed at the look of admiration. "Yes, actually it was one of mine."

"Who in the world is Randi Lawson?" Mr. Tyler piped up.

"She's one of my favorite makeup influencers."

Dan grunted something from his place and Jen rolled her eyes at him annoyedly. "Don't pay them any attention. Everyone on that side of the table thinks an app is something on a menu."

"Hey." Sean protested and Michael laughed arrogantly, mostly because he was sitting on the *cool* side of the table.

"Did you get to meet her?" Jen asked.

"Jen, let Kate eat," Colleen reprimanded with a gentle smile.

"It's okay." Kate turned to Jen with a huge smile. "Not only did I meet her, but she did my makeup and hair during downtime."

"Nuh uh"

"Uh Huh."

"Oh ... my... word!!! Tell me more. How does she get her skin so clear?" Michael leaned over with his face resting on his hands, talking in an accent that Kate assumed was meant to be a mock version of his sister. Jen pushed his arm out from under him and his head fell off its resting place, causing Kate to laugh.

"Now *that* is a nice sound to hear," Colleen commented. "I've missed you at this table, Katie."

"Yeah... me too." She said it quietly, but sincerely. It felt nice to be a part of a family, even if it would be short lived.

Dan cleared his throat loudly. "Mom, this roast is amazing."

"Yes, Mrs. Tyler. I agree. It's very good," Staci reiterated.

With that conversation turned to a mix of topics and Kate felt able to relax and enjoy her lunch. She let her eyes rest on each person at the table and marveled at how seven years had changed them. The boys were now handsome men. Little Jen who was ten when she left, was now a beautiful young woman. Mr. and Mrs. Tyler were grayer with some white at their temples and the crows' feet around their eyes were deeper than she remembered. Yet nothing changed the love and warmth in their eyes. Kate caught herself smiling but quickly schooled her features when she happened to glance at Dan. He was staring at her, at first stoically then softening his expression to a warm nostalgic look of friendship as if he were remembering their history as well.

"Kate, I am so deeply sorry to hear about your father. He is so precious to all of us," Staci said out of nowhere as she put her head on Dan's shoulder. "It wasn't long ago that he was giving me some much-needed fatherly wisdom."

Something akin to anger started rising in Kate's core. "Are we talking about the same man? Tom Benson?"

"Oh, my yes! I moved here to attend Bible College and he has been so sweet. Not a Sunday goes by that I don't go get a dad hug from Mr. Tom."

Dan squeezed her hand at that point, a familiar move he made with Kate several times when they had dated. It was a silent prod to get Staci to stop. He most likely intended to be discreet, quickly shaking his head and furrowing his brow in an attempt to cease the direction of the conversation.

"Well, how nice for you," Kate said quietly as she buried a little carrot under the mashed potatoes on her plate. Not everything about Kate had changed. Carrots were still not her favorite.

"I didn't even know Tom had a daughter until recently." Staci didn't get Dan's message.

"Finally, something that *doesn't* surprise me," Kate laughed ruefully.

Staci finally ceased her spouting, possibly due to the expressions of those at the table.

"Not to change the subject..." Kate lightened her tone and directed her conversation to Mr. Tyler. "How much do I owe you for the damages to your property? If you have a money app I can send it now or if you prefer I can write a check."

Mr. Tyler knit his brow. "I don't have a …a money app. Really, Katie, I'm not worried about it. We don't have to discuss it now."

"I really would like to get it all squared away. I intend on leaving tomorrow after I talk to my father's doctor and I can rent a car."

The table was silent.

"I'll have to return to pick up my car at some point. If you want to get estimates in the meantime, I can just bring you money then…"

"*Tomorrow?*" Dan asked. "How can you get everything settled that quickly?"

John shifted uncomfortably in his seat. "We can discuss it another time, Katie Bug. The fence was Dan's handiwork. He'd know the prices better than I would."

"Kate, I'm not worried about the fence. We don't need money for it." Dan stated quietly. "I just think maybe you should wait around until …"

Kate's phone rang from her pocket. "Excuse me. I need to take this."

Kate excused herself, grabbed her jacket from the coat tree, and went to sit on the front porch. The caller ID said it was Mark, but she didn't move to answer it. She'd call him back later. The solitude of the porch was what she needed at that moment and the call gave her a good excuse to remove herself from the awkwardness at the table. A brisk breeze sent a few leaves free from their branches. She put her hands in her pocket and felt the crumpled note the nurse had transcribed for her father.

She pulled it out and read the cryptic words all over again. *Go find Bunny.* The only bunny Kate knew of was her beloved stuffed rabbit that Grandma Lydia had made for her. It had been her best friend since birth. She hadn't seen that battered old stuffed animal since she moved out at eighteen years old. Curiosity rose up in Kate. She had wanted to go to the old house anyway to see it one more time. Maybe it was a good idea to go and have a look around. At the very least, Kate imagined she would need to find her father's important papers to settle his estate. Hopefully, she could take it all with her and settle it from Boston.

The screen door opened and Staci came out followed by Dan.

"Headed home?" Kate knew she sounded a little too happy at the thought of their leaving.

"I have some work I need to do before tomorrow. I'm student teaching at the elementary school."

Kate nodded and tried not to make eye contact with Dan. "It's a good school. I have a lot of good memories there."

"Are you going to go back to the hospital?" This came from Dan as he pushed the unlock button on his truck's key fob.

"No. I was going to head to the house and look for Dad's papers."

Dan paused. "If you wait, I can send someone over with you."

Well, that's a bit high-handed. It's not like you own the place, Kate thought to herself. "Why would I need you to do that? Doesn't your mom still have a key?"

"Yes, but it's a mess over there and it's not really safe."

Kate laughed. "I'm a big girl. I think I can handle my father's clutter."

"Dan, come on. I have to study," Staci called as she climbed into his truck.

He looked over his shoulder at his girlfriend but redirected his attention to Kate with a stern expression. "Just wait until I get back... please."

Kate didn't answer him, but he nodded as if she had agreed to his nonsensical suggestion. She stared as he pulled out of the driveway with Staci before moving into the house to request the key from Colleen. *Who does he think he is? I do not need his protection in my own house.*

When she entered the kitchen, Colleen was busy instructing her boys on washing dishes. Kate smiled at the familiar bantering. Mr. Tyler dozed in his recliner and Jen had disappeared, most likely to her room. Kate glanced at the pantry door and saw exactly what she had expected to see hanging on the inside. Several sets of keys. One set had the label *Benson* above the hook. Quietly, she took the keys, told Colleen she was going to get some fresh air, and left the house.

The path that wound through the wooded boundary on the western end of the Tyler property still looked very much as it did when she was a child. Between her and the Tyler boys, the path was always well worn. The trees formed a colorful canopy above her head and Kate got lost in the beauty of it all. Up ahead on the path would be the old cabin they used as a fort.

As she approached it, she stopped abruptly. It didn't look the same. Years ago the cabin had been in such disrepair that one could see between the slats in the walls. This cabin appeared to be new. It had a small porch that housed a pair of work boots. There were blinds in the windows and a door with a lock. Kate snuck up on the side of the cabin and peeked in the window. The inside looked lived in. There was a table, a counter with a coffee pot, and a small fridge. A bed was in one corner and a small recliner facing a television in the other. Who turned their fort into an actual place to live? Maybe one of the people who worked for the Tylers? Kate all of a sudden grew self-conscious. She didn't want to get caught peeking in some strange person's window.

She hurried further down the pathway until the trees started clearing. As expected, there was Grandma Lydia's bird bath. There weren't vibrant flowers growing around the base as there once were. In fact, it looked like weeds took over a long time ago. The wind caused the old tire swing to move in the breeze, catching her eye. It would never hold her weight now, but it still hung from the tree where Grandpa Bob placed it. Then there was the house.

She approached the steps cautiously. It looked like there were a few boards replaced recently, but other spots looked sketchy, to say the least. With every step she tentatively placed her foot down until she was sure it would hold her weight. The old screen door cried on its hinges as she opened it to unlock the door.

The smell of cleaning agents hit her nose and Kate imagined Colleen had been there to aid her father. It was dim inside but the outside light coming from behind the blinds allowed enough light to see around her. She blinked at the sight of a bathroom where a closet used to be. Other things looked different as well. The furnishings looked the same as they did when she left, but the kitchen looked nicer... newer. An old recliner caught Kate's eye. Her father's chair. Next to it on a side table were pictures. She picked up the photos and couldn't believe her eyes. They were of her! *Peter*! Of course, her father must've had him reporting back rather than reaching out himself.

She shook her head and moved away towards the stairs and stopped when she saw hardware and tools in a pile at the base of the steps. Confused she stepped over them and headed up the stairs carefully. It was when she noticed one of the middle steps was missing that she wondered if she should've waited for someone to come along with her after all. Pushing that crazy idea out of her head, she held tightly to the banister and pulled herself up along the edges of the steps. If Kate was anything, she was independent.

When she made it to the upstairs hallway she felt familiar sadness. If she stood still long enough, she was sure she would hear her grandmother humming from her bedroom at the end of the hall. All the doors were shut and as tempted as Kate was to reminisce about happier times, she knew that the dark times would also threaten to come to the forefront. Kate walked to her dad's room and opened the door.

He wasn't one to like change and everything was just as she remembered it. On the bedside table was her mother's urn. Kate gently ran a finger over the name engraved on the dust covered, golden plate. *Rose Eileen Benson*. It hurt Kate that she remembered very little of her mother's voice. If only she had been allowed to talk about her mother more when she was a child. Maybe then she'd have been reminded from time to time about the special attributes that made her mother so amazing.

Remembering the fireproof safety box in the closet, Kate assumed that was where her father still kept his important papers. She opened the closet and as expected she saw the box on a shelf. She also spotted a small arsenal of guns and rifles. She didn't remember those. Her brows furrowed but she chose to keep on task and pay no attention to the weapons. She grabbed the box realizing it was locked and she wasn't sure where to look for the key. She'd take it back to the house with her and hope that Mr. Tyler had a way of opening it.

Kate moved down the hall to her old room. She wasn't sure what she had expected to see when she entered. Kate thought maybe her father had used her room for storage like he had threatened when she left. However, when she opened the door it was like she was stepping back in time seven years. Yellowed tape on the walls still held photos of her, the Tylers, and various high school friends. A small smile lifted the corners of her mouth as she took in the old images. One, in particular, caught her attention. She and Dan sat on a brick wall and in the background was Lake Ontario. They held hands and looked so deliriously happy. She tugged the picture down and stuffed it in the same jacket pocket as the note, reminding Kate of the original reason for coming to the house.

Find Bunny. Kate scanned her room until her eyes rested on her bed. She sat on the old quilt and spotted a familiar fluffy leg from behind the corner of a pillow sham. She pulled it free and held it for a moment in her hands. At one time, it had been pink. Now it was a dirty gray. Instinctively, she held it to her face like she did as a child. Something bulky inside caught her attention. It felt small and stick-like. Maybe a key? One of the seams looked as if it had been opened and hastily sewn shut. It wasn't the same as Grandma Lydia's handiwork, that was for sure. *Why so mysterious, Dad?* Kate tucked the bunny in her other pocket and got up to leave when she looked back at where she had pulled the bunny from.

Moving the pillow away Kate revealed a stack of folded notes. There had to be hundreds of notes, some with more pages than others. She opened one and saw her father's handwriting. The letter started like he was continuing an ongoing conversation with someone. It talked of how he had cleaned out part of the garage and found a stash of her Barbie dolls hidden behind a large tool chest. *I remember how you loved playing where you weren't supposed to. I miss that about you.*

Kate refolded the letter quickly and opened another. This one contained many pages and was stapled together. It started with the words: *I've been putting off telling you this but you need to know everything I've done.* Her eyes scanned down the page, but she couldn't bring herself to read it all. She felt tears threatening. Spotting her old backpack, Kate threw the locked box and the notes inside. Later she would read them. Maybe much later.

It was as Kate put the backpack over her shoulder that she heard noises outside. The sun was sinking lower in the late afternoon hour. She moved to the window and looked out to see two men getting out of an unfamiliar truck. Her breath caught in her throat as she watched them moving closer to the house. She had left the front door unlocked. Instinctively, she moved her hand to her cell phone in her jeans pocket. If she called 911, would the police even arrive in time?

Maybe she was overreacting. Maybe they were just friends who didn't know her father was in the hospital. Kate texted the one person who she thought she could count on to get to her quickly. Dan.

"There are men at Dad's house. Don't know them."

A moment later her phone vibrated with the words, "Why are you there? Stay put. On my way."

Kate didn't have time to feel put out with Dan's overbearingness. The door downstairs swung open and raucous laughter and talking announced the strangers' entry. Springing into action, Kate ran to her father's room and grabbed the rifle she had noticed earlier. Easing the bedroom door shut, she held her breath listening to the men below. She didn't know if the blasted thing was even loaded and she didn't know how to shoot even if it was. Something told her she was about to get a crash course.

7

Kate held her breath and stood motionless behind the bedroom door as she heard the men walk past her hiding place. She waited for the sound of the creaky floorboards down the hall to alert her that she had the all-clear. With rifle in hand and backpack awkwardly slung over her shoulder, she swung the door open and bolted to the stairs.

She heard the gruff voices shouting behind her, but she didn't stop. As she hit the top of the steps, she remembered their poor condition and did her best to maneuver the tricky spots. On any other day, she would've been proud of herself for the prowess it took to make it to the landing safely. However, there was no time to pat herself on the back. The smell of heavy cigarette smoke and the sound of an angry man shouting propelled her forward. The front door was in sight. If she could get to the woods, she could hide.

"Hey, you! Stop!" The man yelled after her. "She's got a gun!"

"Don't let her go!" said the other.

She ran through the door and blinked as her eyes tried to adjust to the light again. Her sneakers hit the grass as she jumped over the weak porch steps and noticed another figure coming up on her right. Where had this person come from? She had only seen two emerge from the truck earlier. He ran towards her with significant speed and she wasn't optimistic she could make it to safety without a fight.

With a loud angry cry, she spun on her heels and tried to get the rifle in what she thought was the right position. Yet before she could attempt to aim the rifle, she felt her legs being kicked out from under her. As she fell, a hand shot out and grabbed the rifle's barrel pointing it upwards and away from any target. From her place on the cold ground, Kate's eyes which had been clenched shut started to pry themselves open. She saw a seething Dan pushing the magazine release on the weapon. Pulling back the bolt of the rifle, Dan let out a choice word and released the chambered round. Then his furious gaze landed on her.

"You could've killed someone! This was *loaded*, Kate!" He raged and dropped the emptied rifle to the ground.

The other two men, out of breath, approached Dan from behind and Kate pointed at them in fear. When Dan turned to see who she was looking at, he didn't seem affected at all.

"They ... They were in my dad's house! In the bedrooms!"

"Do you know this lady, Boss?" The one managed to wheeze out the words, while the other was bent over with his hands on his knees gasping for air.

Kate's eyes darted to Dan. *"Boss?"*

"She's Tom's daughter," Dan told the man while reaching down a hand to help Kate up off the ground. It was the act of a gentleman, but his eyes shot flames at her.

Kate hit his hand away as she attempted to get up on her own. She forgot she still had the backpack on her shoulder, however, and the weight caused her to fall right back down in a humiliating heap. Dan attempted once more to help by lifting the backpack off her shoulder, but Kate hissed and slapped at his hand repeatedly like a feral animal. "I don't need your help!"

While she struggled to get to her feet in a mighty ungraceful way, Kate heard the stranger laugh and say, "Yep. That's Tom's daughter all right."

"Charles, can you take this inside, please? I have no idea where she found it. Just put it in the coat closet. I'll deal with it later," Dan instructed.

As Kate got to her feet, albeit unsteadily, she looked at the man who had been a threat just moments before. His expression was one of amusement. Kate felt her chin raise in indignation.

"I'll make sure everything is locked up after I help Bud find his phone." Charles then nodded at Kate politely and pulled on Bud's arm as he walked back towards the house.

"What was so crazy important that you couldn't wait?" The way Dan demanded the information as if he had any right or reason to know her plans, caused Kate's ire to rise.

Kate turned on her heels and limped her way to the path towards the Tylers' house, ignoring him altogether.

"Kate!" She heard his footfall behind her and soon he was in step next to her, eyes staring at the side of her head as if he expected an answer.

"I don't need your permission to go into my own house. I told you I needed to get my father's papers."

"Wait... *Your* house?" He put his hand on her arm to stop her and she shrugged him off.

"Yes. *My* house. Why is that so hard to grasp?"

She started moving forward, realizing he was still standing behind her with his mouth open like an ugly widemouthed bass.

"He didn't tell you." The words caused Kate to pause again and she spun on her heel to face her old friend.

"Tell me what?"

It was Dan's turn to walk ahead now and he ran his hand through his hair in frustration. Kate could tell he was trying to measure his words.

"Tell me what?" Kate repeated loudly.

"Your father promised he had told you."

"Just spit it out already."

Dan turned to her, his expression soft and tender a dramatic change from moments before. Kate felt her insides twist. "He sold the house to me."

Kate stood and stared blankly ahead as the news sunk in.

"I was doing repairs for him because he couldn't keep up with everything that was falling apart. He asked me if I was interested. I said yes ... as long as *you* were okay with it." Dan's brow furrowed as he searched her face. "Kate, say something. I thought you knew. I'm sorry if ..."

They approached the cabin she had passed on the way to her father's house and Dan stood still. "I can show you the deed if you don't believe me. Wait here for a minute."

"The deed?"

"Yes. It's in my cabin."

"Your cabin," Kate repeated his words numbly as she realized the cabin was Dan's home. *Well, one of them.* "No. I don't need to see it. I believe you."

Kate continued to move down the path.

"Kate, please talk to me. I need to know that you understand I didn't try to ..."

"Why am I surprised?" Kate laughed sardonically as her pace picked up. Dan followed uncomfortably at her side, like a scolded puppy. "Of course, he sold you the house. It's just one last way for him to dig the knife into my heart. One last twist of the blade."

"It's not like that... Not at all."

She didn't want to hear anyone come to Tom Benson's defense. Why was everyone so blind to his actions? Tears stung her eyes.

"He thought you'd be able to use the money. He never thought you'd want to live there again."

"I *don't*. You can have that stupid house." Kate marched ahead of Dan as they came back to the clearing and the Tyler house came into view. "I hope you and ... and .... Shelly ... have a great life in that house. Fill it with kids for all I care!"

"Staci."

"What?" Kate spat.

"Staci. Her name is Staci."

Kate turned around to face Dan waving her hands wildly in the air. "I don't care! Have a wonderful life!"

With that, Kate left Dan in the dust and entered the house letting the door slam behind her. Mr. Tyler startled himself awake as she passed him to go to her guestroom. Colleen looked up from her book, stunned. Kate paid them no mind and continued her rant until she was safely away from everyone else. "I don't care if I have to hitchhike. Tomorrow I am gone. Back to Mark. Back to Boston ... and back to *my* life."

Throwing the backpack onto the bed, Kate threw herself down next to it. The image of Dan and his future family living inside her house drove her crazy. The fact that her father thought that it was a good idea made her even more so. Reaching for her phone Kate dialed Mark and when he didn't answer she landed back on her pillow with a thud and let herself cry. Kate sobbed herself into a fitful sleep. She slept so deeply that she never even realized her phone started buzzing next to her on the bed, illuminating Mark's name in the twilight of the room.

*****

Tony followed the instructions he was given to the lake house, parking in a secluded wooded area rather than driving down the long drive to the house. Someday he wanted to own a place like this, surrounded by nature and no people for miles. Only the rich could afford vacation homes like this. Doctors. Politicians. *Judges*.

The Sunday sun was setting as Tony approached the end of the vacant drive. One of his uncle's men had dropped Eddie and James off at Judge Blocker's house earlier that day. Tony could only assume they had completed what they set out to do. He looked past the grand house with the wrap around porch to the lake in the background. A stratum of colors hovered above the waters as a witness to what was transpiring below. On the dock, two men in wet suits lifted another man onto a boat.

"What took you so long? Hurry up!" James hissed as his nephew approached. "Grab that fishing pole and hand it to me."

Tony complied quickly. "I have news. I know where she is!"

"Grab that tackle box, too." James handed the fishing pole to Eddie. "Make this look like it was cast."

"Did you hear me? I know where Benson's daughter is. And I'm pretty sure *Daddy* is there too."

"Put that wet suit on. Can you swim?"

Tony just stood staring at the two men incredulously. Eddie had a smile of superiority on his smug face and Tony's uncle let out a sigh before saying. "Yeah ... she's in Deer Creek, New York. We already know. Can you swim? I don't have time to rescue you if..."

"How did you know?" Tony demanded as he grabbed the folded wetsuit lying on a bench.

"Eddie did some digging into the Benson's past. Are you going to just stand there? Get up here already and be useful for once."

Numbly, Tony complied, stripping from his clothes and putting on the wetsuit before joining his uncle and his nemesis on the dock. His mind reeled and inside he seethed. How could Eddie have gotten that information? He had to kill for it and this smug ...

"Sit down, Tony Boy," Eddie smirked, interrupting Tony's hate filled ponderings. "You don't want us to capsize, do you?"

Tony looked down at the man lying on the floor of the boat. He was much older than he had expected. He was wearing waders and looked ready for a leisurely day of fishing on the lake. Somehow, Tony doubted this was what he had had in mind. "Is he ..."

"Not yet, but if you keep wasting time and he wakes up, you both will be." James glared at his nephew before giving Eddie the go ahead to undo the ropes. They shoved off from the pier and James nodded to the paddles on either side of the boat's interior. "Paddle us to the center."

Once Eddie and Tony got them to the center of the lake as instructed, James double checked the pulse of their target.

He was still breathing. There was a faint heartbeat and the chloroform would wear off soon. During the planning stages, his uncle explained that to make it look like a fishing accident, the man needed to have his lungs fill up with the lake water. Therefore, when they threw the judge in the water, he needed to be alive. Eddie got to his feet and threw the fishing pole into the water before turning to Tony. "Grab his legs."

Cursing under his breath, Tony carefully got to his feet trying to ensure his balance didn't cause the boat to dip to one side more than the other. "I don't take orders from you."

"Really? 'Cause it kinda looks like you do." Eddie smiled as he bent down to grab the upper torso.

Stand up for yourself, Kid! Don't let him talk to you like that.

"I can't," Tony muttered. He brought his hand to his forehead and rubbed an invisible spot with great aggravation.

"What's your problem? Who are you talking to? What's this kid doing, James?" Eddie was amused.

"Quit screwing around. We have to get going," James hissed at both of them.

The men began swinging the body of the old man over the edge of the boat. "One … two … three…"

With a splash, the man landed in the lake.

"Goodbye, Judge Blocker," James muttered. The list had its first name crossed off. The plan was now in motion and Tony knew there was no going back now.

The judge's waders did their intended job to pull him down into the murky lake, but what they didn't expect was for the man's eyes to fly open and begin to flail his arms wildly. He began gasping. His calls for help were getting a little too loud and Tony watched as his uncle glanced around the shoreline. James fixated on something and sighed in exasperation. Tony instantly noticed what got his uncle's attention. Further down the water's edge was another house. His uncle turned to him and said, "Finish him."

"I've got it." Eddie dove into the water without hesitation, causing the boat to rock like crazy.

Tony watched with part hatred and part admiration as Eddie wrapped his arms and legs around the man, bringing his face under the waves. The old man sputtered and gasped several times and they rose and sank into the water repeatedly. Then the thrashing ceased and only Eddie emerged with his obnoxious look of satisfaction.

Uncle James thumped him on the chest, drawing him from his thoughts. "Come on. Help me get the boat overturned."

They put all of the weight to one side and Eddie aided from his place in the water, pulling on the side that dipped low. Soon the boat capsized, plunging Tony and his uncle into the brisk lake. The coldness took his breath and, at first, he was immobilized. Eddie grabbed onto his arm to help him to shore, but Tony shook him off and began to swim on his own. They made it to the pier, pulling themselves out of the water only to be met by the chilly autumn breeze.

"Hurry up and get changed. You better not leave anything behind." James instructed his two accomplices. "Did you park where I told you?"

"Yes."

James grabbed a duffel bag from the underside of a bush and led the way back to the road. Once at the truck, Tony noticed that Eddie paused and turned back to the house, his cell phone in his hand. "Come on! What are you doing? Let's go."

"Hold your horses, Little Man. Just get the truck started." Tony looked at James with shock wondering if his uncle had even heard what was happening, but his uncle was smiling and climbing into the back seat.

Then as if a fire was lit under him, Eddie jumped in the front seat and yelled, "Go! Go! Go! Everything is back online in two minutes."

Tony pushed his foot down to the floor and sped out of the cover of trees onto the asphalt and down the road back to civilization. "What was that about?"

"Eddie hacked into the houses' system to make sure the power was off and the cameras were disengaged until we could get out of there," James said with pride from the backseat.

"Smart houses aren't always that smart." Eddie rested his head against the seat rest and looked at Tony. "It's okay, Tony. You'll catch on eventually."

Playfully Eddie reached over to muss Tony's hair, but Tony grabbed his wrist and bent it at an angle that surprised the arrogant passenger. "Nice grip, Kid."

"Don't mess with me. You don't know what I'm capable of." An image of the lifeless woman's body on the kitchen floor floated to the forefront of Tony's thoughts. He released Eddie's wrist and watched in satisfaction as the man rubbed it.

"Well, let's hope we'll finally get to see what you're capable of because we're not done yet," James asserted. Tony looked in the rearview mirror at his uncle, letting his words take root.

Oh, James will see exactly what you are capable of.

Tony nodded at his father's voice echoing in his head. There was no doubt about that. Tony felt something shift in his thinking as he grew weary of seeking the approval of someone else. When the moment was right, James and Eddie would both see just exactly what Tony could do... without them.

8

"Dan Tyler came today to begin construction on a bathroom downstairs. I'm finally to the point where I can't go up and down the stairs without risking the chance I might fall. I really wished you two would get married someday. I know he loves you. He still does and it's been years since you left us. Someday he's going to have to move on. I think I'm going to ask if he wants to buy this place. It makes sense. He can live close to his parents and raise a family. They'll get to be close to their grandkids. I know I don't deserve the right to wish I could've had the same, but I can't help but wish I would get to be a part of your life and someday get to hold my own grandbabies. Even if you were still here, I know I wouldn't be alive much longer anyway. I'll sell Dan the house and you'll get the money. At least that way something I did has contributed some value to your life..."

Kate sat on the porch's wicker couch and placed the finished note on top of the pile of letters she had already read that morning. Kate found herself wide awake before the sun rose with swollen and achy eyes. No one else was awake in the house so in the serene early morning hours Kate read her father's thoughts. He seemed to use the letters to his daughter as a journal. Some letters were short, others were long. In some notes, he just expressed his disgust at the world's condition. In other letters, he recounted memories from Kate's childhood that she thought he had totally been absent from.

"I was thinking about the homecoming game from your junior year tonight. Remember that floozy Sandi Williams hurt her knee and you got to be the one they tossed in the air? I hate crowds and I didn't stay long, but I got to see

them hold you up so high. I thought my heart would burst. You looked like an angel ..." That was Kate's favorite letter. It caused her to openly weep.

The next letter was the thick one she had only scanned at her father's house. Yet as she sat in the early morning light, she felt the air leave her lungs. Words like *planted evidence* and *he killed your mother* left her in stunned silence. Her mind was spinning with each page she flipped. Her father's handwriting grew erratic in certain spots and so did her heartbeat. Page by page she was learning who her father was and why.

"The pastor told me I needed to let go of the past and that Christ forgave me. Granted he said this not knowing the whole truth. I don't know if you'll ever read these, but this is my confession and my recognition that I hurt you. I'm sorry, Kate. I know I became a monster. I'm not making excuses. I should never have started drinking. I know it made me mean, but it wasn't the alcohol that kept me distant from you. I was trying to keep you safe. Even now I don't know if it worked..."

The front door opened to the house and Kate jumped, knocking the papers onto the porch.

"I'm sorry. I didn't mean to scare you. Wasn't expecting to see anyone out here this early," Mr. Tyler said as he bent down to pick up the scattered papers. It was when he handed them back to her and saw her tears that he sat next to her on the couch.

They sat in silence for what felt like an eternity and Kate surprised both she and Mr. Tyler when she put her head on his shoulder. In that moment, she was that nine year old girl all over again needing a fatherly touch. Needing comfort. Needing reassurance.

"I'm sorry." Her voice sounded pathetic to her own ears. "I was horrible last night."

Kate felt Mr. Tyler nod and she looked up at him expecting to see reproof. Instead, she saw such compassion.

"I know you are hurting, Katie Bug. No one is upset with you, just worried."

"Why couldn't *you* have been my father?"

"Well, I think the good Lord had other ideas in mind." John chuckled. "You might not see it yet, but God isn't done with you, Kate. He uses everything we go through for a reason, even the painful things."

"I think God left me a long time ago."

"You think so?" Mr. Tyler shifted on the couch to face Kate with a smile on his face that told her she was going to hear a thing or two. "Do you think He wasn't there when you crashed? That could've gone way worse than it did. What about when you grabbed a loaded rifle and nearly killed yourself?"

Kate looked at him, shocked.

"Didn't think I would hear about that, did you? After the way you came into the house last night, we called Dan."

"Dad sold him the house."

Mr. Tyler nodded. "I know. I'm sorry *you* didn't. I don't agree with how Tom handled a lot of his life, Kate, but I *do* like what I've seen God doing in his life these last several months."

Kate looked at John skeptically and he continued his thoughts. "Parents fail. Some more than others. Yet, we *all* fail our kids. There's only one Father who doesn't, Kate. He's the one you should be clinging to right now, not me."

Kate scoffed. "You're talking about *God* again, aren't you?"

"I am." He got to his feet and smiled down at Kate, probably much like he smiled at his own daughter. "I've got to get my day started, but I think Colleen is inside getting breakfast ready. You may want to talk to her. I know she was pretty worried about you."

Kate nodded contritely and John Tyler winked at her before walking off the porch and towards his barns. Kate pondered on what he had said to her for a moment when she felt her phone vibrate in her pocket. *Uncle Pete!*

"Uncle Pete, you and I have a lot to chat about," Kate answered her cell phone ready to hash it all out with her father's oldest and only friend.

"Where are you?" he demanded.

"No. I'm going to ask the questions right now. When were you going to tell me about what happened with you and Dad?"

"Are you with him? Are you in New York?"

"Don't change the subject…"

"Kate, there's a woman on your kitchen floor … dead. Just tell me where you are. Tell me you're safe."

Kate felt all the color drain from her face. Had she heard him correctly? "*Dead?*"

"Yes, dead. She was identified as your aunt's neighbor, Mrs. Angie Simpson. Her husband came looking for her when he couldn't find her. Her throat was slit. Your aunt is flying back today. I just need to know where *you* are."

"I'm in Deer Creek. Dad is in the hospital."

"Stay there. Under *no* circumstances are you to come back here. Do you hear me?"

"Mrs. Simpson! She was feeding the cat for me until I got home. I told her it was just for a couple of days. I was supposed to be back today."

"I'm getting in touch with the local police there. They're going to ask you questions and collaborate with the officers here. You stay put, Kate. Do not set one foot back in Boston until things are all clear, do you understand?"

"Was it a break-in? Who would do that to her?" The silence on the other end made Kate's blood grow cold. "Peter, who did this?"

"Did your father talk to you?"

"He's on oxygen and it's hard for him to get words out. He left me letters. I know what you and he did."

"The local police think this is a break-in, but I'm telling you it wasn't. Kate, they were coming for you."

*****

He didn't know what he had expected to find when he walked over to his parents that Monday morning, but it definitely wasn't the police car parked in front of the house. He ran up the steps and into the house to find Colleen with her arm wrapped around a very pale, shaking Kate. His father sat in his recliner taking everything in quietly, scrutinizing every word. Detective Martin sat in a chair facing Kate, his face intense as usual. Luke Martin attended church with them every Sunday. People who knew him also knew he was an overgrown teddy bear. However, those who were on the wrong side of the law saw his less than amicable qualities. He was a detective in the major crimes unit for the county. The fact he sat in his parents' home for a reason other than a social call meant something was seriously wrong.

"Do you know of anyone that would want to hurt you? Detective McKinney is requesting a lot of men and resources to keep an eye on you, Miss Benson. I need to know why."

"What's going on?" Dan finally asked. Colleen motioned for her son to sit down and to hush.

"No one wants to hurt me. I don't know why he requested that."

Kate's eyes met Dan's and that is when he knew she was holding something back.

"Why would he request surveillance on you at this house, Miss. Benson? It's an odd request considering it's a robbery gone wrong. In another state, I might add. He must feel there is some threat to you to suggest you need protection."

"He's always been over-protective of me. Uncle Peter thinks it's possibly someone my father put away a long time ago. My dad has had him watching me since I left Deer Creek after high school. I swear, no one wants to hurt me." There it was again. *The swallow*. It was Kate's tell. As kids, when they played games she always gave herself away. What was she hiding?

"What can you tell me about Mrs. Simpson, the deceased?"

Deceased? Dan's eyes flew to Kate.

"She was very nice. No one ever said anything bad about her. She was willing to help me feed my aunt's cat even though it was short notice. I don't know who would do this." Kate cried into a tissue.

"If this was an interrupted robbery, can you think of anything that someone would want in your aunt's house?" The detective scribbled notes onto his pad of paper before looking Kate straight in the eye.

"No. My aunt isn't rich. Maybe someone saw me leave the house early in the morning with suitcases. I don't know. I'm trying to make sense of this myself."

The Detective Martin got to his feet. He handed Kate a card and said, "If you remember anything else, reach out."

Kate nodded and stared blankly at the card.

"Miss Benson, I know your father isn't doing well. I assume that means you will be here for the foreseeable future to handle his affairs?"

"I… I was planning on going home today."

"I recommend you hang around a bit. Especially while they sort things out at your aunt's place. I'm sure Colleen wouldn't mind keeping you around a little longer."

Colleen smiled sweetly. "She knows very well that she's welcome here."

"Your father doesn't talk much," Detective Martin said to Kate. "But when he did say something, it was normally about you. I know he's proud of you."

Kate smiled weakly. "Thank you."

"If you need anything, please let me know. I don't know what's going on back in Boston, but if I can help you while you are here I expect a call."

"I'll walk you out, Luke." John Tyler finally spoke up and followed his friend out the door.

"I need to get to the hospital," Kate stated. Then she slapped her head as if remembering something. "I forgot to call into work."

"You need to eat something. You go get ready and call work. I'll make you something to take with you to the hospital," Colleen directed. Kate looked genuinely appreciative at that moment. Whatever was going on, Kate was unnerved.

The door opened and his father reappeared. After he made sure no one else was within earshot, he approached his son.

"Luke said he wants us to keep an eye on Kate, not letting her go out alone. He's not certain that this is about someone Tom put away, but he wants to be careful."

"So now we're babysitters."

"Something like that. I'll talk to your brothers as well. You don't have to hover. He's not completely convinced it's that serious, but until we know for sure, maybe you could take her to the hospital today?"

Dan sighed. "That's going to go over well with Staci, I'm sure."

"I can see if your mom will go with her. She was going to try to get things ready for that class trip that's supposed to come by Wednesday."

"It's okay. I can talk to Staci and let her know what's happening. I don't think Kate should be driving anywhere by herself anyway. She doesn't look like she's doing too good right now."

His father agreed with a nod. Shortly after that was said, Kate emerged from the guest room looking more put together, though definitely not up to her usual self-imposed standard. No makeup. Dressed simply in jeans and a sweatshirt. Her hair was pulled up in a messy bun and Dan had to look away. She was more beautiful than he had ever seen her. *Help me, Lord. My mind can't go there.*

"Kate, Dan will take you to see your dad at the hospital. When you get back, I have the number of a lawyer who will help you weed through Tom's papers. I think Luke was right, you need to stay around a while longer."

To Dan's surprise, Kate didn't put up a fight. She nodded quietly. "I just called the office. I have quite a buildup of paid time off and they're going to let me use that."

"That's good! Now you're talking sensible!" John pressed a kiss to her forehead and went to find his wife before he went back to his work.

"You ready?" Dan asked. Kate nodded and followed him to his truck.

The trip was painfully silent until Kate out of the blue blurted, "I'm sorry for yesterday. This isn't what I ... This entire trip hasn't gone how it was supposed to."

His heart constricted at the pain in her voice. "Yeah. I get that. I'm sorry, too. I really thought your dad told you about the house, Kate."

"Can you tell your friends I'm sorry... you know ... for almost killing them?" There was something in the way she said it, mostly serious yet with a hint of mischievousness, that broke through his defenses.

Dan smiled and turned to his passenger. "I think they were entertained by you more than fearful. But ... might I recommend having someone go over gun safety with you if you ever plan on even *looking* at a gun in the future?"

"Are you volunteering?" Kate smiled back playfully. Then as if she caught herself she grew silent again and quickly looked out the window.

Her cell phone rang and she fumbled awkwardly to answer it.

"Mark! I'm so sorry. It's good to hear your voice, too. Yes, I know you've been worried."

It wasn't as if he was trying to listen in, but the man on the other line spoke loud enough that Dan could hear what he was saying. "What is going on? I was watching the news and I saw your place... I drove by and saw police everywhere."

"Yeah. I'm not sure what happened. My aunt is coming back early. I think I'll be staying here longer. Dad is still alive and I should probably ..."

"Of course. That makes sense. I'm worried about you taking on all of this by yourself."

"I'm not really alone. I have good friends."

Dan gave her a side glance.

"Well, some of them are good. Others are more annoying than anything." She smiled and Dan felt his own expression lighten. How could she still have this effect on him?

They turned into the hospital parking lot.

"Mark, I'm getting ready to head into the hospital. I'll call you tonight at six. See? I'm telling you the exact time so we can stop missing each other's calls. You better answer this time," Kate teased.

Dan wanted to gag when he heard the voice on her phone say, "I'll be living for six o'clock then."

Dan pulled the truck up to the visitor's entrance and turned to Kate. "You told him you don't know what happened. Why?"

"Why *what*?" Kate wasn't making eye contact. "I *don't* know what happened."

"It was an attempted burglary, right?" Dan prodded and waited for her response.

"Right."

"Kate, does this have something to do with why your dad was so panicked to get to you?"

Kate cleared her throat and Dan watched as the wheels in her head started spinning. "He's on morphine. The nurse said it can make him agitated."

"But that's not it, is it? I saw your expression when you were talking to Luke. What's going on?"

"I can't ..." She shook her head. For a moment Dan saw her wall start to crumple, but then just as quickly she built it back up. "It was a robbery. That's all it was."

He stared at her a moment longer. She knew *he* knew there was more to it. She raised her chin before she finally said, "Thank you for the ride. I don't know how long I will be."

"It's okay. Take your time. I've got some calls to make and then I may pop up to see Tom as well." Dan assured her as she got out of the truck. *Calls to make*. One call in particular. He dialed Staci's number after he parked, praying as he did that she would be understanding of the latest events, Luke's request, and that it looked like Kate Benson was going to be around a little while longer.

9

The doors of the elevator closed and Kate tried to keep her hands from shaking. How could Dan read her so well even after all those years? When she kept back a few details from her statement to the detective she thought she was pulling off a confident laissez faire attitude. She needed to work on her poker face. There was a lot more than her safety at stake.

Peter's words from their phone conversation earlier echoed in her head.

"Kate, listen to me. Now that you know about what happened ... what you say when the police question you can hurt both your father and me. You might be mad at your dad, but I have a lot to lose, and I have been there for you all these years. Haven't I?"

"Uncle Peter.."

"Haven't I?"

"Yes. Of course."

"You have to act like this is all brand new to you. Say nothing, Kate. All anyone needs to know is that someone your dad put away is now out of jail. You don't need to say anything more."

Now as Kate walked numbly to her father's room she felt her insides quiver. She had agreed to keep their secret. Just as she had as a little girl. She remembered that time in her life well. She had woken up for school that day to find her father passed out on the couch in the living room. Beer cans and bottles lay on the floor around him. It was one of many times her father couldn't get her to school. Kate had to forge letters to the school to explain her absence. If her father had gotten in trouble, they might've taken her away so Kate just learned to make sure she was up early enough to ride with the Tyler kids.

With a sigh, Kate entered the room and the television played a national news channel, presumably for background noise. She was surprised to see a man in a suit sitting next to her father. He held a Bible and as she got closer she recognized the kind demeanor of Pastor Munson.

"Oh, my word! The rumors are true! You *are* home," he said with a wide grin and rose to his feet to greet Kate.

"Hello, Pastor Al. It's been a while."

"Yes, it has. I'm so happy to see you here, but I wish it was under different circumstances."

Kate stood awkwardly and stared down at her sleeping father. His mouth was wide open as he struggled for breath and his eyes were clenched shut as if he was in discomfort. It was a pitiful sight. Kate brought her attention back to the man before her.

"How are Mrs. Munson, Ana, and Alexis?"

"The girls are off doing their own thing. Mary's cancer seems to be in remission."

"I'm so sorry. I didn't know she had been sick."

Pastor Munson smiled in appreciation before changing the subject. "I'm sorry I wore him out. We were discussing some of his wishes. I think we have things in place for when…"

"Good. That's good. I wasn't really sure about all of that." Kate fidgeted in her spot and started wringing her hands. The silence that followed was painful, to say the least. She racked her brain for what to say at that moment. The timing might have seemed abrupt but Kate had a question and the pastor was the only one, other than her father, who would know the answer. "They tell me he got *saved*. Do you think it was real?"

"Did it *take*, you mean?" He chuckled softly before looking back at Tom. "Yes, Kate. It took. When I first started visiting your father, he met me at his door with some very rough words. More like threats. Then after a few visits, he shocked me by asking when I would come back and talk with him, almost like he was enjoying it. We had lots of conversations in that old living room, mostly superficial stuff about sports and the weather. Then, one day he surprised everyone and showed up at church. A few weeks later he came forward for prayer and to ask the Lord to come into his life."

"When you talked with him all those times ... what did he tell you?"

"That's for him to tell you, not me. What I can tell you is that he loves you and that he has grown so much in the last several months. I'm genuinely going to miss him."

Kate saw the sincerity in the man's eyes.

"I hope I'll see you at church Sunday. I know there will be a lot of people excited to see you."

"I don't know. Maybe. It's been a while since I've gone to church."

"Well, you'd be very welcome. Your father prayed for you often." She wanted to laugh out loud. Her father *praying* was not something she envisioned easily. The pastor patted her arm in a goodbye as he left the room and Kate took the vacant chair near the bedside.

She felt conflicted when she looked at the man who had been the object of her hatred for so long. He deserved everything he got. As a father, he was abysmal. Apparently, he had violated quite a few laws as an officer. Yet maybe he *had* changed. Was that even possible? Could people change that dramatically? *God changes lives.* That had been something she heard all the time as a child between the Tylers and her grandparents. It was a common theme in all of the Sunday school classes and summer Bible camps she had attended as a little girl. A long time ago, she thought she had believed that as well. Now, she wasn't so sure. However, everyone seemed to think the world of him. Perhaps they knew this version of her father better than she did.

Tom's eyes fluttered open and scanned the room until they rested on Kate. He blinked several times as if he doubted his vision.

"Hi." Kate scooted her chair closer and spoke softly. Tom struggled to sit up and, clearly, there was something on his mind. "I read your letters."

His body rested back against the bed. He nodded and slid his eyes shut momentarily before opening them again with tears in his eyes. He spoke finally, but the words were raspier than before. "I'm sorry."

"I'm not going to tell anyone. I'll keep the secret. You can rest easy."

"No.... it's not yours to carry." He looked frustrated. What was it he wanted from her? She gave him her word she'd stay silent. She came home despite everything in her resisting the trip. What more did he want?

"I don't get it."

"It's not yours ... My sin is not yours."

Now it was Kate's turn to blink.

"I protect *you* .. not you ... protect *me*." He wheezed and then coughed. His coughs continued to escalate and he motioned to the cup near his bed on a side table.

"Why are you so stubborn?"

His eyes were soft as she brought the cup to his lips and Kate stiffened when he put his hand over hers. Kate gulped and knew she needed to get to the main point of her visit. "I need to know what you want. Everyone is asking me about... end of life things. I don't know how to answer them."

He rested his head back against the pillow and smiled. "Just let me go. I have you. That's all I need."

"What if they want to put you on a ventilator?"

"No! I'm ready to go home." His tone was emphatic. "Give the police my letter."

"But Peter said..."

"We did wrong."

"But what does it matter now? That man is dead. Surely whoever is left in that family has the sense not to get themselves in trouble." Even as she said the words, she pictured the body of her neighbor on the floor of the kitchen. She couldn't tell her father about that. She wanted to believe it was a robbery and she was going to keep telling herself it was nothing more.

"Quit arguing. Just do it."

Kate sat in awkward silence until her father asked, "Did you find the key?"

"To your firebox?"

He nodded.

"It's in the bunny, right?"

He nodded again.

"Very clever, 007." Kate smiled and looked down at her hands. "I haven't opened it yet. There aren't any more surprises, are there? Please tell me now if there are. I can't keep doing this roller coaster. There's nothing more, right? You're not going to tell me that you're a spy or something, are you?"

"Just open it. Follow the directions."

Tom's eyes darted from Kate's face to something behind her. She heard someone clear their throat and Kate turned to see Dan standing there. Admittedly, since her arrival in Deer Creek, he hadn't seemed too thrilled at her presence. Yet, there were moments when he was the same Dan she knew over seven years ago. There were glimpses of his humor and warmth. At that moment, however, as he stood in the doorway his expression was unreadable.

Without looking her in the eye, he said the doctor was at the nurse's station asking for her. With a nod, Kate got up and Dan took the chair next to her father. She found the doctor leaning over a patient's file on the nurse's station.

"Miss Benson? I'm Dr. Carlson. I've been attending your father." The man in the white coat shook Kate's hand. "We've been pleased with this rally he's taken in the last couple of days."

"Do you think he's improving? Is there a chance he could pull out of this?" She wasn't sure why the thought brought her hope, even relief.

"It's common in end of life scenarios for the people to perk up a little bit. Some people start eating, drinking, and communicating better. Most times it's short lived, so I'm going to urge you not to get too excited." The doctor smiled warmly before pulling out a pamphlet. "Since your father is responsive and alert at the moment, we want you to consider transferring him to a hospice facility."

Kate's brow furrowed. "Move him?"

"This facility is great. They are trained in end of life care and he'd have one on one attention. Our ICU is limited on space and…"

"You're kicking him out?"

"The insurance won't cover his stay if it goes on indefinitely, but they might cover hospice…"

"*Might?*"

Just then the conversation was interrupted by the sounds of loud beeping and a flashing light from down the hall. The doctor dashed from her side and ran past her, followed by nurses. Kate turned to see where the activity came from and her heart sank. Her father's room. Joining the rush of people she got into the room just in time for Dan to pull her into his arms to get her out of the way so the medical professionals could do their jobs.

"Come on out here. Let them do what they need to do." He spoke into her hair as he tried to lead her from the room, but she wasn't having it.

Her father convulsed and every gasp and cough produced blood from his mouth.

"No. He was fine. What happened?" Kate demanded loudly to the room.

"Kate, come on."

"No. I'm not leaving. What happened? He was fine!"

Dan managed to pull her out of the room, but not before she saw the doctor and nurses suctioning her father's lungs and injecting medications into his IV line.

"What happened?" Kate looked up at the dazed and confused expression on Dan's face.

"I don't know. He was talking to me then something on the news caught his attention. Then he started breathing funny."

Kate didn't want to cry. She tried to keep it at bay, but she couldn't. She wanted to block the sight of her father spewing blood from her mind forever, but she knew it would haunt her. Even as Dan pulled her close, she began to shake. Soon a nurse came out and directed them to a waiting area.

"He's sedated, but his vitals are erratic. After the nurses get him cleaned up and change his bedding you can go in and be with him. I'm so sorry."

"I don't understand..." Kate whispered.

"I don't understand, Daddy." Kate held her father's hand and looked up into his face. "Where is she?"

Her father stayed stoically silent. He had just returned from the hospital where his wife had been rushed after the shooting. Kate's grandparents wasted no time getting there to be by their side as soon as her father called. Grandma Lydia came and knelt next to her and said gently, "Mommy is with Jesus, Katie."

"But, Daddy, you were just at the hospital with her, right? Can't the doctors make her better?" Her father sank into a chair, letting go of her hand. "They made my broken arm better. They'll make Mommy better, too."

"Sometimes things can't be made better, Katie. Sometimes doctors can't fix people." His words were spoken monotone and his eyes stared straight ahead.

"But Jesus can. Mommy told me so. We can just pray. Right, Grandma?"

Grandma Lydia pulled Katie into her arms. "Sometimes Jesus heals us by taking us home to Heaven, Katie. Your mommy loved Jesus so much and she knew that when Jesus told her it was time she'd get to go be in Heaven with Him."

"Jesus told her it was time?" Kate started crying then. "But I want to go with her."

Tom sobbed then. "Me too. Oh, God, just let me go with her. I can't live this life without her. Take me, too."

*****

The ride home was deafeningly silent. Dan tried to process what had just happened. One minute he was sulking over a conversation with Staci that went horribly wrong. Then he was holding Kate in his arms as she went through the trauma of seeing her father fight to breathe. He went over the details of the past hours over and over in his mind. When he sat down next to Tom's bedside, the man thanked him for being with Kate and watching over her. Dan hadn't wanted to tell him that just moments before he had been forced by Staci to promise that he would avoid Kate from there on.

Then Tom, whose color was already a sickening yellow, seemed to pale as he watched something on the television.

"What's wrong? Tom, are you okay?" Dan looked at the TV screen to see what had caught his attention. The anchor said something about a well known judge being mourned after drowning. A fisherman found his body along the shoreline of a lake. Tom had acted frantic and tried to speak, but words weren't coming. Then he started gasping for air and spitting up blood. Dan pushed the emergency button to get help as the heart monitor beeped and went wild.

He looked over at his quiet passenger. Kate sat staring at a pamphlet for a hospice facility the entire drive home. His heart twisted in his chest and he prayed that God would show him what to do. What could he say? Tom's death was inevitable. It had been inevitable since the doctor gave him the diagnosis years back. What part was *Dan* to play in helping Kate through the pain? Was it worth hurting the relationship he had with Staci to be a friend to Katie at that moment? Did he even see a future with Staci? As Dan pulled the truck into the driveway he had no answers. Kate got out and walked mutely to the house and he stayed where he was. Suddenly, he put the truck in reverse knowing he had to talk to Staci, praying as he drove that God would give him words to say and Staci the ability to understand.

10

Peter McKinney muttered under his breath as he tried to get the cap off the oil well of his engine. It wouldn't budge and he felt the pressure to get on the road quickly. He and his wife had a long drive ahead of them. The news that morning spoke in depth on Judge Blocker's accidental drowning death. Peter knew very well it was not accidental. James had a very long time to make a hit list while sitting in his jail cell. It didn't surprise Peter that Judge Blocker would be near the top of that list. He had been the judge to sentence him to the maximum time possible and even mocked James when he had tried to insinuate his brother had been killed wrongfully. Peter assumed the next on that list would've been the lawyers involved but both had passed away before he was released. Only two people remained on that list… he and Tom.

He wouldn't be able to relax until he and Hannah were safely out of the area. Once they got to Florida, he could make sure they lived in a modern day Fort Knox. Until then, he felt like a sitting duck. A noise caught his attention and he looked around the corner of his car's hood to see a familiar face walking towards the garage with a smile. He relaxed a little.

"Mark! I wasn't expecting to see you here. How are you?" He hoped he didn't sound as unstable as he felt. He needed to hold himself together.

"Hey, Peter! I'm doing great. Are you heading out somewhere?"

"If I can get this cap off." Peter tried to come across as lighthearted.

"Let me give it a try." Mark moved to the engine alongside Peter to give his strength a try. "Has Kate talked to you lately?"

"Uh, no. I know she's busy trying to sort out her father's things."

"Yeah, she's told me that. I just feel bad that she is all by herself. I was thinking of going to see her." Mark struggled with the cap. "Do you have a wrench? This is pretty tight."

"I packed everything away. The movers took it all. Let me go check in the trunk if I still have something useful."

Peter moved to the back of the car and struggled with what to tell Mark. If Kate wanted him involved, she would've talked to him about the situation. Mark seemed like a great guy. Maybe it would be good to send Kate some support, he thought.

"Never mind, I got it." Mark held up the cap in his hand with a look of victory. "I don't go to the gym for nothing, you know."

"I miss being your age. I'm hoping Florida will bring some of my youthfulness back."

Mark laughed with a nod. "I'm sure it will. You look good on oil. See?"

Peter looked at the dipstick and felt himself relax. He shouldn't need to stop anytime soon. The calm he felt made him feel generous. "I'll tell you what, let me call Kate and see if she'd like company before I send you down there. You and I both know how she is. She doesn't really go for surprises."

"Even if it's me?"

Peter laughed at the feigned shocked expression on Mark's face. Mark broke into a dimpled smile. It was easy to see why Kate was drawn to this young man. He possessed a certain charm about him.

"I'll call her and then text you her address, okay?" Peter started moving towards the entrance to the house. "I have no idea what is keeping Hannah. The movers came yesterday and got all of our stuff. There's nothing left inside to pack. She's probably having a good cry in every room before we leave."

"You all have a safe trip, Peter. Tell Hannah I said goodbye." Mark waved as he headed back to his car.

As if on cue, Hannah came out of the house. Just as he had suspected, there were tears in her eyes.

"Did you say goodbye to all the rooms?" He said softly as he led her to the passenger seat.

"I'm going to miss this house," she sniffed.

"Well, another family will get to enjoy making memories here while we are living it up in the Sunshine State," Peter said as he got into the driver's seat. He pulled the car out of the garage and reached up to push the button on the garage door opener, only to remember that it was no longer there.

"Old habits die hard." Hannah smiled. "It wouldn't have worked anyway. The electricity was turned off yesterday."

"I guess I have to do this old school."

Peter felt a twinge of nostalgia as he brought down the garage door manually. They raised three kids in that house. There were cookouts out back by the pool and Christmases that made those sappy holiday movies look like rubbish. He would miss this house, but there was nothing that mattered more than the chance to live out the rest of his years away from danger. He just wished Tom could have the same privilege.

With a heartfelt sigh, Peter looked one last time at his house and got back into the car. He held his wife's hand and gave it a squeeze before they drove down the driveway for the very last time.

"Here we go, Hannah. Florida or bust!"

*****

Eddie watched from his place in a secluded driveway as a gray sedan sped past him. He pulled out slowly behind the car, making sure to keep enough of a distance so as not to be noticed. His phone on the seat next to him lit up and with a glance, he saw it was a text from Tony Jr. "Is it done?"

He ignored it and kept his focus where it needed to be. Truthfully, Eddie had no idea why James kept giving that kid chances. He was a liability, not an asset. He was sloppy and impetuous. Loyalty to family was going to ruin everything James had planned. He'd better still pay him if his little vendetta didn't pan out the way he wanted. He had sunk a lot of time and energy into this and he was a professional. He had turned down jobs to see this to completion.

Up ahead was his target area. It was isolated and wooded. Reaching into his jacket pocket he found the burner phone and held his finger over the number that would detonate the device he had stuck on the side of the engine. It all was too easy. Maybe after this job was done he'd look for something more challenging. One ... Two ... Three ... Eddie pressed down on the phone and pushed his brakes to allow himself safety from what was about to happen. A split second later the expected explosion erupted from what used to be a gray sedan.

Eddie knew there wasn't much time, but he needed to make sure the job was complete. Just in case he grabbed the gun in between the driver's seat and middle console, screwing on the silencer before exiting his car. The device in the engine mount should've burned up with the explosion leaving little to no evidence. At least, that is what its designer promised. It didn't really matter if it looked like an accident at this point anyway. Not to him, that is.

The smoke subsided as the breeze shifted. Eddie looked into the car. He didn't have a lot of time before the flames would reach the gas tank and finish the disposal of his handiwork. The wife was gone. That was clear. Somehow, Peter still stirred. Eddie shook his head and sighed in annoyance as he pulled up his gun.

Peter turned his severely injured face towards him and Eddie couldn't help but smirk as the truth registered on the dying man's face. *"Mark?"*

"Goodbye, Peter. Have a safe trip." He fired once into Peter's head, and once into Hannah's ... just in case.

*****

Distraction was good. At least that is what Kate concluded. Tuesday morning dawned and her father was still unconscious. There was nothing she could do for him at the hospital, so Kate decided to dive into the paperwork that needed to be weeded through. Mr. Tyler helped her get in touch with a friend who was a lawyer. Her mind was spinning with all the legalities and paperwork that needed to be signed. Michael's shift ended early and, since Dan disappeared after they got back, he agreed to take Kate anywhere she needed to go. The bank. The lawyer's office.

The notary's office. She appreciated the busyness, while also keeping an eye on her phone for any updates.

"Anywhere else, Milady?" Michael asked in a truly horrible British accent after Kate had gotten back into his truck.

"I don't know. My brain truly feels numb."

"Might I suggest we go home and eat? Everything looks better when you're not hungry."

"Might I suggest you stop talking in that accent? It's really bad, Mike." Kate smirked at her friend. His presence was exactly what she needed. Comic relief.

He laughed and put his hand to his heart as if she had wounded him greatly. "I'll have you know, many young ladies have melted at that accent."

Kate laughed out loud. "They were probably humoring you and didn't want to crush your sweet little spirit."

"You think I'm sweet?" He batted his eyelashes at her.

"Just drive…. Please."

"Home then?"

She nodded. *Home.* It wasn't her home, but at that moment it was the closest thing she had.

Colleen was putting everything on the table as they arrived. Jen was setting the table and Kate noticed it was one plate short. Sean carried in a plate of food and placed it on a trivet. Where was Dan?

"You're just in time. Chicken pot pie right from the oven," Sean said with a warm smile. He came over to Kate and put a gentle arm around her shoulder. "I heard about what happened today at the hospital. I'm sorry, Kate. Let me know if I can help with anything."

"Thank you, Sean." She truly wished she could have a family just like the Tylers in Boston.

He smiled again before going to his place at the table and sitting down. Everyone else took their seats and Mr. Tyler blessed the food. She knew she should've been listening, but Kate squinted through half shut eyes at the empty place at the table. The prayer ended and Michael helped Kate solve the mystery.

"Where's Dan?" He asked scooping an astronomical amount of pot pie onto his plate.

"He called and said he wouldn't be joining us tonight." Colleen's soft tone made Kate think there was more to the story, but it wasn't any of her business.

"He's probably with Staci," Jen surmised. Then after a moment of reflection, the younger Tyler asked, "If they get married, will she be here every day?"

Michael laughed out loud, almost choking on his food. "It won't get to that, believe me."

Colleen cleared her throat and gave her son a stern look. "I don't think we need to hear your input on the matter, Michael."

Kate glanced around the table and noticed Sean's look of amusement as well, but he knew better than to open his mouth.

"Jen, I got a call today from Mrs. Smith. She wanted to know if you might reconsider entering the Fall Days Pageant."

"Ugh, Mom. No. I told you, I'm supposed to be helping Ben with the photo booth."

"They still have the Fall Days Pageant?" Kate was shocked. Somewhere in her storage unit in Boston, stuffed in a box, was her tiara and sash from her junior year.

"Hey! Jen, you can get Kate to help you. She knows all about it, don't you?" Michael nudged Kate in the arm.

"Since when do we encourage pageants?" Mr. Tyler asked from his place at the table.

"Since we discovered there's a scholarship involved." Colleen winked at her husband.

"There's no bathing suits or anything?"

"No, Dear. It's *fall*. October is a little cold for that."

"Scholarships are good." Mr. Tyler nodded.

"It doesn't matter," Jen muttered as she pushed her food around on the plate. "It's not like I'd win."

"Why would you say that? You have as good a chance as anyone," Sean stated sincerely and Kate smiled at the brotherly encouragement.

"Not when Kristi is running, too."

"Who is she?" Kate asked.

"Only the prettiest girl in our school. Probably three sizes smaller than me."

Kate didn't like the look on Jen's face. Jen was a beautiful girl. Her brown hair, though it was always up in a ponytail or a messy bun, was a beautiful color that complimented her pretty blue eyes. Her complexion was like porcelain with an adorable sprinkling of freckles across the bridge of her nose.

"If you wanted … I could help."

Jen's eyes flew up from her plate and looked at Kate with tempered excitement. "Really?"

"*Really?*" Colleen echoed in surprise.

"Sure. It looks like I may be here a little longer than I thought and it might be nice to have something else to think about for a bit."

"Kate, you don't need to do that. You have so much going on," Colleen pointed out.

"I can at least give you some pointers. Maybe help you with some makeup and dress suggestions before I go back."

"I'll think about it." Jen smiled at Kate appreciatively.

The matter was dropped and the conversation turned to the school group that was coming to the farm the next day for a field trip. Colleen reminded Sean that he was in charge of driving the tractor that pulled the hay wagon to the pumpkin field. Michael was in charge of crowd control while Colleen and John taught the kids a lesson on the benefits of local farms. It was all so heartwarming and wholesome to listen to. In another world and another time, Kate could see herself living there.

The phone in her pocket vibrated and Kate was pulled back to reality. Mark was calling. Relief flooded through her as she excused herself from the table to answer. If she allowed herself to listen any longer, Kate may just find herself wanting to stay in Deer Creek indefinitely. She curled up on the wicker loveseat on the porch and burrowed into her sweatshirt to keep cozy despite the chill.

"Hey, Beautiful." Mark's voice made her smile. "How are you holding up?"

"I'm tired. It's just so much, Mark. I didn't think this would be so hard."

"I'm sorry, Honey." He was quiet for a moment before continuing. "I don't want you to get mad at me, but..."

"Oh no. What did you do?"

"I took a few days off work. I'm going to come to you."

"Mark..." Kate was going to protest but then she saw Dan's truck pull up the driveway. He parked and got out. She waved at him, but he walked down the path to his cabin without even looking in her direction.

"Are you still there?"

"Uh, yeah. I'm here. I don't think you can stay where I am. It's kind of crowded."

"Is there a hotel in Deer Creek?"

Kate smiled at the thought. "I think maybe one or two, but they aren't exactly five stars."

"It doesn't matter. I just want to be there with you."

"What would I do without you?" Kate sighed. Maybe their relationship was better than she thought. Maybe this would be the turning point for them.

Mark chuckled softly. "Don't worry, Kate. I'll be there soon."

11

"Thank you for coming so quickly, Luke. I don't know what it was they were looking for. As far as I could tell we cleared out Miss Benson's car of anything personal before towing it from the Tyler's place."

The morning sun did nothing to ease the growing chill that was creeping into the area. Fall was in full force now. It didn't surprise Luke Martin that kids were out pranking or getting into trouble. Something about October seemed to spawn mischievousness in their area. Most likely the closer to Halloween they got, the more calls like this the local police would get. However, because this pertained to the infamous Kate Benson, who seemed to be the subject of not one but two break-ins now, Luke felt the need to see for himself what had transpired in the wee hours of the morning. He had promised that detective in Boston he'd keep an eye on her and the fact that it was *her* car out of a whole slew of others that was broken into raised his curiosity.

"You said you think there were *two* men?" The detective asked as he approached the candy apple red Audi with a scrutinizing gaze.

"Yes, two. Definitely. My wife installed a trail cam at the back of the garage because she put out new feeders. She likes to watch the deer. I don't think this was the wildlife she was wanting to see."

"You saved the video?"

"Yes. She sent it to my phone. I'll pull it up."

The detective looked at the inside of the car while O'Brien fumbled with his phone. The glovebox was open and the side storage compartments were rummaged through. A pair of sunglasses, a tube of lipstick, and a small packet of tissues were strewn around the front passenger seat. It could have just been an addict looking for spare coins to score a hit in town. Car break-ins weren't uncommon in that area. With the rise of opioid addiction, came the rise of crime. It was possible someone saw the Audi, which stuck out like a sore thumb among the other older cars in O'Brien's garage, and thought they'd find something of use to sell or trade. Yet, Luke couldn't shake the uneasy feeling. Normally, when those feelings popped up he knew to pay attention.

He exited the car and looked at the phone screen O'Brien showed him. The clock showed the event occurred at 3:23 AM. There were definitely two men trying to pry the door open of the Audi, but a detail on the suspects' car caught Luke's attention.

"Rewind to when they pulled up."

O'Brien complied and Luke squinted at the image. The sun made seeing the details he wanted to see difficult on the phone screen, but if he was correct there may be a serious problem. "Can you send this to me on my phone?"

"Sure."

The detective let the local officers do their jobs and nodded his goodbyes to the garage owner. His cell phone chimed as O'Brien's message arrived with a copy of the video. He'd need to have the feed pulled up onto a bigger computer screen and see if he could zoom in better to the license plate. If his gut was correct, those plates weren't New York issued. He did a quick google of Massachusetts license plate images and his stomach sank. Of course, he'd be one hundred percent sure before he called Detective

McKinney of his concerns, but it was quite possible Kate's coincidental home robbery was not coincidental after all.

*****

Kate sat numbly next to her father's side. Tuesday night into Wednesday, he'd taken a turn for the worse and he had been unresponsive. The raspy breathing she had heard earlier in her father's lungs had become a steady rattling sound. His color had gone from sallow yellow to a sickening grayish hue. Tom's eyes were shut and Kate realized that she wished they would open and look at her once more. It was an odd feeling that was very different from when she arrived a few days prior. She knew when she made the trip to Deer Creek the purpose was to say goodbye and finalize her father's affairs. She knew he was dying and she had been just fine with that then. Why was it so hard for her now to accept it? Where were her defenses? Had that much changed in a few days?

In her hands, she held one of his letters. By the date scribbled at the top of the paper, it appeared to be the last one he had written in that stack of missives she retrieved from the house. She wanted him to wake up so she could talk to him about what was written in it. The man who wrote that letter wasn't the man she knew as a child. She wanted to know this *new* Tom Benson. It wasn't fair that it looked like she wouldn't get the chance to.

She dropped her head to re-read it for the tenth time and a stray tear landed on the paper, smearing the ink.

"I had a great father. He wasn't what I would call affectionate. He let Mom handle that stuff. Dad was always there though. When your mother died and I fell apart, he held me. When I needed him, he was there. I never did get to thank him. I wish he could've been here when I got sober. I know he and Mom prayed for my soul every night. I bet

they never thought I would become a Christian. I wonder what they will say when they see me walk through Heaven's gates. Good thing they can't die again because I know Dad would have a heart attack.

I know I wasn't a good father. I wasn't the example to you that my dad was to me, Kate. And this silly letter - that you may never even read - isn't a substitution for all the times I should have said these things in person. I was a bad father, but there is a Father waiting for you that is perfect. You learned about Him as a kid. I know your mom, my parents, and Colleen tried to teach you about Him. I should have taught you about Him and I guess I am hoping this letter is enough. I used to doubt He was real. Until one night, I knew He was not only real but He was calling to me. He showed me everything I did that was wrong and then offered me hope that someone as lousy as me could be saved. I wish I could tell you what that moment felt like. It was like a weight lifted off my shoulders. I knew He loved me and forgave me.

Kate, I want that for you. I don't know if you ever tried to follow Jesus or if you read your Bible. But in my last days and until my dying breath, I am praying you experience this too. Let God be the Father I wasn't. He disciplines, but He loves. He changes our plans, but He makes them far better than anything we could've imagined. Let Him do in you what He did in me. I deserved Hell and because of Christ, I'm getting Heaven. It doesn't make sense. I don't deserve it, but it's true. Let Him be your Father. He won't fail you like I did. I love you. I know you might not believe that, but you are forever my little girl. And as much as I love you, He loves you more. Infinitely more. Oh, Katie, I hope you know Him."

Kate leaned in close to the head of her father's bed and whispered into his ear. "Who are you? Why couldn't the man who wrote this letter be the man who raised me?"

The only sound in the room was the sound of her father's death rattle.

"I don't know what kind of experience you had that made you change like this. But I want you to know … if you can hear me … I forgive you."

She allowed her tears to flow freely and didn't attempt to swipe them away as she had in the past.

"You need to wake up so you can tell me how this happened. How did you change? I want you back so we can try this again. Then you can teach me about what you said in this letter."

She held up the letter as if he could see. There was no response.

"Please wake up," she whispered. She sat there for hours, looking for any sign of improvement. None came.

In the quietness of her mind, she did something she hadn't done since she was a child. She prayed. *I don't know if I'm doing this right. It's been a hot minute, God. I don't even know if you are real. I don't even know what it is I want to say. There's a lot I don't know. But if you are real … could you show me somehow?*

At some point in her prayer attempt, Kate dozed off in her chair. She didn't know how long she had been asleep, but she jolted upright when she felt a hand on her shoulder. Was it a dream, she wondered, when she saw Mark standing beside her? She jumped to her feet and threw her arms around his shoulder.

"You came! I didn't think I'd see you until tomorrow at the very least." She cried against his chest and enjoyed the feeling of being in strong arms.

"I knew you needed me so I left as soon as we hung up last night. I checked into the hotel and came right here."

Kate looked up into Mark's face, hoping for a kiss, but instead saw him watching her father as he slept. "It won't be long now. The doctor said he took a bad turn overnight."

Mark sighed and Kate watched his expression quizzically.

"I was hoping to meet him."

"I feel like *I* just met him."

"What do you mean?" Mark pulled up another chair and the two sat next to Tom's bedside.

"He's not the man I thought he was. He is so different. I actually *like* this man." Kate smiled and looked up at Mark, grabbing his hand. "I feel like maybe I was given a gift. I don't know how to explain it."

Kate couldn't read the expression on Mark's face as he looked between her and her father.

"I know it's weird. I don't even know if I believe in God, but it almost feels like He brought me here to be with Dad so I could know him. You know ... before he died."

"*God?*" The word came out of Mark's mouth as if he had tasted something vile. "Since when do you believe in *God?*"

"I said I don't know if I do." Kate felt defensive all of a sudden. This was not what she had expected to come from Mark. It hurt that he wasn't hearing her heart.

As if he picked up on her thoughts, he quickly backtracked. "I'm sorry, Kate. I'm just tired from the drive. I'm glad you feel some type of relief."

She squeezed his hand. "It's okay."

"Are they still thinking of moving him? You had mentioned in one of our calls that they wanted to move him to a facility?"

"I don't think that's an option at this point. The move might kill him quicker."

Mark nodded and stood up. He looked like he had something on his mind and she was about to question him when a couple of nurses came in to check on her father.

"Hi, Miss Benson. We are your father's hospice nurses. We will be coming in from time to time to check on him and to make sure you have what you need."

Kate nodded solemnly and felt somewhat comforted by their presence. These were different nurses than the ones that had been attending to her father. These came with an end-of-life skillset. It was a realization that hit Kate in a way she hadn't expected.

The nurses proceeded to tell her what signs they were looking for that indicated he was near the end. They answered her questions and left. Mark quickly closed the door behind them.

"It's so noisy. Too many people milling around." He pointed out as he resumed pacing.

"Mark, do you want to go to the hotel and rest? We can catch up later. I'll let you know if anything changes here."

"No… of course not." He smiled then, but it wasn't his normal smile. Kate felt uneasy.

She was about to insist Mark leave to get lunch for them both when the door opened again and Colleen, followed by Dan, walked in. Kate made the introductions and instantly wished she could wave a magic wand to make all of them disappear. Dan looked grumpy. Mark looked unlike anything she had ever seen before. Then, there was sweet Colleen. She just wanted to be helpful.

"So, you're Mark. Kate has said such wonderful things about you." Colleen attempted a conversation. "It's nice to know she has someone watching out for her."

Kate smiled softly at Mark and linked her arm in his, resting her head on his forearm. Dan looked agitated and it didn't surprise her when he leaned down to his mother and said, "I will come back for you shortly. I need to run an errand in town."

Dan nodded at Kate and turned to Mark. "I'm sorry to leave so quickly, but it's nice to meet you. I'm sure we'll get to see each other again."

"How about tonight?" Colleen said to Mark with a warm smile. "Maybe between the two of us, we can convince Kate to eat something. I have a lasagna in the oven."

Kate concluded that Colleen's suggestion sounded horrible as she watched Dan's expression turn stormy and Mark looked physically ill. She didn't like this new awkward feeling. There was enough going on at that moment in her life.

"I appreciate the offer, but I …"

"I wouldn't argue. Mom is persistent if nothing else." Dan forced a sardonic smile and dismissed himself.

"Well, I guess lasagna it is then." Mark conceded and patted Kate's hand on his arm. "If it's okay with you, I think I *will* go to the hotel and freshen up first. I do have a few phone calls I need to make. I'll be back."

Kate nodded and leaned into a hasty, emotionless kiss. She tried not to overthink it as he left the room, but Kate felt hurt. She took her seat near her father and continued her vigil at his side. Colleen sat next to her in comforting silence. Kate's mind wasn't silent, however. Her thoughts roiled with questions that didn't seem to have answers. Soon it would all be over, but would her life go back to normal? Did she want it to? Kate wrapped her arms around herself as she realized something was changing in her. Whether that was a good thing, she just didn't know.

*****

"What do you want me to do? I'm telling you, this is stupid. The man is almost dead already. Let's just drop this and get out of here." Eddie had waited until Dan was well ahead of him before getting on the hospital elevator alone.

"Am I paying for your advice?" James hissed over the other end of the phone. "Your job is to finish Benson."

"Yeah, I get that. What you don't seem to understand is the man is not *conscious*. It's not worth it. This is ridiculous."

"Finish him in his room and bring her here like we discussed."

"Are you kidding me?" Eddie felt his blood pressure rise. "I'm not going to get caught and go down for you and your stupid nephew. This hospital has cameras and people everywhere. It's not the same as breaking into that backward garage from this morning."

"You're a professional, right? Then, don't get caught. Smother him. I don't care how… just do it." James paused waiting for Eddie's response. When it wasn't forthcoming, he continued. "Finish him. Send a picture when he is gone and bring her here. She'll take his place."

"It's not worth it."

"Is it worth the money you're due?"

There was a pause and the voice of Tony piped up. "Forget him, James. If he can't get it done, let me. I'm the one who spotted her car at that garage. He would've driven right by it not even knowing it was there."

Eddie laughed out loud at the audacity of the idiotic moron. "Great skills, Jr. You picked out a sports car in the middle of a junkyard full of trucks. Believe me, I can do this. I can take this whole hospital out if I wanted to..."

"Then do it."

"I'm supposed to have dinner with Kate and the people she's staying with. If I can get her away from these people ..."

"I don't care how you do it, just do it."

James hung up abruptly, leaving Eddie to his thoughts. He obviously had to adjust the plan. Money was money. He may think it was stupid and a waste of time, but it would be easy cash. He casually strode to the car and began reworking his strategy. Tom would be easy if he timed it right. The daughter would be harder. He needed to get her away from those Tylers. After all those months of pretending to be in love, he never even got to enjoy the perks of being the *boyfriend*. Maybe he could take her somewhere remote for some fun before delivering her. At least it would make these last few moments of the job a little more enjoyable.

Eddie pulled the car out of the parking lot to go get the supplies he would need to bring Kate in. He found a hardware store and set about checking items off his mental shopping list. He turned into an aisle of the store and stopped short. Dan Tyler. He had to get out of there before he was spotted, but it was too late. Dan looked up and waved as recognition hit.

"Hey. What are you doing here?"

Eddie racked his brain and tried to push his cart behind him, out of the eyesight of the prying Tyler. "Oh, I had to pick up a few things to fix my car. I wanted to get it taken care of before I took Kate home. What about you? What are you doing here?"

"I'm a contractor. I'm picking up supplies for a job I'm working on." Dan's eyes tried to scan Eddie's cart. "What type of repair? Maybe I can help."

"I think I have it. Thank you." Eddie backed the cart up, still trying to keep it out of Dan's sight. "I guess I'll be seeing you tonight."

Eddie did not like the look on the other man's face. Something in his eyes. The way his brow furrowed. Surely, he didn't know his plans. The sooner Eddie got out of that little town the better. The sooner he delivered Kate the better. Making sure Dan wasn't nearby, Eddie hastily checked out what he had in the cart and drove away. He hated small towns. Everyone knew everything about everyone, and strangers stuck out like sore thumbs. It would all be over that night. Tomorrow Eddie would be long gone and Mark would no longer exist.

*****

The smell of lasagna permeated the entire house and Colleen bustled to get the tray put on the table. Jen brought out the breadsticks to the hungry people gathered around. Mark sat next to Kate and was unusually quiet. He wasn't what she would deem an introvert. In fact, when he went with her to gatherings with her coworkers he was the life of the party. She knew that he wanted to be with her alone. He had come back to the hospital after resting at the hotel and running errands, only to find Colleen still sitting alongside her in her father's room. She never knew Mark to be unpleasant towards anyone, but he seemed almost as if he were sulking. Colleen had done her best to make polite and friendly conversation, but Mark answered in short words and grunts. When Dan couldn't come right away to get his mother, Katie offered Colleen to drive back to the house with her and Mark. His expression was one she had never seen before. It was almost frightening. It had to be exhaustion. This wasn't the Mark she knew.

"Let's bless the food." Mr. Tyler spoke up and everyone bowed their heads, except for Mark. Kate squeezed his hand and smiled gently at him. She knew he must feel out of place. He soon followed along, albeit uncomfortably.

Soon the food was passed, and conversation of various kinds began at the table. Kate felt a nudge and turned to see Jen had her phone out and was pulling up a picture.

"What do you think of this dress? *If* I do the pageant, I was thinking of something like this," she said moving her phone to where Kate could see it.

"That's very nice. Maybe something in this style in a plum color? I think you would look stunning."

"Pageant?" Dan asked, his fork halfway to his mouth. "Since when do you like pageants?"

"Since Kate agreed to help spruce her up." Mike smiled from his spot next to Dan.

"She doesn't *need* sprucing up." Dan looked confused and Kate rolled her eyes as he went into big brother mode. "When did you decide to do the pageant?"

Jen didn't get a chance to answer. Sean piped up from the other side of Dan. "Last night while you were out with Staci."

"Speaking of…" Jen asked trying to deflect attention from herself. "Where is she?"

Dan's face turned red. "We decided to break up."

Kate was not expecting to hear that, but when she glanced at Mike next to him he mouthed the words, "Told you so". He feigned an innocent expression when his brother turned his head to look at him.

"Oh, Dan. I am so sorry," Colleen soothed. "Why didn't you say something sooner?"

"I didn't want to get into it. I still don't."

Kate's heart broke for him. She wondered if her presence at the farm had something to do with it. However, if she were to believe Sean and Michael the night before, the relationship was doomed prior to her arrival. The table was engulfed in a most uncomfortable silence. Kate decided after a bit to change the topic of the subject. "Colleen, I didn't get to ask you how the visiting field trip went today. Did the kids have fun?"

"It was tiring, but fun. The teacher wanted information to take back to the schools, but I realized we don't have anything like that setup."

"You're the advertising woman, Kate," John Tyler spoke from his end of the table. "What would be involved in getting together brochures or pamphlets? It might be a good idea to open up the farm to more schools and maybe advertise our pick your own produce in the spring and summer."

Kate's mind started whirring and ideas started hitting left and right. "Let me think about it and see if I can come up with a few suggestions."

"Pageants. Public relations. You're quite a multifaceted woman." Mark smiled at her rather roguishly. He leaned in closer to whisper for her ears only, "Maybe we can go for a drive. Just the two of us. No chaperone."

Dan cleared his throat from across the table. "Did you get your car fixed, Mark?"

Kate felt Mark tense up next to her and she turned to him curiously. "Is something wrong with the car? It's a rental. Shouldn't the rental agency be the ones to fix it?"

Mark didn't get to answer. A knock sounded on the door, a very aggressive knock. John got up from the table to answer and Mark quietly excused himself from his seat. He said he was going to the restroom. As soon as the front door opened, three or four policemen, armed with weapons drawn entered the house.

"Everyone stay where you are with your hands where we can see them," one yelled. "Who's the driver of the black sedan?"

The police fanned out and went through every room, calling "*Clear*" after each.

Kate's insides went cold when from outside she heard a commotion and an officer yelled, "I've got him! Tried to go through the back door."

Luke Martin entered, scanning the room. His eyes landed on Kate before he asked, "Was there anyone with him?"

"No. What is happening? Where's Mark?"

He softened his gaze before motioning her to come. Numbly she obeyed, but her legs felt like Jello and she wasn't sure if they would hold her up.

"Sit down here on the couch, Miss Benson. I have a lot to tell you and I think you need to be prepared."

12

"Kate, say something." She could hear Dan's voice, but it sounded muffled. It was as if she were in a tin can and she could hear the people around her, but she couldn't discern what they were saying.

"I'm sorry. Did you just say Mark… is not Mark?" she managed to ask in a whisper.

"His real name is Eddie Barrow. He's what you might call a hitman. We're still working out the details on him and the man who hired him." Luke Martin repeated the information, probably for the third time.

"And Uncle Peter and Hannah … they're *dead*?" Kate couldn't breathe. It was as if someone turned everything in her world upside down. She felt something warm being pressed into her hands and she forced herself to focus. Colleen gave Kate a mug of what smelled like tea. She uttered a thank you.

"I tried to get information to Detective McKinney about your car being broken into at O'Brien's. That's when they told me the news. I was wondering why he hadn't been answering my calls or texts."

"And you think … Mark did that? And that he was going to hurt me?" Kate forced herself to look into the face of the detective at that point. The cup in her hand shook and while Kate felt the hot liquid on her fingers around the dainty teacup, she didn't react. Colleen must've thought better of giving it to Kate because she took it back from her, placing it on a side table for safekeeping.

"Mr. Barrows has quite a history. And, yes, I believe he was planning on doing more than hurting you, Miss

Benson." Luke waited a moment before prodding. "Are you sure you haven't seen him with anyone else today? Was he talking to anyone else?"

"He said he needed to make calls. When he left me at the hospital ... that's what he said he was going to do." Even to her own ears, she sounded pitiful.

"Luke, he stopped into the hardware store shortly after I got there. He said he was picking up things to fix his car," Dan spoke up as if just remembering.

"Not unless he was going to fix his car with duct tape, industrial garbage bags, and rope. We found those items in his car... along with a loaded gun. After I found out the suspects' car at the garage this morning had Massachusetts license plates, I made sure the local police were on the lookout. Then we received a tip regarding another crime that was tied to a car with Massachusetts plates. When I found out a car matching that description was seen leaving the hospital and headed toward your location, I knew we needed to move on it."

"I feel sick." Kate got to her feet and stumbled as she turned abruptly back to face the detective. Mike and Dan were there to grab her arms and steady her. She pushed them away and stumbled to the bathroom with Colleen not far behind.

Between the trembling and the feeling of having burning lava in her stomach, Kate lost everything she had eaten that day. Reality hit. Peter and Hannah were gone. Was there really another man? Could Mark have actually been guilty of what Detective Martin was saying? Kate splashed water on her face. Then it hit her. Was her father safe?

She left the bathroom almost pushing Colleen out of the way before walking back into the living room. "My father… who is with him? If there's another person out there…"

"I posted two policemen at his door. They're keeping me up to date if anything happens."

Kate gulped and started wringing her hands. "There's something I didn't tell you when you were here before. Peter had told me not to."

"I figured," Luke responded flatly, and all eyes were on her expectantly.

"I have letters that my father wants you to have. They'll tell you everything." Kate disappeared into the spare room and returned with the stack of letters and the firebox that had become precious to her. She handed them to the bewildered detective.

"What are these?" He asked.

"My father wrote these letters explaining how he and Peter had planted evidence at a scene. I promise, I just found all of this out myself. My father and I haven't talked in years. I had no idea about any of this until he told me to read these." Kate cried openly. "When Peter found out that I knew, he told me to stay quiet. He was retiring. He and Hannah were supposed to be in Florida right now."

Luke didn't answer. Kate continued. "He also wanted me to hand this over."

She pulled a key from her pocket and opened the box. "This is banking information to a special account where my father kept all his retirement payments. He didn't feel right using it, so he banked it away and lived off of social security and odd jobs. He wants me to give it back on his behalf."

Luke Martin shook his head slowly. "Tom, you fool. I knew he had secrets, but…"

The detective's cell rang, and he answered it, getting up abruptly and going to where he had privacy. Kate tried to calm her rapid heartbeat as she anticipated him returning with more bad news.

"Kate, sit down." Colleen put a loving arm around her and guided her back to the couch.

"I'm so sorry. You don't deserve any of this. I don't want to put you in danger, too."

"Stop it now. You didn't know." John Tyler stated in a matter-of-fact tone. "I'm just glad nothing happened. God is trying to get your attention, Kate."

"If you had left with him tonight..." Dan said the words more to himself as the realization hit everyone in the room.

Luke came back in and directed another officer to retrieve the letters and firebox. "I will take these things into evidence. I don't know if and when you can have these back. You're not going to be in trouble, Kate. That is, as long as you're being open and honest with us now."

Kate nodded in understanding, but it didn't take away the pain. If she had spoken up earlier, Peter and Hannah may still have been alive. He would've had to answer for his actions, but he'd be alive at least.

"Was that call something to do about Mark?"

Detective Martin's expression was guarded. "I can't give details, but I think it is safe to say you don't need to worry anymore."

Kate let out a big rush of air as relief set in. "I'm safe? My father is safe?"

"So it would seem. I'll know more after Mr. Barrows is questioned. Meanwhile, stay close. I'll keep the police at Tom's door. Get rest. I'll probably call with questions."

Kate nodded again. She had no idea how she was supposed to feel at that moment. Betrayal. Sadness. Grief. Relief. All she knew was that she needed to be close to her father at that moment.

"Could I go to my father? I know it's getting late, but the hospice nurses said I could come whenever I wanted."

"I'll get you in," the detective stated. The man was gruff, but Kate also saw such kindness.

She gathered a few things to take with her, including her laptop. Colleen wrapped up some lasagna to take along in case she got hungry. She knew she didn't deserve the compassion that the Tyler family showed her. She had brought danger right to their dining room table.

"I don't know if you are religious, Kate, but I'm going to be bold and tell you right now that God had his hand on you today," Luke Martin said as he got into the driver's seat and began the drive to the hospital.

Kate flashed back to the prayer she attempted to pray earlier at her father's bedside. She had asked God to prove Himself to her. Was this God's doing? Or was it a lucky coincidence? Something inside her perked up at the thought. Kate narrowly escaped danger three times now that she could recount. It could've been her on the kitchen floor at Aunt Lilly's house. She could've been hurt severely in that accident. Mark could've gotten her in his car alone and then what would've happened to her? Kate shuddered at all the times she had been alone with Mark in the past, trusting his words and believing he cared for her. Had it been God who protected her all those times?

Luke accompanied Kate up to her father's room and she was grateful to see two officers standing at her father's door. Quizzical nurses watched as she and the detective entered his room. He looked the same as the last time she had seen him earlier that day. It wouldn't be long.

"I wished I had gotten to know him better. I hate that he carried that guilt all this time," Luke said quietly as he stared down at Tom. "I've sat next to him at church, never knowing what he carried."

"I wish I had gotten to know him, too. I've been angry at him for so long."

"You know, human dads fail. They screw up and make mistakes. Sometimes they can make things right again, but sometimes they can't. Mine wasn't such a winner either. It wasn't until after I followed Christ that I learned what a good father was."

"Do you have kids?"

Detective Martin laughed. It was a pleasant sound after the night she'd just had. "Not biological. My wife and I have the tendency of taking in strays. We have several people we've *adopted* over the years."

Kate smiled at the man warmly.

"Well, I'll leave you. If you need a ride back to the Tylers' tonight, call me." He handed her a card with his number on it. "I'll have someone escort you back."

"Thank you, but I think I'll probably stay here tonight."

Luke nodded his goodbye and left her to her thoughts. Her phone lit up and Kate instinctively thought it was a text from Mark. There would be no more of those texts, she realized. It was as if another of her loved ones had died.

The text was from Dan. "I'll be up a while if you need anything."

Kate sighed and scooted up close to her father's bed near his head. "It's safe now, Dad. No more worries. They caught the bad guy. You can rest now."

There was no response. She hadn't expected one. She rested her head against his bed and allowed herself to doze off.

*****

Tony popped open a beer and settled into the hotel bed with a contented smile. Things had not gone according to plan, but that was okay with him. It had never been *his* plan to begin with. From now on things would be done *his* way. *He* was now the boss. No one was going to demean him again.

"You did what you had to do, Son. He was a traitor, allowing that stranger to take your rightful place."

Tony nodded at his father's words as he heard his voice in his mind. He'd been less lonely since his father had come back to him. It was proof that the pills his mother made him take were just to erase his father. That hateful witch.

"James forgot who his family was! Eddie is a low life and isn't loyal to anyone but himself. James should've known better," Tony spat.

"Shh. Don't get yourself upset. We need to regroup and finish what we started. Don't waste any more thought on them. They're not important."

Tony put the beer on the bedside table and sat up straighter as he thought he saw his father's figure start to take form in the corner of the hotel room. Nothing was there in the dim flickering of the TV light, but it was almost as if he could show himself to his son at any time. He had tried to appear earlier that night when Tony had killed again.

Instinctively, Tony looked down at his hands. For a split second they were still wet with blood, but as soon as he blinked they were back to normal.

"I had to do it. He was messing everything up," Tony whispered under his breath.

"He was threatening our mission. And no one treats my son that way! He'll never do that again. Who's stupid now?"

Tony rubbed his head aggressively as he remembered the night's events. James, Eddie, and Tony had checked into a dive motel on the outskirts of town. They were all exhausted after driving through the night and tensions were already hot. They thought maybe they had lucked out when Tony spotted Kate's car at the garage, parked to the side in a crumpled mess. Yet, there was nothing in the car that offered any new information on where she was staying.

Most of their trip had been spent fighting over how to carry out their plan at the hospital. Tony was to go with Eddie, kill Benson in front of his daughter, and bring her back to James. That had *always* been the plan.

"Plans change, Kid," James had said as he threw his bag onto one of the beds. "It's better if Eddie takes care of this himself. We're less likely to get caught if there's only one of you present."

"But Benson killed *my* father!"

"And *my* brother... but you don't see me wanting to rush in and act stupid and sloppy, do you?"

"He doesn't care about us, Tony. If he did, he'd want to be there to see it. He thinks you're stupid. He thinks you're a

joke. Don't let him talk that way to you." Tony rubbed his temples as the words registered.

Eddie started laughing. "Why does he keep doing that?"

"I don't know. Leave the kid alone. Just do what we agreed and bring her back here. He could use the practice and then help get rid of the girl." James laid down on his bed as if the subject was done. Eddie continued smiling at Tony, clearly entertained by his distress.

"You think I'm stupid. You think I can't do what I need to?"

"Calm down, Kid," James said without opening his eyes.

"Yeah, calm down. I'll let you have some of the fun. You just got to let the big people do their job first." Eddie's patronizing tone rang in Tony's ears long after he left the room for the hospital.

Tony had sat on the bed watching his uncle sleep, listening to his obnoxious unconcerned snores.

"See? He doesn't care. Do you remember the day I died? I bet you remember every detail..."

"I remember. I remember." Tony nodded as the image replayed itself in his mind.

"James doesn't care because he didn't see. You saw my blood turning into a puddle under my head. You remember looking into my eyes."

"You were looking at me, but you didn't blink."

"And Benson and McKinney thought you didn't see them grab my gun from the car and put it in my hand. They thought you were stupid, too. Quit letting everyone think you're stupid. Show them what you can do. It's time for you to take over."

Tony nodded confidently. "This is my time."

"Kill him. Kill them both."

Tony looked around the room wildly as he tried to formulate a plan. Eddie's bag lay open nearby. A gun was nestled between the clothing. Too loud. It would draw attention. He could smother him with a pillow. Maybe strangle him with his bare hands? Tony didn't know if he had the physical strength and if he started it, he had better finish it. There, sticking out of Eddie's bag was a sheathed knife. He had success with the knife last time. Why mess with a good thing?

Just as Tony got to his feet, James' cell phone rang, and the sleeping man woke up. It was Eddie calling to voice his opinion on how things should be done. Maybe his uncle would wise up and cut Eddie loose before Tony had to take drastic action. All James did was threaten to keep the money promised to Eddie if the job didn't get done. Where was his power? His authority?

"You should've let me go. He was my father," Tony muttered when James finally looked at him.

"Are you still on this? It's done. Get over it."

Rage seethed below the surface and Tony felt his hands tremble.

"Put yourself to use and go get us dinner," James said going into his bag and throwing some money at Tony. "That should be enough for a couple of burgers. I'm going to take a shower."

Tony watched as his uncle went into the bathroom and noticed the door didn't latch behind him. He heard rustling and then the shower water started. He looked over at the knife and sprang into action. Grabbing the knife and removing the sheath, Tony let his impulse take over. He moved stealthily into the bathroom and when the moment felt right he threw back the shower curtain, bringing his knife down in rapid and heavy thrusts.

He didn't know how long he stood staring at the crimson streaks as they mingled with the shower water traveling down the bathroom wall tiles. His uncle lay in a heap in the tub, bleeding out down the drain. He caught sight of his reflection and froze. His image was splattered with blood, both on his face and on the mirror itself. He looked down at his hands and marveled at how the color of blood changed as it began drying. It was almost mesmerizing.

Snap out of it. Get moving. His father's voice brought him to attention as he quickly grabbed a towel and started removing the blood from his hands and face. He wiped the knife clean and replaced the sheath. He had to move quickly but knew he couldn't leave looking the way he did.

Tony set about washing himself in the shower water that continued to fall over his uncle's lifeless body. He changed his clothes before rummaging through Eddie's and James' bags for anything useful and stuffing it all into his backpack. He took the knife, a gun with ammo, a few pre-paid phones, cash and credit cards, and the fake ID his uncle had made for him. As he was about to leave the room, he glanced over at Eddie's sunglasses on the bedside table and put them on with a smug smile. Tony wished he could see Eddie's expression when he realized it was over.

As he walked from the motel, Tony pulled out the burner phone and dialed 911.

"Hello. I'm staying at the Carlisle Motel ... I just heard a fight in the room next door. It sounded bad. It got quiet and then a man left and drove away. He's in a black Toyota sedan with Massachusetts license plates. I could've sworn I saw him with a gun. Please hurry."

Tony hung up and threw the phone into the wooded area off the side of the road. For the first time, he felt free. He went across the way to grab a bite to eat at a fast-food place and started formulating his next moves. He'd have to keep moving and keep his head down for a little while. Deer Creek wasn't a huge town and no doubt a murder would draw some attention to strangers in the area.

As Tony lay in his new hotel room, courtesy of the credit cards supplied by his generous uncle, he smiled as the local news started with breaking news. "Deer Creek has seen its first murder in ten years. A suspect is in custody tonight."

"Good job, Son. Now finish what you started."

13

A ray of sunlight broke through the slits in the pulled vertical blinds on the window and Kate moaned at the pain in her stiff neck as she turned to look at the clock on the wall. 8 AM. Sometime in the middle of the night, her father's breathing went from raspy and ragged to sporadic. Kate had fallen asleep with her head resting on the edge of her father's pillow and woke up only to realize she hadn't heard anything. No wheezing. No death rattle. Just when she thought Tom had slipped away one lone, fragile breath would emerge to ensure he was still there.

"Is this ... normal?" Kate asked the hospice nurse when she came in to check on her father.

"Yes. It shouldn't be long now. I'll turn off this monitor," the nurse said softly. "It's not really helpful at this point. Would you like me to stay with you for a little while?"

Kate shook her head and reached for her father's hand. It was cold to touch, and she sandwiched his between her own two warm hands.

The nurse had left the room but re-entered a moment later.

"I'm sorry to bother you, Miss Benson. There is someone in the hall asking to come in."

"Who is it?"

"The same man that was here yesterday. He brought breakfast." The nurse smiled. "Do you want me to send him away or allow him in?"

Kate's brow furrowed. Mark? No, he would never be back. He never even *existed*, Kate realized. Rising to her feet, she leaned over to look out the partly opened door to see Dan standing in the hall with a brown sack and a cup holder with coffees and orange juices. He looked as exhausted as she felt.

"He can come in."

The nurse smiled gently and motioned for him to enter.

"I thought you might be hungry." Dan glanced at Tom and cleared his throat. "I didn't know what you might be in the mood for, so I just got a little of everything."

Kate didn't know what to say or do. She wanted to hug him and be hugged, to draw strength from the comfort of his arms. At the same time, she wanted to recoil and forget the events of the night before. So, she stood still, numbly motionless, staring blankly at the coffee in his hands.

"I'll be at the nurses' station if you need anything," the nurse said as she excused herself from the room.

"Oh, wait," Dan spoke up, pausing her exit. "Here. Take some of these before you go. Have a coffee."

"You're so thoughtful. Thank you."

Kate's eyes misted watching Dan hand the nurse a cup of coffee and holding open the bag of breakfast treats for her to choose from. How did he still manage to break through her defenses? She turned away and refocused her attention on her father but felt Dan's warmth next to her a moment later.

"I assume you still like your French vanilla creamer with a tiny bit of coffee?" He held out a cup to her and she gratefully took it. An unexpected, unintentional, soft laugh managed to escape through the tough wall she thought she had erected.

"You remembered."

Without looking at him she could hear the smile in his voice. "You haven't changed *that* much."

The hot liquid did wonders. Kate didn't realize how cold she truly felt until the coffee soothed its way down her throat and into her stomach. In trying to warm her father's rapidly dropping body temperature, her own felt depleted.

"Do you mind if I open this?" Dan motioned to the window. "The sunrise was amazing this morning."

He didn't wait for Kate's permission and the golden sunlight cascaded onto the stark white hospital floor. Kate squinted like a mole exposed to daylight but noticed for the first time the beautiful view from her father's window. She moved closer to take it in. The trees in the park nearby radiated glorious hues of red, orange, and yellow. They were alive and vibrant in the light of the sun. A gentle breeze blew through their branches and a few stray leaves floated free from their confines like feathers falling to the ground.

"I forgot how much I loved fall here," Kate said quietly.

"I'm sure fall is beautiful in Boston, too."

Kate gave Dan a side glance, but he was staring straight ahead at the scene outside. "It is, but there's something special about this place. I spent so long telling myself I hated it here that I guess I forgot all the wonderful parts."

Dan didn't say anything, but Kate thought she saw the corner of his lip twitch up in a slight smile. Just then her father let out another breath and both moved to his bedside.

"Is he…" Dan's brow furrowed as he leaned closer to Tom.

"No. I don't think so," Kate said sadly. "He's been doing that for a couple of hours now. When I think he's gone, he takes a breath."

Instinctively, Kate reached down and grabbed her father's hand again.

"I don't hate him, you know."

"I know."

"I thought I did. I wanted to." Kate fought back a sob. "I.. love.. him."

She felt Dan's hand on her shoulder, and it was her undoing. Tears crept down her cheeks unchecked. And with her free hand, she swiped at them aggressively.

"This is stupid. I shouldn't cry. It's not like I didn't know he was dying. I've gone so long without him anyway. Nothing has really changed."

"It's not stupid. He's your father. And…" Dan leaned closer to her ear. "I think a lot has changed."

Without warning, Tom's eyes opened. For a moment, it looked as if he stared right at her with loving recognition and he pushed out a rush of air from his lungs. Then the momentary light in his eyes faded and he was gone.

"Dad?" She squeezed his hand and gave it a shake. "*Daddy?*"

Nothing. Kate started hyperventilating and Dan pulled her into his arms, letting her sob into his chest while he reached down and pushed the nurse's call button. It didn't take long for two nurses to come in and go right to Tom with stethoscopes, first one and then the other. They nodded and one said softly to the other, "Time of death 8:36 AM".

Kate wept harder and Dan brought his head down and rested his cheek against her temple. He whispered softly into her hair, "He's okay now, Kate."

"Take as long as you need with your father, Miss Benson. When you're ready, we'll call the funeral home to arrange transport."

"I'm ready now." Kate pushed away from Dan and instantly wished she could burrow her face back into his jacket. She couldn't bring her eyes to look at her father, so she moved to gather her belongings.

"Kate, there's no rush."

"I said I'm ready. I'm tired." Kate finally looked at Dan and almost melted at the concern in his expression, but she had to pull herself together. "Could you take me back to the house?"

"Of course, but …"

"I'll just gather my stuff. You can wait in the hall." She didn't mean to sound stoic as she dismissed Dan as if he were nothing more than a servant. Kate needed a moment alone.

Dan sighed and followed the nurses out of the room, closing the door behind him. As soon as she was alone again, Kate forced herself to look at her father's lifeless body. His head still looked toward the window side of the room where she had been standing moments before. She put her things down in her chair and walked back to look into his face one more time. Leaning down, Kate pressed a kiss to his forehead and whispered, "Goodbye".

When she had finally composed herself, Kate walked out into the hallway. The police officer posted by her father's door was on the phone filling in the detective on Tom's passing and finding out whether he was cleared to leave. The nurses walked Kate through the next steps and allowed her to talk directly to the funeral director on the phone, giving consent to do what must be done. Finally, Dan stood patiently and waited to take her back to his family's house. Kate felt numb as she moved through the hall, down the elevator, and out to the truck in the parking lot.

Dan would occasionally try to get her to talk, but Kate answered with few words. Kate felt on the verge of collapse. In the span of a week, she had been through danger and death. Her mind couldn't take it all in. As soon as Dan helped her inside the house, Kate allowed Colleen to hug her and politely excused herself to the guestroom. Kate crawled into the bed, allowed the dam of tears to burst, and fell fast asleep.

*****

"I'm telling you the truth! I did not kill James McCullough."

Luke Martin ran an agitated hand through what was left of his hair as he went over his notes from interrogating Eddie Barrows. All witness claims mentioned only *two* men. O'Brien's surveillance video showed *two* men. The images were grainy but they fit the description of James McCullough and Eddie Barrows. The motel front desk clerk only saw *two* men. Yet, Barrows insisted there was another man, Tony McCullough Jr. It could very well be that he was trying to deflect guilt by trying to invent another person to take the fall. Before any real valuable information could be attained, his court appointed lawyer showed up and he went silent.

Normally, Luke didn't take criminals at their word, but there was an emphatic flair to his statement that rang true. His searches came up empty. According to family records, there was no Tony McCullough Jr. The deceased Tony McCullough, brother of James, was not married when he died. If he was someone's father, the mother did not put his name on a birth certificate. Those who could've known if a Tony Jr. existed were now all dead as of that morning.

"Are you going home tonight, Martin?" Another detective asked as he put on his jacket, readying to leave for the night. "I'm sure Patty has something good going for dinner."

"She always does." Luke attempted a smile.

"What's on your mind?"

"Barrows and this ghost named Tony McCullough."

The other man laughed. "There is no other man. It's done. One bad guy is dead, the other is in our holding cell. Go home."

"But what if he's right? What if I tell Kate Benson everything is okay and there is another guy out there?" Luke couldn't handle that possibility.

Eventually, the other detective left and Luke was about to as well when he caught sight of something in the file box he was about to return to evidence. A stack of letters written by Tom Benson's own hand. Luke pulled them out and turned on his desk lamp. He owed it to Kate to be thorough. He pulled out his cell and called his wife, letting her know he'd be home later. There would be no rest until Luke was satisfied that there was no remaining threat running loose in his county.

*****

It was dark when Kate finally woke up with a start, sitting up quickly in bed. Her first thought was that she needed to get to the hospital. Then she remembered. Her father was gone. Kate reached for her phone and saw that it was after 10 p.m. She had missed quite a few calls while she had slept. She listened to her voicemail and sighed as the funeral director requested a meeting in the morning to work out arrangements. He needed a picture of her father. She didn't have a picture of her father. Grief washed over her once again. This time it was mourning the possible relationship she *could've* had with her father. If things had been different, she'd have framed pictures with her and her father all over the place and candid shots in her phone of them together. But Kate would never have that. At one point, she had been resigned to that knowledge.

Her stomach growled and she realized how hungry she was. Maybe Colleen had something in the refrigerator that she could warm up. Kate cringed at every sound she made as she tried to move stealthily through the downstairs of the Tyler home. The doorknob rattled in her hand. The door creaked open. The floorboards groaned under her weight as she made her way towards the kitchen. Her hand was on the door of the refrigerator when a light clicked on in the stairway that led upstairs. Someone descended.

It didn't surprise her to see Colleen making her way into the room a moment later.

"I'm sorry. I was hoping I wouldn't wake anyone."

"I was still awake." Colleen's motherly smile warmed Kate despite the chill that had crept into her since her father's death. "I imagine you're starving. We had debated whether to wake you for dinner, but when I checked in on you it was clear you were out for the count."

"I didn't realize how tired I was."

"Hmm. Well, let's see what we can come up with." Colleen started moving around the kitchen and motioned Kate to sit at the table. "Do you want a meal or a snack?"

Kate chuckled. "Probably just a snack."

Moments later Colleen produced a ham and cheese sandwich. Kate's eyes went big. "This is a snack?"

"It is when you haven't eaten anything for a whole day. Eat." Colleen sat across from her and Kate ate, enjoying the silent company.

"The funeral director wants a recent picture of my father," Kate blurted out after several moments. "I don't have any."

Colleen looked contemplative for a moment and got to her feet. "Stay here. I'll be back."

Kate sat back in the kitchen chair as she wondered what Mrs. Tyler was up to. That woman had the amazing gift of making everything okay. Even just sitting in the dimly lit kitchen was soothing to Kate's soul. The windows all had electric candles illuminating the old farmhouse. The aroma of cinnamon came from some unknown source, maybe a candle that had been lit earlier in the evening. The ticking of the grandfather clock and an occasional hoot owl from outside were the only sounds. It was a precious change from the hospital's sights and sounds, yet her heart ached to be sitting by her father's side. She ached to see him alive and telling her how they could start over.

Colleen reappeared with a decorative container, the size of a shoebox. She took her seat and pulled off the lid.

"Let's see what I can find in here. These are pictures I've taken at various church events. I know there must be at least one or two in here."

Kate was glad Colleen's eyes were busy looking at photos and not seeing the tears filling her own eyes. Would she *ever* stop crying?

"Ah! Here we go." Colleen placed a photo in front of Kate and continued rummaging.

"When was this?"

"Church picnic in May of this year. He didn't really like his picture taken, but he seemed genuinely happy that day."

Kate looked down at the image of her father. He was wearing the same baseball cap he had worn when she was living at home, it had the name of the garage he had worked for. His eyes looked especially blue in the picture ... and mischievous. His smile almost dared her to take the picture. He had a plate of food on his lap, and he was sitting in a lawn chair next to Mr. Tyler.

"Here's another. This one was at Christmas. We caroled at his house." Colleen smiled wistfully as she looked at the picture before handing it to Kate.

The picture showed her father holding a gift basket filled with various goodies and a large Christmasy red ribbon. He looked uncomfortable to be the center of attention, but he smiled politely in the picture with the pastor standing next to him. Kate felt a lump in her throat.

"That was before he started coming to church. Before he got saved. He put up with us invading his space." Colleen smiled. "Oh, Kate. These are priceless."

Kate looked up to see what Colleen found. One image was her father beaming. The sun was shining over his shoulder, and he was standing in front of a treelined river. The other image was her father in the river with Sean and Pastor Munson.

"Those are from his baptism not that long ago."

A tear slipped from Kate's cheek onto the picture in her hand and she quickly tried to wipe it off. "Oh no. I'm so sorry. I don't want to hurt your pictures."

"*Your* pictures. These are yours, Sweet Girl." Colleen reached across the table and squeezed Kate's arm lovingly.

Kate couldn't find her voice, but she managed an appreciative nod.

"I think these will do nicely to give Mr. Johnson at the funeral home a good idea of who Tom is," Colleen concluded as she wiped her own tears away.

"The man in these pictures … is so different than the man I knew."

"He *was* different."

"Because he became a Christian?"

"Because when Jesus pulled at His heart, he responded. He truly loved Christ. Some people ask the Lord into their hearts to escape Hell. Your father came to God knowing he was unworthy and that he needed God's grace and mercy. When he accepted that gift from God, well, the joy and freedom he felt afterward was evident. It was a night and day difference."

Kate sighed contentedly at the sweet description of her father's change.

"And, Kate, he's more alive now than he ever was here on earth. I can imagine him dancing in the presence of God with your mother and grandparents."

"That's a beautiful thing to imagine." Kate choked out the words.

"It is. You can have that, too."

Colleen paused to see if Kate would respond. Kate nodded but didn't want to talk about that right then. "Can I take these to my room?"

"Of course. Like I said, those are your pictures now. If I find more, I'll pull them out for you."

Kate gathered up the photos and hugged Colleen before disappearing back into the guestroom. She arranged the pictures on the nightstand next to the bed, propped up against the lamp. She fixated on the image of her father's smiling face being illuminated by the sunshine. He looked ethereal. Was that what he looked like in Heaven, Kate wondered as she fell back into a deep sleep.

14

"Also, we will need clothing for Mr. Benson." Mr. Johnson, the funeral director, informed Kate the next morning at their meeting. "There is an option, if you'd prefer, to rent a suit for the viewing. It would be removed prior to locking the casket before interment."

"A *rented* suit?"

The man nodded.

"...that will be *removed*?" Kate found the idea oddly funny, but then again, she had a knack for finding the wrong things humorous at the most inopportune times.

"Many of our clients like this option to keep all of their loved ones' belongings rather than burying them."

"So, my dad would be buried ... naked?"

Kate and Mr. Johnson just stared at each other for a moment.

"I think I can come up with some clothes for him, Mr. Johnson."

"Very well. Could you drop those off for us along with his undergarments before Sunday evening since we are looking at a Monday afternoon viewing and service?"

"*Undergarments*. There's not really a middle ground is there? Either he goes naked or dressed to the nines." Kate chuckled awkwardly, but Mr. Johnson didn't seem to find it amusing.

She cleared her throat, shook the man's hand, and left quickly. Maybe she should've accepted Sean's offer to help her through the funeral planning process after all. Kate pulled out of the funeral home parking lot with her mind spinning with details pertaining to caskets, flowers, and limos. At her age, she never really thought about all of the details that went into a funeral. She could almost hear her father's voice in her head, saying "*It's a rip off*". Would he want a mahogany casket or something in blue metallic? Did she want the little keepsake roses that come off of the four corners of the casket? Plants or flowers? Did she want one limo for herself or more limos to accommodate guests that would follow behind the hearse to the cemetery? Then there was the headstone….

Kate's cell phone rang and she glanced down to see the name of her condominium complex on the screen. Her stomach sank. It was Friday. She was supposed to go sign the lease *that day*. In fact, she was supposed to be there right at that moment. Pulling Colleen's car over to the side, Kate fumbled to answer the call before the leasing agent hung up.

"Hello, Miss Benson?"

"Yes. I am so sorry. I know I missed the appointment to sign the lease today. It's just that …"

"Are you nearby? I can wait here until noon for you, but after that, we'll have to reschedule for Monday," the no nonsense woman informed her.

"You see, my father just passed away. I'm in New York handling his affairs and I am not sure how long it will take to get everything squared away before I return to Boston." Even as Kate said the words conflict started in her heart.

This condo meant the world to her. At least, it had a couple of weeks ago when she decided to put a deposit down. Everything about this place exuded elegance. From the marble countertops to the wireless features that she could control from her phone, Kate wanted this condo. The views of the city at night were amazing. She was closer to work. Closer to Mark. A knife tore into her heart. None of it seemed important anymore.

"I suppose you can sign the documents online, but we will need the security deposit and first month's rent in order to proceed. I can send you the link to pay that online today."

"Wait..." Kate's brow furrowed. "Is there any way I can just handle all of this when I get back?"

"We have a long waiting list, Miss Benson. If you'd like, we can put your name back on the list and contact you if there is another opening."

"No. I really liked that corner condo." What was her hesitation? She could do it all online and return to Boston to a fresh new home. It should've been a no-brainer.

"So, you would like me to send you the link then?"

Something didn't feel right. Kate would go back to *what* exactly? What was waiting for her in Boston? Her job waited, but she hadn't been happy working for the advertising firm. When she got back, she'd have to answer all of Lilly's questions and be reminded of the horror that happened in that house. Horror intended for her. Even this new wonderful, luxurious home with the hefty price tag came with a jagged pill. She had toured it with Mark, with the hope maybe they would share it. Boston's appeal was lessening, and Kate knew she had some major decisions to make quickly because she was going to run out of paid time off.

"Are you still there, Miss Benson?" The voice on the other line brought her back to reality.

"I'm here." Kate swallowed hard before she continued. "You may go ahead and contact the next person on the waiting list. I'm withdrawing."

There was a pause on the other line. "Are you sure? These corner units rarely open up and I can't guarantee when another one does open that the price will remain the same."

"I'm sure. I'm no longer ... interested." The words were painful to say and even more so to realize.

"You do understand that the deposit is non-refundable, correct?"

Kate wanted to cry. What was she doing? She swallowed hard before answering. "I understand."

"Very well. We wish you the best and offer our condolences on your father's passing."

With that, the phone call ended, and Kate made her way back to the Tyler house. Deep down she knew she had made the right decision to walk away from the condo. The woman who had plunked her money down and dreamed of cityscapes and high-end finishes was gone. She died sometime over the past week in between rediscovering her father and losing the man she knew as Mark. This new Kate Benson was someone she had never met before.

As a very discouraged Kate pulled into the Tyler driveway, she spotted Jen moving a wheelbarrow full of pumpkins to the newly erected *Tyler Family Farm* sign. Dan was on a ladder, painting the letters black and bold. The expression on his face when he noticed Kate behind the wheel of the car, made Kate laugh out loud despite the turmoil she felt inside. She slowed the car and lowered the window.

"You keep on driving down to the house... slowly and carefully," he ordered while waving the paintbrush in her direction.

"Stop! You're getting paint on the pumpkins," Jen complained below.

The scene was entertaining for sure, and Kate couldn't resist to call out, "Can I help?"

The brother and sister both answered back emphatically, Jen with a yes and Dan with a no. The temptation was too much, and Kate pulled the car to the side of the driveway and parked. She felt Dan's eyes on her as she walked below his perch on the ladder.

"What can I do?" she asked looking up the ladder and squinting against the mid-morning sunlight.

He pointed to a tree and said, "Go stand over there and don't touch anything."

"Grab some pumpkins and help me make this look pretty." Jen smiled and motioned to the array of hay bales and mums lying around in disorganized heaps.

"It's the least I could do considering I kind of hurt the first display."

"*Kind of?*" Daniel repeated. "You should come with a warning label."

Jen laughed and Kate scowled.

"*You should come with a warning label.*" Under her breath, Kate mimicked Dan's tone with a little extra drama as she reached the wheelbarrow of pumpkins. "Should we clean these off first? They're dirty."

"They're pumpkins." Jen ignored Kate's observation and continued moving whole bales of hay to where she wanted them. "The rain will clean them."

Kate's brow furrowed as she contemplated how to lift the pumpkins without getting herself dirty or hurting her manicure. She found one that had a decent handle and lifted it only for the stem to break completely off. The pumpkin fell back into the pile with a thud. She brushed her hands on her jeans and self-consciously looked up in Dan's general direction. He had paused his painting to watch her, an amused smile on his face.

"Try lifting from the bottom of the pumpkin. Use your legs when you lift so you don't hurt your back," he called down to her.

"Thank you, Sir, for *mansplaining* how to accurately lift a pumpkin! How ever would I manage without you?" Kate rolled her eyes but followed his suggestion, nonetheless.

After a few minutes of working side by side with Jen, she realized it was Friday, a school day.

"Skipping school today, Jen?"

"It's a long weekend since Monday is Columbus Day. We have off today and Monday."

"And you're spending your day off arranging pumpkins?"

Jen smiled at Kate and stated, "I wouldn't have to if someone hadn't hit the other display with her car."

"Touché."

A few more moments of silent work passed and Kate noticed Jen kept looking in her direction as if she was bothered. "Am I doing something wrong?"

"No. You're doing great. Good pumpkin to mum ratio. Nice use of small pumpkin to larger. Good mix of different colored gourds," Jen rambled.

Kate stopped what she was doing and looked at the younger girl who obviously had something on her mind despite the overly glowing description of Kate's pumpkin placement. "There's clearly something in that head of yours that you want to say. What's up?"

Jen flushed and looked down at her shoes. "I think I want to do the pageant."

At first, Kate didn't think she heard correctly. "You decided to do the pageant?"

Jen nodded shyly.

"That's great, Jen. I have good memories of being in the Fall Days pageant." Kate tried to keep herself from looking up at Dan.

"It's just that … I know you have a lot going on right now. I don't feel right asking…"

"Then don't!" Dan's voice sounded from above and Jen snapped her lips closed in agitation.

"You paint! We talk." Kate glared at him and returned her attention to Jen. "Jen, I would be honored to help. I need a distraction right now. It's not been a fun couple of days, but maybe girl time would help me out just as much as it would you."

"Are you sure, Kate?" The girl looked excited, and Kate started creating a mental to-do list.

"I'm sure. Now, how long do we have? When is the pageant?"

"It's towards the end of October. The Friday before Halloween."

"Okay. So we have about three weeks."

"Do you think... I mean, will you still be here? Will you stay for the pageant?" As Jen asked the question Kate noticed Dan had stopped painting again. While he pretended to inspect his work, Kate knew he was keenly aware of their conversation.

She cleared her throat. "I guess I will stay until my paid time off runs out at least. I should still be here."

"Didn't you win the pageant when you were in it?"

"I did! I think I wore my red dress. I loved that dress."

"It was green," Dan said as he started descending the ladder.

"No, it wasn't. It was a red dress. I remember it like it was yesterday."

Dan laughed knowingly. "Well, you are remembering wrong because it was green."

Jen stood awkwardly between her brother and Kate as they now stood a few feet apart with conflicting memories.

"I think I would remember my own dress, Dan. I worked hard to earn enough money for that dress."

"I remember the red dress, too. That was the Christmas dance. I remember it well because I had to cancel the order with the florist after you found out I had the corsage made with red roses and not white. Remember? You said it was too much red?"

Kate's brow furrowed and she sighed in defeat. She did her best not to make eye contact with Dan. How did he remember all of that? "Anyway, *Jen*, maybe tomorrow we can go shopping."

Dan lowered his head to hide the smug smile on his face and he moved away to collect his painting tools.

"That sounds great. I'll double check with Mom since she's the one buying the dress," Jen laughed nervously and ran down the slight hill to the house, leaving the now empty wheelbarrow.

Dan shook his head and put his paint bucket and brushes inside as he began to push the abandoned wheelbarrow down towards the house.

"Dan…" Kate called out and he turned towards her.

All of a sudden she felt silly inside. His eyes held a mysterious combination of softness and amusement in them. "I … I was wondering if you would mind helping me with something."

"I'm not picking out any dresses…"

Kate laughed and his chagrined smile put her at ease. "No. Believe me, I would *not* put Jen through that."

"What can I help you with?"

"The funeral director said I need to bring clothes for my father…"

Why was it so hard to put what she needed into words? Why couldn't she admit Dan knew him better than she did, that he'd know better what to bury him in? Thankfully Dan was able to see the direction her words were headed.

"You want me to help you pick something out," he surmised.

Kate nodded.

"Okay. I can do that. Do you want to go over to the house now and we can see what we can find?"

"*Now*?" She had been hoping he would just go himself and pull an outfit together on his own. She didn't think she could handle being in the house again, not with Dan's watchful eyes.

"I imagine Mr. Johnson wants those sooner than later... Especially if the funeral is Monday." Dan's voice was gentle but insistent. Did he know she wanted to run and hide from reality? Was she not doing a good enough job masking her intentions?

"I guess you're right."

Dan motioned to the car still parked to the side of the driveway. "Hop in. I'll drive."

"Wow. You really don't trust my driving. It's less than a quarter mile to my father's driveway."

Dan's smile said it all.

"It was a rainy day and *your* dog was in the street. Anyone could've crashed into your sign, you know," Kate asserted, but Dan wouldn't budge.

With a sigh, Kate got in the passenger side and the two drove in silence. It was when they pulled in front of the house, that Dan spoke. "I should probably tell you before we go in, we moved the furniture to the side so we could work on the stairs. We were careful, I promise."

"You fixed the stairs?"

He nodded and she almost thanked him. Then, she remembered it was *his* house now. Her father had sold it to him. He was fixing his *own* property. An ache settled into Kate's heart at the realization. Why did she suddenly feel homeless? The condo was gone. Her father's home belonged to Dan.

Pushing the growing melancholy aside, she followed Dan up the porch steps. She watched him unlock the door with a key on a ring he took from his pocket. This wasn't her home. It was Dan's. Would that realization ever stop stinging?

"Hey, are you okay? Do you need a minute alone inside first?" Dan paused and put a tender hand on her arm. He must've read something in her expression.

Kate squared her shoulders and pushed past him into the house. "I'm fine. Let's just get this done."

Just as he had said, the furniture was moved to one side of the room and covered in sheets. It cast an eerie feeling to the home. When her grandparents lived there it was alive and vibrant. Even when it was just her and her father, there was *some* activity. Now it sat like an empty shell. Hollow, dark, and cold. Kate shuddered.

"I'm sorry. I turned the heat down after your dad went into the hospital. Do you want my jacket?"

"No. Thank you though."

"Suit or casual clothes? I think most of his casual clothes are still down here somewhere. He slept in his recliner when lying flat became uncomfortable. He didn't go upstairs much at that point."

"Maybe a suit?" Kate didn't honestly know.

"Okay. If there is a suit, I would guess it's in his bedroom closet."

Kate nodded and Dan moved towards the stairs. She didn't know whether to follow him or stay where she was.

Her grandmother would roll over in her grave if she knew Kate had a gentleman upstairs with her alone. She wondered if he sensed her hesitation because Dan turned to her and said, "I'll see what I can find and bring it down for your approval, how's that?"

She smiled, but let it fade as soon as he disappeared. Kate went over to the old fireplace and stood staring at the spot where the Christmas tree would go every year. The mantel was cluttered with matchbooks and nonsense, but back in the day, Grandma Lydia had little knickknacks decorating every inch. Something bright blue hiding behind a mishmash of junk caught her attention. It was the blue jay she had made in art class.

Taking it into her hands she remembered how hard she tried to sculpt the clay into a bird-shaped object. At the time she was so proud of it though it really didn't resemble a bird at all. One night when her father was in one of his drunken moods, he threw it and it shattered. Obviously, at some point, he must've glued it back together. There were places where she could see it had been broken. The cracks were still there, but it was restored. Kate turned it around in her hands and noticed there was writing on the bottom of the bird that she didn't remember. It said, "*Katie, 4th grade*" in her father's handwriting.

Dan came back downstairs and she quickly tried to put the bird back on the mantel before she was caught. However, in her hurry, she almost dropped it and ended up just keeping the bird tucked in her palm.

"What did you find?" she asked trying to cover her temporary showing of emotion.

He smiled gently. "You first?"

"Oh, this?" Kate held up the bird. "It's just something I made as a kid."

"Mrs. Nash's art class? She had everyone make birds. Mine was a cardinal. Didn't turn out as cute as yours though."

"Now you… what did you find?"

Dan held up a suit with a look of uncertainty. "It's the only suit he had."

"Ooh." Kate winced. "I think he wore that to my grandparents' funerals."

"Both of them?"

"And maybe even my mother's." Kate cringed. "It's a bit…"

"It's old, for sure." Dan looked down at the old navy blue striped suit. "You know, Kate. The choice is yours, but I never saw your dad in anything but jeans and flannel."

"Then I guess that's what I take to him," Kate said softly. "Where are his other clothes?"

Dan motioned to a few storage containers piled up near the furniture graveyard and the two sorted through the ragged clothes.

"I guess he didn't go clothes shopping very often." Kate attempted humor.

"I don't think he liked going out at all, let alone clothes shopping."

"Let's do these jeans and…" Kate paused when a piece of fabric caught her attention. She pulled out a blue plaid flannel shirt. "Is this the shirt he wore when he was baptized?"

"I don't remember what he wore, but it's possible." Dan looked at Kate puzzled.

"Your mom gave me pictures of him. One was taken at his baptism."

He nodded with a small smile. "That was a nice day. He looked happy."

"Then I guess we have a winning outfit. I hope he'd like it."

"I think he'd like anything you pick, Kate."

Kate straightened up and looked around the room. "There sure is a lot of stuff here to go through. I'll have to figure out how to either move this to a storage unit or get a dumpster before I go."

"There's no rush."

"Yes, there is. This is your house now. I doubt you want to wait until I get my act together before getting in here to do whatever it is you're wanting to do." She hated how wistful she sounded.

Dan looked as if he were searching his mind for words to say so Kate decided to rescue him from the awkwardness... with more awkwardness. "*Underwear*. Did you happen to see any in these containers? Ones in good shape?"

"I wasn't looking."

Kate chuckled at the look of confusion on Dan's face and shrugged. "I guess it's a thing. The funeral director had asked me to bring them for Dad. Who knew, huh?"

The two found what they needed and were about to head out the door when Dan stopped Kate at the front entry wall.

"Hey, Kate." He nodded toward the wall with a mischievous smile.

"What? Why are you …" Her eye caught what it was he was trying to show her as he turned on his heels and headed out of the house with an obnoxious smirk.

There on the wall, among dozens of framed pictures, were two side by side. One was Kate in a red dress, wearing a white rose corsage. The other was Kate in her green dress standing with a brilliant tiara of rhinestones and a sash with the words *Miss Fall Days* over her shoulder. Kate smiled and conceded that she had indeed been wrong. Then her smile wavered and tears threatened to mist her eyes as she realized what those two precious memories had in common. In both pictures, Dan Tyler stood by her side.

15

Sleep deprived, Dan left his cabin and squinted at the Saturday morning sunshine. It was a chilly, crisp day. He made his way to the main house, hoping that his family had left a cinnamon roll for him. On weekends Colleen loved to bake and she had promised him that this Saturday would be cinnamon roll day. After the night he had, a cup of coffee and that roll would do wonders for his outlook.

Every time he thought just maybe sleep would claim him, he saw Kate's face. He had grown lax lately trying to keep a safe distance between himself and Kate. When she had asked him for help the day before he didn't even hesitate. How could he have said no when she was grieving her father?

"Morning, Dan." His dad called out when Dan rounded the corner of the house. John and Sean were leaning over the tractor engine, hands dirtied with grease.

"Good morning. Where's Michael? Why isn't he helping?"

"He had an overnight shift. He's sleeping," The second oldest Tyler son said as he wiped his hands on a rag.

"Looks like you guys have your hands full. Let me get a cinnamon roll and I'll come help you."

"What cinnamon roll? We have cinnamon rolls?" Sean asked looking at his father as though he was holding out on him.

John laughed at the faces of his sons. "Sorry, Boys. There are no cinnamon rolls. Your mom is taking a much needed break today."

"Do we have coffee?" Dan tried to hide his disappointment.

"Now *that* we have."

Dan was about to walk into the house, but he turned back to his father and brother and asked, "Is Kate up yet?"

"Kate? Why would you want to know about her?" His father winked at Sean. "The ladies are out having a *girl's day*. They said something about shopping for dresses, buying makeup, and eating out. Your mother looked very excited."

Sean couldn't help but notice the keen disappointment on his brother's face. "Did you need her for something?"

"No. I was just wondering." Dan disappeared into the house and moments later returned with a cup of coffee in one hand and a bagel in the other.

"You look tired," Sean commented when his brother rejoined them. "Everything okay?"

"Didn't sleep well."

John smirked at his oldest. "Be careful, Dan. You've been down this road before with Kate Benson."

"Am I that obvious?"

Sean laughed, "Were you *trying* to hide it, Man?"

Dan replied with a punch to the shoulder strong enough to move Sean from where he stood, but it didn't get rid of the smile on his face.

"I'm sorry. I shouldn't tease."

"No, actually, you shouldn't. Especially when there is a certain waitress in town that you harass every other day."

"I do not harass her. I like Marty's turkey club."

"I bet you've gained ten pounds since Tessa moved to town. Marty's doesn't have *that* great of a menu." Dan knew he had better be careful where he went with his argument. Tessa was a believer and a wonderful person from what he could tell. Kate didn't share his faith in God and had a history of leaving him, therefore, a heartache waiting to happen.

"You've been eating at Marty's every other day?" John questioned Sean.

"Dan's exaggerating." Sean shot Dan a warning look and Dan smiled a menacing smile right back at him.

Not many people could say their siblings were their best friends, but Sean and Michael had been Dan's closest friends since birth. They bantered back and forth and knew how to push each other's buttons, but he also knew Sean prayed for him and had his back.

"Seriously, Dan, you know we all love Kate but…" John Tyler looked at his son with compassion mixed with warning.

"I know. I know. She's not saved and she's going back to Boston as soon as she's done here."

"We don't want to see you hurt again," Sean said with sincerity. "Especially since you and Staci just ended things…"

"Did I tell you she texted me yesterday?"

Both John and Sean looked up at Dan at the same time. "Staci?"

"Yes. She was lonely and wanted to get together for coffee."

"And you said what?" Sean pried.

"That I didn't think it was a good idea." Dan sighed loudly and rubbed his temple. "Ever since Kate came back I can't think straight. I've been praying God would show me who it is that's the right one for me and then Kate comes back. Is this some type of test? Should I have tried to work things out with Staci?"

"Son, I don't need to tell you that you need to go with what you know God is telling you. I wasn't too fond of Staci, but I also know God wouldn't have you commit to someone who isn't following His ways. Maybe it's neither of them. Maybe He's seeing if you'll stay consistent and keep praying and seeking Him."

"She'll be gone soon anyway. Kate doesn't plan on staying past her paid time off. She said so yesterday." Dan hated the melancholy tone in his voice.

"Maybe that's for the best. In the meantime, we'll just keep praying," Sean affirmed. What his father and brother were saying was true, but it didn't take away the sting of reality. Ever since they started dating as teens, Kate was the one that Dan imagined sharing his life with. She was the one he compared all other women to. Even worse, Katie Benson was the one who could hurt him more than any other woman on Earth.

*****

Kate didn't realize how starved she had been for female companionship. In Boston, she had a few work friends, but no one that she could see herself going on an excursion with. The environment in her office was competitive at best. Most of the women were busy trying to prove themselves to those in authority rather than building friendships. Outside of work, Kate had only Aunt Lilly. Recognizing all of that made the Saturday morning trip with Colleen and Jen even more special.

After the past week, something as simple as looking at dresses for Jen was a balm to her soul. What was even better was watching Jen, who was painfully shy, develop confidence and a better view of herself with each gown she tried on. At first, Jen relied on Kate to tell her what looked good on her. Then Kate encouraged her to decide for herself what made her feel pretty and what was most comfortable to her. Soon a new sassy Jen emerged. Kate's heart swelled as the girl exited one of the dressing rooms in a trumpet style gown. Everything about the dress, from the cut to the deep Aubergine color, made Jen stand out in all the right ways.

"Oh, Jen!" Colleen gasped. The maternal pride in the older woman's eyes warmed Kate's heart.

Jen stood on the pedestal and moved in a full circle to see herself from every angle, catching the few sparkles that peppered the top of the dress in the light. The smile on her face grew wider as Kate lifted her hair up to show how an up-do would look.

"What do you think?" Kate asked watching the younger woman's expression of awe.

"I feel so beautiful."

"You *are* beautiful, Jen. You were beautiful before you even put this dress on."

Jen smiled sweetly at Kate before doing one more spin.

"I think we have our dress." Colleen nodded to the sales associate.

"Now we need to accessorize and figure out a good makeup palette." Kate went into planning mode and spotted a display of glimmering and shimmering jewelry. "Do you see anything that speaks to you?"

"Speaks to me?" Jen chuckled. "Not really. It's kind of gaudy. Too much."

"I agree. Good eye, Jen. You don't need a lot of extra glitz. In pageants, there's a temptation to be something you're not. The win means more when you're dressing and acting like yourself."

"I was thinking a simple necklace and earring studs.

Kate nodded in agreement. "I still need to find a dress for the funeral. Maybe we'll see something in another store that's more your style."

Three stores later, all three women were tired but everything that they had set out to do had been achieved. Kate found a black dress and even an outfit that she could wear the next day to church, which thrilled Colleen to no end. Jen found a classy tear drop shaped crystal necklace with matching earrings, which Kate insisted on gifting to her. Even Colleen picked up a few items for herself. Before lunch, they went into a cosmetics store to purchase everything needed to finish Jen's look.

"Girls, I'm exhausted." Colleen chuckled as they piled into a booth at the burger joint. "I'm not as young as I want to think I am. You both could shop circles around me."

"I don't know about that, Momma T. You're pretty spry." Kate smiled at the older woman.

"This was fun. Let's do this every weekend," Jen suggested.

Colleen laughed at her daughter's enthusiasm. "I'd go broke if we did this every weekend, my Dear."

"I'm going to go to the bathroom before the food gets here," Kate said excusing herself from the booth.

As Kate made her way to the back corner of the restaurant where the bathrooms were, someone bumped into her.

"I'm so sorry," she said quickly and brought her eyes up to meet those of a man staring at her intently. Did she know him? He didn't immediately move out of the way and his hands were on her arms. It seemed as though he was frozen in place, glaring down at her with a look that unnerved her. "Excuse me."

The man finally dropped his hands and side stepped to allow her to pass, but he never took his eyes from her face. Kate quickly moved away and glanced back over her shoulder at the man. He stood in the same spot, watching her. A chill crept up Kate's spine and she forced herself into the safety of the bathroom.

"Stop. It's nothing. He's just a strange man," she told herself.

There was something about his expression. It felt cold... hateful. Kate reminded herself that she was still recovering from the events of the week. She had to be careful not to make villains and monsters out of everyone as a result of her father's enemies. Is this how she was going to be from now on? Fine one moment, and untrusting and scared the next?

Kate waited until another woman exited the restroom before leaving the room as well. At least that way she'd not be completely alone should she bump into that man again. Her fear was unfounded, however, as the man was gone. Her head was on a swivel as she scanned the restaurant, but she did not see him.

"Kate, are you okay?" Colleen asked curiously. "You look upset."

Quickly composing her features, Kate forced a buoyant smile. "I'm great. I think today is catching up with me."

"I think we will all enjoy a quiet night at home tonight." Colleen agreed.

The conversation turned to the events of the upcoming week and church the next day. Even though Kate contributed a few words here and there, her eyes were perusing every person who walked by their table. Was she making too much of that interchange? Maybe he was a harmless man who was just as caught off guard as she was. She was no longer in danger. It was done. It was time to move on… to let go… to heal.

*****

That was a close one! You almost gave yourself away.

"I know. I'm sorry. I ... didn't expect to see her there," Tony muttered under his breath as he walked along the side of the road. "I've never actually been that close to her before."

Bide your time and get the plan fine-tuned before you make any moves. It's up to you now.

Tony nodded and fumbled with his phone as he tried to pull up the directions to his next destination. The hotel had gotten too risky. Earlier that day, he had forgotten to put the *do not disturb* sign on the door and a maid tried to enter his room. If he hadn't blocked her, she would've seen his open bag that contained his gun and knife. Thankfully, he had a new lead on a place to stay. It was a stroke of great luck that he sat near a group of loud speaking people at the restaurant because what he overheard changed his whole outlook.

"I hate to hear things have gotten so bad between you and Carol. You are more than welcome to stay at our house while we're gone."

Tony glanced over at two men and a woman sitting in a booth near him. The female talked in a sympathetic tone to the man sitting across from her and her husband.

"I appreciate the offer, but I'm staying with my brother for a little bit. I'm hoping Carol will come around and let me come home."

"Well, if you change your mind we keep a spare key under the dog statue." The husband reiterated his wife's offer.

"If I get tired of my brother, I just may take you up on that." The man on the receiving end of the offer laughed. "You're in the house with black shutters, right?"

"Yes, 330 Culvert Street. You can stay the whole month we're gone if you need to."

"I will keep it in mind, but I have to say... I've enjoyed staying with my brother. It reminds me of college all over again.... Playing video games and eating whatever I want without someone watching over my shoulder."

The couple laughed politely, but the woman piped up and cut the frivolity short. "If we don't leave now, we will be late for our flight, Honey."

"Enjoy London and thanks for taking me to lunch. You're good friends."

With that, the conversation had ended and Tony quickly googled the address he had overheard on his phone. He'd have a long walk ahead, but the reward was a secure place to stay for a decent amount of time. Now as he walked towards the house, Tony shook his head at how irresponsible people could be. No one thinks others might possibly be listening in on their conversations. He learned a long time ago to trust no one and definitely to not overshare information in public.

He brought his head up from his phone's screen. He had been walking an hour at least and his feet hurt, but up ahead was his prize. Culvert Street. The reason behind the name was obvious. The Black River was not far away and a large culvert helped divert water under the main highway he had traveled on. Culvert Street was dark and appeared to only have two houses. One house looked derelict and abandoned. But down the street further was a stately looking home with porch lights shining their welcome for him. Luxury *and* privacy.

He carefully approached the house at the bottom of the dead end street. The one thing he did learn from his time with Eddie was to look for any type of home surveillance. A porch camera would ruin his chance at free, uninterrupted lodging. From the shadows, he scanned the house for any type of security camera and finally felt safe in proceeding after seeing nothing threatening.

Near the garage was a statue of a Doberman pinscher. Tipping the heavy statue to one side, Tony saw the silver key glisten. He quickly retrieved it and went to the main door and entered with no resistance.

"We're home, Dad," he whispered to himself as he used his phone as a flashlight to get a look at his surroundings. He didn't feel bold enough to turn on lights that weren't already on. A light in the kitchen above the stove was lit and a small lamp in what appeared to be a family room was also illuminated. Those would have to do just in case someone happened to see and got suspicious.

From what he could tell, the house was very well kept and homey. There was a living room with a fireplace that seemed to be more formal. To the left was a dining room, set up with an elaborate centerpiece. Tony imagined holidays and family dinners sitting around that table. Something he never had. Passing the staircase, he went into the kitchen and was thrilled to see a pantry full of food. The refrigerator was pretty empty, probably since the owners were planning on traveling for a month. The freezer had frozen meals which would work out just fine for Tony. Off of the kitchen was the family room and Tony found the TV. Being at the back of the house, he could watch it without fear of someone outside seeing. This part of the house abutted the woods.

Family pictures adorned the walls. The family appeared to consist of a father, a mother, and two kids. The portraits seemed to document their history as they evolved from being a young family to one with adult children. A few other photos contained various faces of all ages and genders. Maybe grandparents or aunts and uncles. They all looked happy. Tony stood staring at the images for quite a while. His eyes stared into those of the father's without blinking.

I know, Son. It's not fair. You were denied a dad. I was taken from you and then your wretch of a mother married that lunatic.

"He was never my father. She may have let him adopt me, but he was no dad!" Tony self-consciously brought his hand to the forehead and felt the raised scar just under his hairline.

If I had been there I would've killed him for hurting you all those times. I would've made him suffer and beg for his life.... Just like he made you beg him to stop.

Tony wept and felt rage burning inside. It started as a low moan of anguish and turned to a scream of fury, loud and guttural. With a sweep of his arm, he knocked every picture from the wall and sent them crashing to the floor. Some shattered and, to the ones that didn't, Tony stomped on them with the heel of his boot. Only when the wall was wiped clean of the happy family did Tony start breathing steadily again. Then, as if nothing had happened, he grabbed a bag of chips from the pantry, settled into the recliner with the TV remote, and watched cartoons until he fell asleep.

16

The reflection staring back at her seemed unfamiliar to her. Kate dressed and readied to go to church with the Tylers, but wondered what she was doing. Why was she going? Was it to appease Colleen? Kate sighed. No, that wasn't it. She felt drawn. It was a place that meant something to her father, a place where he experienced a life changing encounter with God. Maybe she was hoping for the same.

A soft tap sounded on her door. "Come in."

The door creaked open and Jen poked her head in. "You're really coming with us?"

"Did you think you'd find me sleeping in?" Kate chuckled as the girl came into the room and sat on the bed.

"I wasn't sure, to be honest. I was hoping you were going to come."

"I'm a woman of my word." Kate turned to the younger woman and asked, "What do you think? Is this outfit church worthy?"

Jen's eyes scanned Kate's attire and she smiled. "You look amazing in anything, but you really don't need to worry. Our church isn't snobby. Well, not *everyone* is."

"That's a comfort, I guess."

"Do you have the makeup we bought yesterday? I thought maybe I could try some of it out. I'm curious what Ben will say."

Kate smiled. "I've heard you mention this Ben fellow a couple times now. Is he...?"

"No. Nothing like what you're thinking." Jen corrected Kate adamantly, a little too forcefully and quickly in Kate's opinion. "He's my best friend."

"Ah, I see."

"Stop smiling like that, Kate." Even as Jen reprimanded Kate, her own smile was huge and very telling.

"Do you want me to do your makeup?"

"Would you?"

"Sure. As long as you understand, you wear makeup because it's something you enjoy. Wear it to make yourself feel confident and good, but don't you ever do it for anyone else. Okay? Don't wear it to please some boy or because you think without it you're not pretty."

Jen rolled her eyes. "Yes, Mom."

Kate ignored the sass and set about showing Jen subtle ways to use the cosmetics they bought the day before.

"When you did that ad for Quasi Cosmetics and worked with Randi, did you like it?" Jen asked as Kate applied mascara.

"It was fun."

"Just *fun*? It sounds so amazing. You must get to meet a lot of famous people in your job."

Kate laughed wryly. "Not really. It's not all that glamorous. In fact, it's a lot of hard work and sometimes people take credit for things I did. It can definitely be stressful to make a perfect sales pitch to some very picky people."

"But you love it, right? You make a lot of money."

Kate shrugged. "It's okay, I guess."

"You don't sound like you like it."

"I used to. Or at least I thought I did," Kate said wistfully.

"What do you *want* to do?"

Kate's brow furrowed as she thought through the question. "I enjoy helping people with ideas to make their business successful. I like public relations, helping people get attention for their businesses and helping them draw the attention of customers."

"Is that what you're doing in Boston?" Kate doubted that Jen knew her questions were incredibly thought provoking. Was she *really* doing that in Boston? No. She wasn't. Her job encompassed a small measure of what she wanted and it definitely paid well, but it left Kate feeling unfulfilled. Once again Kate felt disillusioned and misplaced.

"I know you must be good. The stuff you gave Dad and Mom about turning the farm into a family fun spot really got them excited."

"Really? What did they say?" Kate paused what she was doing to look Jen in the eye. While she had spent the overnight hours in the hospital, Kate had played around on her laptop with logos and ideas for the farm. John said he'd look at it, but Kate didn't know if he actually did.

"Why don't you ask him?" Jen laughed. "All I remember is him saying they needed someone like you."

"Girls! Are we ready? The first Tylor shuttle to church is leaving the station." Colleen called from the living room.

"We'd better go. What do you think?" Kate asked as Jen looked at herself in the mirror.

"Whoa! I love it. Thanks, Kate."

Jen bounded out of the room and Kate followed behind her at a slower, less confident pace. She caught sight of her reflection one last time as she left the room. She was even more unsure about her life than she had been when she woke up.

"Kate did that to you?" Kate heard a masculine voice ask in a low rumble. She rolled her eyes and walked out to the living room, not surprised to see Dan scrutinizing his sister.

"She looks stunning!" Colleen smiled, amused by her sons' reactions. All three sported a different expression. Dan looked concerned. Sean had a proud smile and Michael's mouth was gaping. "It's about time everyone recognizes Jen is a beautiful young woman and not just a tomboy."

John Tyler kissed the top of his daughter's head. "Don't go getting a big head, Gorgeous. Now come on or we'll be late for church."

Everyone filed out of the house to their respective rides and Kate noticed Dan's face was still sour.

"What is it? You have something against makeup all of a sudden?"

"No, not at all. But she's ..." Dan fumbled with his words.

"She's 17... and smiling. Did you see that smile?"

Dan snapped his mouth shut and sighed. Kate smiled and started walking to the door.

"It's just ... could you stop changing things please?"

Kate stopped and turned back around at her old friend, expecting to see a teasing smile. She didn't know what to think of the dark expression on Dan's face.

"Excuse me?"

"You come here and change things. You meddle. Then you leave and ..." He was flustered and Kate had no idea what she had done to cause such anger at her.

"It's just makeup."

"No, it's not just that. You... you..." He threw his hands up in frustration.

"You know what? You're being a jerk right now. Maybe you should just stop whatever *this* is..." Kate waved her hands at him, feeling the heat rising in her cheeks. "...and get to church, *Joe Christian*, because I think you need some Jesus."

With that, she spun on her heels and left Dan standing in the living room staring at her as if she had slapped him. *Good*, she thought to herself. She had enough turmoil going on in her heart and mind than to put up with Dan Tyler's up and down mood.

*****

"Lord, you have to help me. I'm losing my mind." Dan prayed on the way to church.

Kate had been perfectly justified in calling him out on his idiocy. What she didn't seem to understand was that he was only an idiot around *her*. Kate made him lose every ounce of common sense. Seeing Jen so happy that morning warmed his heart. His sister actually glowed. It was something he didn't see very often if ever. Kate invested in Jen and his sister came alive. Just like he did. The horrible truth was that she would be gone and where would Jen be then? Where would *he* be?

He made it to church a few minutes late and quietly made his way to an unoccupied seat next to Michael in the Sunday school room. His eyes scanned the room and he found Kate, sitting in a back row in a far corner a few seats down from Tessa. She looked uncomfortable and out of place. He did nothing to help her feel at peace about coming that morning. *I'm so sorry, God. Forgive me. Help me to find a way to reign in these feelings so I can act like the man you want me to be.*

Kate looked up and for a moment their eyes met. She turned away quickly, her jaw set and rigid. He recognized that look oh so well from their dating years. Dan tried to focus on Sean, who was teaching the class that morning, but all he heard were words. He was about to sneak out of the room to get a cup of coffee to clear the cobwebs from his mind when Staci entered the room.

She approached slowly and sat next to him with a hesitant smile. Dan straightened in his chair unsure of how to respond and heard Michael let out a quiet groan. He glanced at Kate and saw her staring curiously before she looked away. Dan did his best to keep his eyes on Sean and not look to his left or to his right. This would go down in Dan's memory as the most awkward Sunday to date. *God, just help me get through this.*

*****

Kate sipped on a cup of coffee she had gotten from the church's coffee bar and watched the people milling around. Sunday school was lost on her. Her mind was on Dan the whole time, unsure of what caused their argument that morning. Then Staci walked in. Why it bothered her so much that she sat next to Dan, Kate did not know. He wasn't hers. Maybe since losing Mark and the death of her father, she had drawn too much strength from Dan. Yet, it felt right to enjoy him. His humor, his black and white way of looking at everything, his care and concern ... those were the things she had always loved about him. *He's not mine.*

"It's always a good Sunday when there's a leftover plain donut." A woman smiled from the coffee bar and held up her donut in apparent triumph. She was a pretty woman with her dark hair pulled up in a claw clip. Kate noticed that on the top of her foot, she sported a peacock feather tattoo with the words *From Death to Life*. "I'm Tessa Grayson."

The woman offered Kate the hand that didn't contain a donut. Reluctantly, Kate shook her hand. "I'm Kate Benson."

"You're Tom's daughter. It's a pleasure to meet you. He was a very interesting man."

Kate laughed wryly. "*Interesting* is a good way to put it."

"He and I used to hang out in this very spot and people watch." The mischievous smile and glint in her eye made Kate smile.

"Oh really?"

Tessa nodded and a softness filled her eyes. "When I started here, I wasn't much of a people person. So I tried to stay out of sight. Turns out that was his plan too. I'll miss him."

Kate tried to imagine her father standing in the very spot where she was standing, doing the very things she was doing. Something about the thought made her feel closer to him. She was grateful to Tessa for sharing it with her.

"Anyway, I wanted to let you know that I will be praying for you tomorrow." Tessa wrapped her arms around herself as if drawing comfort from the oversized cardigan she wore. "And I really mean that. I know some people just say it to say it, but I promise I am praying."

Kate decided she genuinely liked Tessa. She had a vulnerability and sweetness to her that not many people possessed.

"I appreciate that, Tessa. Things were ... different ... between Dad and me. We didn't have a great relationship, so I kind of feel... I just feel a lot of things." Kate couldn't put it into words and she didn't even know why she felt comfortable sharing with this stranger. Yet, it was nice to have someone care. If she didn't watch she might start crying, something she didn't want to do in public.

There was a look in Tessa's eyes, a type of comprehension and understanding. So Kate believed her when she softly said, "I totally get that."

Across the fellowship room, Kate spotted Dan talking to Staci. They were deep in conversation and it was hard to tell by Dan's facial expression if it was one of reconciliation or something else. Kate didn't like how the scene made her feel so she looked back at Tessa. Tessa also stared wistfully but at a different Tyler family member. *Sean?* The woman looked as though Kate had read her inmost private thoughts and blushed, looking down at her shoes. As she had done earlier, Tessa wrapped herself further into her sweater.

Music started playing from the sound system and people started moving towards the sanctuary. Tessa smiled and started to lead the way with Kate following behind her. Too bad she was going to leave after her father's affairs were taken care of. Kate could see Tessa being a good friend.

Walking into the sanctuary was like taking a step back in time. In her head, she could almost hear her grandparents singing *Amazing Grace* from their favorite pew. A few things had changed in the seven years she had been gone. The hard benches were replaced with soft, padded pews.

The carpet looked different. Up in front was a drum set and musicians. When had that happened?

Kate looked uncertain as to where to go and where to sit. The Tylers had taken a pew close to the front. Kate smiled slightly when she noticed Jen sat next to a boy her age. She assumed that was the Ben that Jen had referred to earlier. Dan hadn't entered yet. Kate saw a possible open spot near them but didn't feel like being so enmeshed with the congregation.

"Do you want to sit with me in the boonies?" Tessa leaned over and whispered as if reading Kate's mind. The woman tugged on Kate's sleeve and led her to a tiny alcove with chairs.

"This is much better. Thank you." Kate smiled and Tessa nodded.

Dan entered the sanctuary, looking tired and emotionally spent. However, he entered alone. Kate didn't see Staci. The alcove where she and Tessa sat afforded Kate the safety to watch without being easily spotted herself. Dan scanned the congregation and Kate wondered if he might be looking for her. Probably not. He took a seat at the end of one of the back pews. Michael, who had been sitting with his family, looked back and caught sight of his brother. It brought a smile to Kate when she saw him get up and join Dan. He leaned over and whispered something in his big brother's ear and gave him a nudge in the arm. Whatever Michael said, Dan must've appreciated it because he smiled at his brother and nodded.

As if he knew he was being watched, Dan turned his head and caught sight of Kate. She quickly pretended to join the congregational singing and glued her eyes to the screen at the front of the sanctuary that displayed the words to the song. It was while she was pretending to be invested in the song, that she actually *read* the words. *I was dead and You brought me to life. I was broken and you mended me with Your love.* The words felt oddly accurate. If she could've expressed how she felt over the past week, dead inside was a perfect description. Broken and shattered to pieces described the majority of her life. Even when things were *good*, she felt as though she were just going through the motions of living her life. Kate didn't expect to respond to the song's words, but tears pooled in her eyes. It was as if her ears were turned on and she was hearing for the first time.

She swallowed hard, grateful when the song ended, only to hear her father's name mentioned.

"As many of you are aware, this week we lost a precious brother in Christ. Tom Benson went home to be with his Lord and Savior on Thursday morning. Visitation and services will be held at Johnson's Funeral home in town tomorrow afternoon. A meal will be held here at the church following burial. Anyone willing to bring a dish is asked to have it here by noon. Please be in prayer for his daughter, Kate Benson, as she navigates this grief."

People turned in their seats as if looking for her. Kate felt like leaving. She didn't like these emotions and felt like a spotlight had been put on her. Then another song began to play and she tried to relax. Yet, the words of this song undid her as well. What was happening to her? Why did she feel so undone? There was a weird feeling in that room. It felt like electricity. It reminded her of her father's words in one of his letters when he described the day he went forward to get saved. He called it the *Holy Spirit*.

Pastor Munson got up and started reading a scripture. Kate relaxed. As a kid, this is where she normally zoned out or started doodling on paper, but if she thought she was going to be able to do that this morning she was mistaken.

"Read with me. Ephesians 2: 'And you were dead in your trespasses and sins ... and were by nature children of wrath... *But God*, being rich in mercy, because of His great love with which He loved us... even when we were dead in our trespasses, made us alive together with Christ.'"

After the Pastor read the words, Kate sat back in her chair and glanced back down at Tessa's tattooed foot. *From Death to Life.* As if she knew Kate's thoughts, Tessa winked with a smile and turned her attention back to the pastor.

"Who's your father?" The Pastor asked abruptly and Kate's head snapped up in attention as if he asked her directly. "We can all answer this in different ways. Some had amazing dads. Some had horrible fathers. But here's something you may not realize, despite who our *earthly* fathers are, we were all born to be children of wrath. What does that mean? Due to the curse of sin, we were born into the family of Satan, God's enemy. We were born sinners. We carried on our family name well, bringing nothing but judgement on ourselves. There's literally nothing we could do to help ourselves. Trying hard doesn't bring us out the pit we all find ourselves in. Our successes or what we accomplish do not somehow miraculously bring us peace or joy, though maybe we may experience small moments of happiness in gaining possessions. So where is our hope if we are spiritual children of Satan?

But God.... Don't you love those words? He loved you and I enough to send Himself in the form of Jesus Christ to live perfectly and to die the death we deserved. He died the death of a man convicted so that we could be adopted. I remember the day I led Tom Benson to the Lord at these very steps. He knew he couldn't save himself from his sins. He knew without saving, he would go to his family home ... which was Hell. That Sunday he cried out to God to become his Father. Tom was taken from one family and put into another. And now ... he's home with his Father. In the moment God becomes our Father, we are no longer dead or broken. We are made into something new altogether. Restored into something beautiful and new. So I ask you again, *who is your father?*"

Kate leaned forward. Her heart raced. What was happening right now? It was as if she were seeing her life in perspective for the first time. She had made her life all about how her father had been horrible to her, how he didn't love her. Kate had felt justified in her anger and rage. However, the real issue was not who her earthly father was, but who her *spiritual* father was. It was real. She knew it was. Not only was she experiencing it in *her* heart at that moment, but she saw it with her own eyes. God the Father transformed her own imperfect father. Kate knew she needed that same transformation, but would God have her? What if God turned her away like her own father had when she was younger? *He didn't turn away my father, why would He turn me away?*

At some point the service ended and the final hymn was being sung, but Kate sat frozen in her seat. Tears streaming down her face, she didn't know how to do what her father had done to get saved. She felt a warm arm around her and smelled a sweet scent of perfume.

"What is it, Kate? How can I pray?" Tessa asked in her ear.

"How do I do this? How do I become a child of God?"

Tessa's smile was watery and she took Kate's hand in hers. "You just ask Him."

"That simple? I feel like it should be more... involved."

"Well, you have to *mean* it. You have to see you're a sinful mess and there's no way to save yourself without Jesus doing it for you. Then you let Him change you. My life changed drastically. I stopped doing things that weren't pleasing to God. Then I actually wanted to please Him. I started reading the Bible every day."

"I don't have a Bible."

"We'll find you one, okay?"

Kate nodded. She felt like a child about to approach her father, but it was different than what she had known all her life. "What do I say?"

"Tell Him what you're feeling. Tell Him you want to be His and you want Him to change your heart. That you'll live for Him and not yourself."

With a nod, Kate put her head down. "God, I'm a sinner. I know I'm lost. I'm dead inside. Please bring me to life. I want You to be my Father. Forgive me the way you forgave my father. I want you to change me into who I am supposed to be like you changed my father. Make me new. Please, Jesus, save me."

She lifted her head into the tear filled eyes of Tessa. "Now what?"

"You talk to Pastor Munson. I was baptized after I got saved."

"Will you come with me?"

Kate was scared to move, but Tessa held her arm. She was a stranger turned lifeline and dear friend. As Kate moved, she could feel eyes on her and resisted the desire to run away. Yet, she knew she couldn't. Something was very different. For once, Kate felt very much alive.

*****

It was late. Outside a breeze blew the tree limbs and Kate imagined the leaves falling to the ground gracefully in a dance. What a day! She was thoroughly exhausted and knew tomorrow would be another emotional day. How could she contain both hope and sadness at the same time? Her hand ran over the cover of a leatherbound Bible on the corner of the dresser in the guestroom. Her father's Bible. Colleen had Dan go find it in the house after everyone became aware of what happened at church.

Tears fell fresh. This time she didn't scold herself for being emotional. It was right to feel this way. Kate looked at her reflection and marveled. Who was this new woman looking back at her? There was a light that didn't exist before that day. Taking the Bible into her arms, Kate held it to her chest and moved to the bed. She would look at a few scriptures Pastor Munson gave her before trying to sleep. While she grieved and missed her father, Kate realized for the first time in her life she was loved by *the* Father.

17

There it was in black and white. Tom Benson's obituary. He found it while eating breakfast Monday morning at the kitchen counter. He had opened the small town paper to have something to read while he ate cereal only to see the familiar name in print. The paper was a couple of days old and Tony's insides sunk. He was already dead. There would be no slow and painful death for that monster. The funeral was to be *that* day.

"I failed you. He's already gone." Tony crumpled up the newspaper and threw it on the floor.

But she's not. His daughter is alive and well, living the life you should've had.

"What good is it going to do to kill her if Benson won't even know?"

Oh, he'll know.

"How? He's dead?"

So am I, but I see you. Take her to his grave and kill her right on top of him. Let her blood soak its way down to him. Then you can join me. I'll come for you.

Tony got up and retrieved the crinkled up newspaper. Johnson's Funeral Home.

"It doesn't say where he will be buried. Just that it's a private location."

Do I have to do all the thinking for you? Follow them. Get going. But, son ... don't get caught.

Tony nodded to the empty room and began getting ready. The day before Tony had discovered what a treasure trove the house actually was. The clothes in the closet in the main bedroom fit him well enough, though slightly bigger than he would've bought. The biggest windfall was the keys hanging on the wall near the garage door off the kitchen. He opened the garage door revealing a dark green Jeep. Pushing the button on the key fob the car lit up and unlocked. Hopefully, in such a small town, no one would see the Jeep and put together that he was not the real owner.

Tony stood in the mirror of the walk in closet and admired his reflection. He chose a simple pair of black pants and a button up shirt. The shoes were a bit snug, but he'd make do. When he was content that he would blend in well enough with the mourners, he headed down the hallway to the stairs. He passed a room and something caught his attention.

In a smaller bedroom with a sign that said *"Nana's Angels"* on the door, Tony caught a glimpse of an old yellow dump truck. It was just like the one he had as a kid. He remembered the day that his dad stopped by his house for his usual visit and he pulled out the big box from the back of his car. His mother groused about spoiling him and accused his father of trying to bribe their son.

She didn't want you to be happy. She sucked all the joy out of your life.

"I remember. She kept taking it away from me. Hiding it in the shed."

Tony entered the smaller bedroom. He sat on one of the twin sized beds and picked up the old truck in his hands. Then as if he were nine years old again, he began driving the truck and making motor noises with his mouth. He remembered sneaking out to the shed and finding a patch of dirt to drive his truck through. He had gotten so lost in the fun, he hadn't heard the sound of heavy footsteps approaching. His stepfather, the man who his mother had married when he was three. The evil monster that made every day of his life like something out of a horror movie. Tony remembered the smile on the man's face as he approached.

"Didn't your mom say not to come out here? You know what happens when you disobey."

The adult Tony winced as he remembered the abuse and trauma that followed that encounter. Then tightened his jaw in anger. He recalled the moment vividly. He was still on the ground writhing in pain when his stepfather called a kid from the neighborhood over and gave him Tony's toy truck. *His* truck. Now in the present moment, Tony looked down at the truck in his hands and rage filled him. He threw it across the room as hard as he could, shattering a mirror above the dresser. In the remaining shards of glass, he saw himself, heaving in uncontrollable rage with tears streaming down his face.

Pull it together.

"If they hadn't taken you, you would've come back for me right? You would've rescued me."

Of course. Don't you remember the night Benson shot me? We were talking in the car about running away together.

"Yes. I remember. Then he killed you and I had to go back."

Finish it, Tony. Follow her, plan it out, and finish this. Then we can be together forever.

*****

Kate held the ceramic blue jay in her hand as she walked into the living room. She knew she must look quite morbid dressed in black, holding that small trinket from her childhood. The mood was somber at the Tyler house. Even Michael and his normal over the top sense of humor was subdued. He pulled her into a brotherly hug, as did Sean.

"Kate, you didn't eat anything for breakfast. Can I get you a bagel or some toast to take with you?"

"No, thank you. I'm fine." Kate smiled gently at Colleen. She was a gem of a woman. How many times had Colleen made sure that little Katie had everything she needed? Now, even though Kate was a grown woman, Colleen still offered her maternal love. It was greatly appreciated, especially that day.

"Well, we'll head out to the car and wait for you. But if you want there is a coffee already poured in that travel mug on the counter." Colleen winked and ushered her crew out the door.

Just when Kate thought she was by herself, she saw Dan come from the kitchen holding the travel mug out to her.

"Here. Take this as a peace offering." He offered it with a contrite smile that nearly melted her defenses.

"Peace offering? Does that mean you're admitting…"

"That I was a jerk yesterday?" He finished her sentence. "Yes. I was… an idiot, Kate. I'm sorry."

Kate took the mug from his hands and smiled warmly. "So we're friends again?"

"Friends, yes." Something in the way he said the word and the look in his eye caught her attention, but he didn't give her a chance to contemplate it much. "I didn't get a chance to talk to you after church. You left with Tessa right after and I didn't get to see you again yesterday. Did you really ..?"

"Did I get saved?" Kate laughed softly. "Yes. I think it took. I feel different. It definitely makes what I'm about to do easier."

Dan's face was unreadable, but it looked akin to happiness.

"I'm getting baptized! Pastor Munson said we can do it at the church picnic Saturday."

"An October baptism? That will be pretty chilly. You must be serious," Dan teased gently.

"It's the same place my father was baptized. I wish he could see it."

"Oh, I don't know. I bet somehow he's very much aware of what's happened in your heart. There's a passage in the Bible that talks about heaven rejoicing when someone comes to Christ."

His words meant a lot to Kate and she felt emotions threatening to come forward. The day threatened to be full of those emotions and she knew she had better pace herself. She was grateful when he motioned for her to go ahead of him out the door.

The ride to the funeral home was quiet, which Kate needed. Everyone allowed Kate space to enter the funeral home first and Mr. Johnson showed her to a room set up for her to have a private moment with her father before opening the room partitions, allowing the assembling visitors outside to enter. She didn't know what she expected to see or feel, but as she entered the room she felt undone. As soon as the funeral director shut the partition behind her, giving her privacy, she let the tears fall.

Up ahead was the mahogany casket, flanked by large ferns on both ends. Her mother's urn was held in the crook of her father's arm. An overhead light cast a glow on her father. She approached carefully, not sure what to expect when she saw him. She had heard so many people at funerals over the years say things like, "He looks so peaceful" or "It looks just like she is sleeping". Now as she stood above him, she wasn't sure if she would say he looked like he was sleeping, but from what she understood so far in her new faith, her father was definitely at peace. He looked as though at any moment he could open his eyes. There was a hint of a small smile on his face.

Kate brought the little bird up as if to show him. "Look what I found at the house. Do you remember it? You had gotten mad and smashed it, but you fixed it apparently. When did you do that?"

She placed the bird next to him. "So, I did a thing yesterday. I went to church and I met Jesus. You were right. He does change people. I guess you and I are like this bird. Broken and then restored."

For a moment, memories of her father before his conversion started coming to mind. His temper. The abusive words. His neglect. All of the things she felt tugged at her healing heart as if trying to re-condemn Tom for his actions. She remembered the nights feeling unloved and scared. She remembered the bitter anger and how she wasn't going to come to give him the satisfaction of her presence while he died. *Was that really just ten days ago?* Then she remembered how he looked at her just the other day, with tenderness and love.

Kate leaned in close to her father and whispered. "The past is the past. You are forgiven and set free. We might not have started so great, but we're going to finish well. Both of us. God made us new. I'll see you again... someday. I love you, Dad."

A moment later, Kate heard the partition separate and Mr. Johnson poked his head in to see if she was ready to receive people. She nodded and turned back to her father, bracing for the onslaught of well-wishers. For the next hour, Kate stood poised and held herself together quite nicely, in her opinion, as people told her tales of her father's ornery personality or how he had touched their lives. She heard many times how people were sorry for her loss and many strangers hugged her neck. A few people she recognized from her past and the church. Luke Martin and his wife attended as well.

It was all becoming quite overwhelming when Kate caught a glimpse of a group of familiar faces approaching her. Tessa, Sean, Michael, and Dan took their turn in the receiving line.

"How are you holding up?" Sean asked thoughtfully.

"I'm tired. So tired."

"I think we are bringing up the end of the line. Can I hug you?" Tessa asked.

Kate walked into her new friend's hug, trying to draw strength.

"Why don't you come sit down, Kate? I don't think anyone will mind." Dan tugged on her arm and led her to the front row of chairs. His timing was just right because Pastor Munson came to her and asked her permission to begin the service.

The service was beautiful and Kate felt her father was honored. More so, she felt encouraged and curious about her newfound faith with each scripture passage the pastor read. She would ask him for a list of the verses so she could read them at a later time. The comfort of having Tessa and the Tyler family sitting next to her was soon short lived, as the funeral director excused everyone out to their awaiting cars. Kate drew from her memories of her grandparents' and mother's funerals how the cars would be lined up outside to follow the hearse to the cemetery.

Colleen wrapped Kate tightly in her arms before heading outside. As soon as she and the others left, Kate felt cold and lonely for the first time that day. It was final. There were no more people coming to pay their respects. The sermon was over. Now it was once again just she and her father.

"Spend as long as you need, Miss Benson. Let us know when you're ready for us to close the casket," Mr. Johnson spoke quietly to Kate as she stood close to her father.

With a hard swallow, she replied, "I'm ready."

"Would you like to leave this with your father or take it home with you?" The funeral director pointed at the blue jay.

"That's his. Leave it with him."

The funeral director nodded and gently took her arm to lead her to the waiting limo. She glanced once more over her shoulder at her father and walked out into the daylight. Kate paused outside as she took a breath. Mr. Johnson was patient as he waited for her to continue down the path to the waiting car. Kate took in the line of cars parked behind her limo without really seeing. Numbly, she got into the vehicle. It was such a big car for just her. She wished she had someone to sit in there with her, someone to distract her.

It was after the car door shut that she caught a glance of a vehicle across the street. The Jeep wasn't in the funeral line, but the man inside was staring at her and her father's awaiting hearse. For a moment, her breath caught in her throat as she thought she recognized the man from the restaurant. Yet, when she looked back the Jeep was gone as was the man. She turned in her seat to look out of the rear window but didn't see it anymore. Was she seeing things? Did she imagine the strange man out of tiredness?

She didn't get much time to ponder because the funeral directors were wheeling her father down the ramp and those designated as pallbearers awaited. Kate watched as all of the Tyler men, the pastor, and Detective Martin carefully lifted and walked her father's casket to the hearse. Then the back door was shut and they drove away to the small cemetery on the outskirts of Benson property.

Kate wondered how so many people would fit in the tiny cemetery. The plot of land was considered a part of her family's land, but it held the graves of founding families of Deer Creek and dated back two hundred years. As children, the Tyler boys and she would sneak there to tell scary stories and play hide and seek.

The cars lined the edge of what used to be Benson corn fields. They hadn't been used for crops since her great grandparents lived on the land. Now the field served as a makeshift parking lot as people exited their cars and walked carefully on the uneven ground to the hill. Kate accepted the arm of who she thought was the funeral director only to realize it was Dan. She whispered a thank you as he led her to an area that had been prepared ahead of time for their arrival. The small lot, which hadn't seen activity other than wildlife since her grandparents' burials, now came alive with people. Dan took Kate to the small row of chairs designated for family, before returning to the hearse to fulfill his responsibility to Tom.

The casket made its way to the lowering device positioned above the freshly dug grave. A small stake with her father's name served as a place marker until the headstone arrived the next month. It would have both her father's and mother's names on it. Kate sighed as she thought of them reunited in Heaven.

She swallowed hard against the emotion as Pastor Munson gave final words over her father. The moment felt surreal. It hadn't been unexpected, but yet she felt grossly unprepared for it. With a closing prayer, it was over. People spoke words to her, but she really didn't hear any of them. Soon she realized she was sitting in the cemetery alone but for Colleen, Dan, and the funeral director.

"Come on, Sweetie." Colleen's words were so tender as she prompted Kate to stand.

"Is it okay if I drive with you and Poppa T? It's kind of lonely in that limo."

"You don't have to ask." Colleen hugged her. She needed the feeling of closeness to somebody at that moment. Despite all of the anger and bitterness she had carried... despite the fact she had survived by pretending her father was already deceased for seven years... Kate felt like an orphan.

18

The days following the funeral were a blur. Kate felt like she was living someone else's life as she went about finalizing her father's affairs. Numbness set in. Just when she thought she was going to give up trying to clear out her father's house, an army of friends showed up with gloves, cleaning supplies, and dollies to move furniture. Dan had helped her secure a dumpster and aided in trips to a storage facility where she decided to keep family heirlooms until she had a permanent place to keep them. An estate auction house took a good portion of the furniture that remained.

Now as she wandered the bedrooms upstairs, Kate allowed herself to cry. She had never seen the house this way, echoey and empty. Her footfall sounded loud and intrusive. It was really over. Her father was gone and she was the remaining Benson. This house would live a new life in the Tyler family and that should've brought her comfort, but it didn't.

"Kate, are you here?" Dan's voice came from downstairs.

"Yes. Coming."

She descended the steps and watched her old friend as he took in the barrenness. Was he feeling the same sadness or was he looking at a clean slate to put his own mark on the house? The thought caused resentment to creep into Kate's heart. Why had her father sold the house without telling her? She knew the reason. He didn't even think she would come back. Goodness knows she hadn't intended to. Was she glad that she did? Kate considered that for a moment. *Yes*, she concluded. Her only regret was not coming sooner, and not resolving her anger toward her father more quickly. Maybe she would have found God earlier. She didn't know what could've been, but there was no undoing the past.

"There you are. I just came to check on you and see if you needed anything. My guys are coming to grab the dumpster."

Kate sighed. "I guess everything is done."

"It looks like it. How are you doing in all of this?" His tone was tender and Kate lost a little of the previous bitterness.

"I don't know. It doesn't feel real, you know?"

Dan nodded and allowed Kate to continue.

"I mean, my name is still written in the closet. Did you know that?" Kate walked over to the coat closet and opened it, revealing her juvenile handwriting in a corner. "It's weird to think that it will be painted over. Or maybe this won't even be a closet anymore after you redesign everything."

Dan stayed silent.

"This is awkward. You're my friend but also kind of the bad guy at the moment." Kate attempted a smile, but she knew it fell flat. "Just promise me this doesn't become some type of guy hangout."

"That's not my intention."

"What *is* your intention, Dan?" The words came out a little harsher than she meant them to.

"I want a family. I want to raise my kids near my parents so they can experience life like I did. I want to turn the old workshop out back into my contractor's office. It'll be nicer than working out of my truck or cabin."

"That sounds wonderful," she said wistfully. Dan actually had a good future waiting for him. Kate should be happy for him. Yet, she had no clue what was happening in her *own* life. She wished she could say she had the same awesome future. Mark had been her future.

"I hope it will be. And I can promise you, Kate, this house will be loved and taken care of."

The sincerity in his eyes caused her to swallow hard and look away. "Maybe you can work things out with ... what's her name?"

"Staci." Dan ran a hand through his hair and turned away. "I don't know who God has for me yet, but I'll be ready."

Kate's cell phone rang in her pocket and she looked down in surprise to see Detective Martin's name pop up. A moment of dread filled her soul.

"I'll call him when I get back to the house. He said he would be there tomorrow at the church picnic. Maybe I'll just talk to him then."

"Call him when you get back to the house," Dan insisted. "Tomorrow is your baptism. What if he has something... *unpleasant*...to tell you? You don't want that hanging over such an important day."

"You think something is wrong? Everyone was caught." Kate was certain she couldn't handle any more bad news.

"I hope not, but I would want to know sooner than later. Come on. I'll give you a lift back."

Dan held out his hand for Kate as they left the house and for a moment, Kate had an image of him and his wife leaving the house to go on some type of fun day trip with their kids. She could imagine him holding out his hand lovingly and his doting wife accepting it happily. The thought hurt. The hurt wasn't just about the house. There was an odd ache that Kate did not have the right to feel. She was the one who had ended their relationship. The house was no longer hers, and neither was Dan Tyler.

*****

People were laughing and enjoying one another's company in the Saturday sunshine. The church picnics along the river were always highlights on the church calendar. Kids splashed along the edges of the water but weren't brave enough to go all the way in due to the autumn chill. The state park offered the perfect location for the event as it had everything they needed: playgrounds, a volleyball court, grills, picnic tables, and bathrooms that were not too far off the path. If the location wasn't inviting enough, October baptisms always drew curious spectators as many wondered who would be crazy enough to get dunked in the river in the fall. Kate would, Dan smiled.

Everyone grew quiet as they watched Pastor Munson and Sean, wearing waders, make their way into the water. Pastor Munson gave a few words of welcome and began explaining the significance of baptism.

"This is a day of celebration. Those who have come forward today have given their lives over to Christ and are now making a public declaration today before all of you. Now it is our responsibility to love, guide, and cheer them on in their walk with the Lord."

He held out his hand and motioned for the first person to join them in the water. A ripple of chatter and snickering erupted through the crowd as the man waded waist-deep and drew in a sharp breath before coming to stand next to the pastor. Pastor Munson encouraged the man to share his testimony and the fellow began to speak. To his shame, Dan found himself distracted from the words the man spoke. He caught sight of Kate standing next to Tessa by the water, as she awaited her turn. Her hands were fidgety and her expression was intense as she watched the man ahead of her go under the water and brought back up with the cheers of the people.

Then it was Kate's turn. Tessa gave her a quick hug and Kate gasped as she entered the cold water and made her way to the pastor and Sean. Dan recognized the look of determination that crossed her face. Kate went into her zone and pushed forward despite the obvious scrutiny and discomfort. Then the pastor encouraged her to speak.

"I came back to Deer Creek not long ago to see my father before he passed away. We... didn't have a good relationship. I wasn't expecting to find him changed. Not just changed, but completely different. God did that. God changed my father. I realized I had become an angry bitter person and I really craved what my father had found. I wanted God to become the father I never had and I wanted Him to change me as well. So I asked Him into my heart last Sunday... and here I am."

Dan felt his heart swell with happiness. Kate clearly didn't like being the center of attention, but something in the way she spoke – despite the awkwardness – was genuine. His heart rejoiced and ached at the same time. She was everything he had ever wanted, but she'd be leaving soon. He had to keep reminding himself of that fact. Kate wasn't permanently in Deer Creek.

The sounds of cheers erupted and Dan snapped back to attention just in time to watch Kate emerge from the water, clinging to Sean's arm. His mother and Tessa ran to the bank to wrap her in a towel and their hugs. She belonged here. This is where she was loved. Why couldn't she see that?

Dan felt eyes boring into the side of his head and turned to find Michael staring at him with a wide mischievous smile. "What's wrong with you, Man? Why are you looking at me like that?"

"This solves everything now. The big drawback was that Kate didn't have a relationship with God, right? Now she does. You and Kate can be together. No more grumpy brother."

"Mike. It's not that simple."

"Well, it should be." Michael's smile lost some of its exuberance. "If you don't move, someone else will. Look."

Dan turned to see what Michael motioned to. A group of people surrounded Kate, among them a few younger guys with dopey smiles.

"Even *I'm* tempted to ask her out," Michael admitted and Dan snapped his attention back to his brother.

"*You?*"

Michael got to his feet with a wink and started moving toward the group circling Kate, propelling Dan to do the same.

"Mike…" He hoped his tone was threatening enough to subdue his younger brother, but he wasn't so sure.

Michael paid him no attention and went right to Kate's side and hugged her. He turned enough so he could look at Dan's reaction, which was one of intense warning.

"We're proud of you, Kate," Michael told her before nudging her towards Dan, causing her to stumble into Dan's arms. "Aren't we, Dan?"

"Uh... of course." He hugged her then, ignoring the look of pure satisfaction on his brother's face. Kate in his arms felt right. He wanted to protect her. To love her. Forever.

When he realized he was holding her a little too long, he let her go and tried to regain his composure. She didn't immediately move away and he forced himself to take a step back.

"How do you feel... you know... after being baptized?" Dan kicked himself mentally. *How do you feel after being baptized? That's the best I could come up with? Smooth, Tyler! Smooth!*

"Good. It feels really ... good." Kate smiled. "And really cold."

"Come on, Girl." Tessa laughed and tugged Kate away from her adoring crowd. "I've got your bag. You can get changed into dry clothes in the bathroom."

Once Kate was away from visibility, Dan punched his brother in the arm as hard as he could.

"Uh oh. What did he do now?" Sean asked, joining his brothers.

"I just tried to nudge Dan in the right direction. That's all." Michael feigned an innocent face.

"Quit interfering." The words were said through gritted teeth and Dan hoped his brother saw that he was serious. "I told you, starting a relationship with Kate is not that simple."

"He's right, Michael. Back off of this one," Sean agreed.

Dan hoped the matter was dropped, however, not twenty minutes later Michael was at it again. He strategically took over assigning sides for the volleyball game, putting Kate on Dan's team and putting the other flirtatious guys on the other. Dan resisted putting his brother in a choke hold when Michael brushed past him saying in a low voice, "Really, Dude, do I have to do everything for you?"

Much to Dan's relief, soon the dinner bell rang and everyone started making their way to the pavilion set up with a wide array of potluck dishes and desserts. He stayed back from the crowds for a while to distance himself from Kate, but she was never out of his line of sight. There was definitely something different in her countenance. There was a peacefulness that hadn't been there before. He smiled as he watched her laugh with Tessa and a few other ladies at a picnic table.

What would happen if she did decide to stay? Maybe the idea wasn't too far-fetched after all. Maybe she'd realize that she could be happy in Deer Creek. She already had a host of new friends. Maybe she could start her own business there. Maybe he and Kate really could have a relationship again, this time not as two love-sick kids, but as adults wanting the same thing. *That's a lot of maybes,* Dan thought to himself.

"That's quite a face." A soft voice snapped Dan back to reality.

Staci stood next to him, looking apprehensive. He sighed and forced a smile. "I didn't know you were coming today. I thought you said you were going home to see your parents."

"I haven't been able to bring myself to tell them about us. They had great expectations. I just didn't want to go home and talk to them about it just yet."

Dan nodded. He wasn't sure what he was supposed to say at that moment.

"Dan, I know it was my idea for us to stop seeing each other, but…"

"Before you finish that sentence…" Dan turned to her and put a gentle hand on her arm, leading her further away from any listening ears. "You were right to suggest our breakup. You deserve someone who is head over heels for you. That wasn't me."

"Oh, I know I was right…" Staci laughed knowingly. "But I want to give you another chance."

Dan stood silent, staring at the petite woman in front of him. "Staci, I still don't think it's me. I'm more conflicted than I was that night we broke up."

"I'd hate for our chance of happiness together to be ruined just because *she* came storming into the area and left chaos in her wake." Staci's voice rose a notch and Dan tried to move them even further out. "She's going to leave, Dan. Then what? Are you still going to obsess over her? Is that what God wants for you?"

"I don't know. I don't know what the answer is."

"I am willing to forgive this mess and move on. We can start fresh." Staci reached down and lovingly took Dan's hand in her own. "What do you say? Will you think about it at least?"

She was right. He knew she was. Kate would leave and then what? But did he have real feelings for Staci? No.

"Staci, you deserve a man that loves you unwaveringly. I don't. I'm so sorry."

Dan knew the words hurt. Staci took a step back as if he had struck her. His own heart ripped in two as tears pooled in her eyes. At that moment, he wished he *could* love her the way she wanted. His life would certainly be easier.

"You're an idiot, do you know that?" Staci backed away and Dan allowed her to say what she needed to, silently taking the verbal beating. "She doesn't love you. She'll be gone and then you'll really regret this, Dan Tyler. Don't try to call me. Don't even look at me."

With that, Staci walked up the stone path to where the cars were parked. He waited a few moments to give her a head start before heading to his own truck. He didn't feel social anymore. Just as he put his hand on the door handle, he looked for Kate one last time. She was standing talking to Luke Martin, her face unreadable. As if she knew his thoughts were of her, she looked in his direction and their eyes met briefly. For a moment, he thought he recognized a flicker of something almost as torturous as what he was feeling. Then as quickly as it appeared it was gone and she was giving Luke her full attention again, nodding at whatever he was telling her. Not for the first time since Kate Benson came crashing back into his life, did he pray the same prayer. *God, if she can't be mine, take these feelings away. I'm in danger of falling in love with Kate Benson all over again.*

*****

Kate tried to be polite to Detective Martin, but she kept catching voices in the wind and glimpses of Dan and Staci in her periphery. There seemed to be a lot of touchy-feely stuff going on. She tried to hear what they were saying but Tessa or Luke would say something that required a response.

"I'm glad to see you and Tessa building a friendship. She's the closest thing I have to a daughter." Luke smiled proudly at Tessa and she looked like a doting child, beaming under the compliment.

"Oh? I didn't know that." Kate smiled warmly and momentarily glanced over his shoulder to see what Dan and Staci were doing.

"The Martins were instrumental in my coming to Deer Creek. I'll have to tell you sometime… when there's not so many *distractions*."

Kate's eyes shot to her friend's face and she saw her smirk. Before Kate could respond, Luke turned to Tessa and said, "Tess, would you mind giving Kate and me a moment to discuss something?"

Like a daughter who knew her father well, she seemed to pick up on the seriousness that was to follow. "Yes. Of course. I'll just be over at the table, Kate."

"I guess this has something to do with your call yesterday?" Kate surmised.

"You didn't call me back." There was a softness in the older man's eyes, but there was still a tone of scolding. "I'm pretty sure I called a few times."

"I'm sorry. It's just … I knew that if you were calling, it probably meant you would say something I didn't want to hear."

Luke surprised Kate by laughing. "At least you're honest."

"What was it that you needed to tell me?" Kate caught sight of Dan leaving and instantly she felt like the sun was going behind a cloud. Whatever Luke was about to tell her, Dan wouldn't be there to comfort her. For a split second Dan looked up and she all but pleaded with him through her expression to stay, but he got in his truck and drove away. Was he going somewhere with Staci?

Luke cleared his throat and brought Kate back to the present.

"I'm sorry. I'm listening."

"I was trying to tell you that after interviewing Eddie Barrow, we have reason to believe there is still another possible threat. Your father mentioned a young son of Tony McCullough in his letters to you. There is no birth record of a son. Did your father mention anything about this to you?"

"Only what he said in the letters. My father didn't really give more information before he died." Kate paused and looked up at Luke. Ignoring the familiar stab of her recent betrayal, she asked, "Did Mark ... Eddie... say another person was *here*?"

"He's not being very forthcoming unless he gets a deal with the prosecutor, but he *did* mention he was not intending on taking the fall for James' nephew. After going through his cell phone there are a few texts to James McCullough referencing this person." Luke looked frustrated about not being able to give more information. "James' phone hasn't been located. I feel like we're chasing a ghost."

The image of the man Kate ran into at the restaurant and then the glimpse she thought she caught at the funeral popped into her mind. "If there was another person... wouldn't he stand out? Isn't there a video somewhere? I don't know, maybe from a gas station or something?"

"Believe me, we're working on it. I have people looking into every past relationship Tony McCullough ever had to see if there was a son. If we find one, we'll make sure we find that person."

Kate nodded numbly.

"Kate, in the meantime, be on guard. If you see someone out of the ordinary or even think something is off, call me."

"How do I know when something is really wrong or if I'm just being paranoid?"

Her tone must've given her away because Luke sighed and shook his head. "You've already experienced something."

"It was a man at a restaurant. It was just the way he stared at me. It made me uncomfortable." Kate wrapped herself in her arms as if protecting herself. "And then at my father's funeral, I thought I saw him in a Jeep, but it was a split second. I blinked and he was gone. I could've imagined it."

"I'd rather not risk that." Luke pulled out his phone and started taking notes. "Now I want you to tell me what restaurant that was, and on what day, and what time."

For the next several minutes, Kate recounted every detail she could remember of the odd encounter and did her best to describe the Jeep. She felt tired, overwhelmed, and anxious by the time Luke finally concluded he had something to go on.

"I'm sorry to have cast a shadow on such a special day, Kate."

"I should've called you yesterday."

"Yes, that would've been much better," the Detective chided. Then his tone softened. "I know that you have to return to Boston at some point, but you have people here who care about you. Our Tess is one."

Kate attempted a smile.

"That Dan Tyler is a good guy. That whole family is pretty great."

Had he picked up on her preoccupation with Dan and Staci earlier? *Of course he did, Idiot. You were obvious.*

"I'm talking as an older father figure now. It might not be a horrible thing to stay close to them for a little while. You're growing as a new Christian and needing healing from everything you've gone through. Maybe you'll find Deer Creek is too wonderful to leave. You wouldn't be the first person who came here and decided to stay."

Luke winked and smiled warmly at Kate as he dismissed himself. The idea of staying in Deer Creek with these amazing people was tempting, to say the least. Not for the first time, Kate realized she had nothing enticing her to go back to Boston. But to stay in Deer Creek? And do what? Moon over Dan? Live off the Tylers' generosity? Hide from an unknown, possibly non-existent, enemy? Kate stood silently staring at where Dan's truck had been parked. *I belong to You now, God. I could use some Fatherly wisdom. What do You want me to do? Staying here feels right, but it's crazy, isn't it? I have a job in Boston. What would I have here? Where do I belong now?*

19

Kate sat on the porch staring numbly down at the phone in her hands. Three phone conversations in a row - in addition to her already troubled thoughts that Monday morning - made her despondent at best. The blast of cold in the October air matched her mood. The leaves started trembling on their branches as another breeze hit, causing them to flitter to the ground. Kate burrowed a little further into her jacket.

The first call came at the breakfast table and she had dismissed herself to answer. O'Brien's garage called to let her know that the insurance company declared her car a total loss and that even if she wanted to repair the car, he was having a tough time getting the right parts for her Audi. It wasn't the best news, but Kate wasn't altogether shocked.

The next call came as she was getting ready to go back inside. This time the call was from Aunt Lilly.

"I'm having an open house this weekend. I decided to sell the house," Lilly had said. "It's hard to be in this neighborhood after what happened."

"I'm so sorry, Aunt Lilly. It's my fault."

"No, it's not, Katie. It's your stupid father's fault. After everything you told me about what happened, I blame him."

"Lilly, it wasn't his fault either. He had no way of knowing what would happen."

"Death follows that man. First my sister, then my neighbor." Kate heard her aunt sniffle on the other line and Kate felt it was best to keep quiet. "I don't want to argue with you. I know you think you found some kind of resolution with Tom before he passed. It's better if we just don't discuss him."

"I guess." It hurt Kate to have someone speak of her father this way.

"The reason I'm calling is to see what your plans are. You've been gone for a little while now and I want to know if you plan to move with me to a new place. Either way, I need you here to pack your things, Katie."

Kate felt the walls closing in on her. Of course, she knew she had to go back, but she didn't feel ready. Not yet. There was so much more that she wanted to know about her walk with the Lord and she didn't even begin to know who to go to in Boston for guidance. In Deer Creek, there were so many people who helped her by giving her scriptures to read, praying with her, and offering their friendship.

"You lost your condo. Do you have another place lined up?" Kate doubted her aunt knew she sounded as harsh as she did, but it stung her. "You're more than welcome to come with me but I'll need you to start paying more in rent. Prices are outrageous right now."

"I…I've been so busy handling Dad's business. Can I have a couple of days to think things through?"

"I'm not trying to be unreasonable, Kate. It's just that I need to choose between a house or a smaller apartment. A lot depends on what you decide." Lilly sighed then. "Do you think you can give me an answer by Sunday?"

Sunday wasn't that far away. She had less than a week to decide whether she was going to live with Lilly or get her own place. *Or I could stay here.* Kate shook her head at the thought. The sentiment popped up more and more frequently lately, but it wasn't realistic. Her job was in Boston.

"Yes, I'll let you know Sunday night."

"Great. Oh, by the way. You had better call work. They left a couple of messages here at the house. Don't they have your cell phone number?"

That was odd. "Yes, they do. What did the messages say?"

"I didn't keep them on the answering machine, but it was something about a new project with some makeup company that was coming up and they needed you to say whether you'd be back in the office."

"When did they call?"

"Oh goodness." Lilly blew a rush of air out as she tried to think. "I think it's been a few days. It might've been last Thursday."

Kate felt her jaw clench and she tried to gracefully get off the phone with her aunt as quickly as possible. Something felt wrong and if her suspicions were correct, she may have just lost the Quasi Cosmetics account, the one she had worked on for a year prior to leaving Boston. The very account that Randi Lawson had requested Kate for specifically.

"Kate?" Colleen's voice cut through the hurtful thoughts. "Are you coming back in? It's awfully cold out here."

"I'll be in shortly. I have a few things I need to address."

"And you can't do that inside where it's warm?" Colleen looked concerned.

Kate didn't answer and Colleen went back inside the house, leaving the younger woman to figure out what was happening. Kate nervously called into her office in Boston and pressed her boss' extension. Maureen offered a few pleasantries and rote condolences regarding Kate's father, but her tone became matter-of-fact when Kate asked about the Quasi Cosmetics account.

"We didn't hear back from you so I assumed you were still busy handling your father's affairs. I gave the account to Scott."

"*Scott*? Randi Lawson requested *me*. I've been leading on this account since she came to our firm over a year ago." Kate felt her blood pressure rise. "Why didn't you call my cell phone? Why did you call my aunt's house? I told you I was in New York. I never got the messages."

"I gave Scott the job of contacting you. I had no idea what number he used to reach you. He just told me he left messages for you and when I never heard back, I had to move on. This account is worth billions. We can't let it fall through the cracks, Kate."

"Maureen, Scott has my cell phone number. He's called it many times."

"Are you accusing him of something, Kate?"

Yes, she was. Kate knew very well how competitive things were in the advertising firm. She was gone and Scott saw an opening and took it. Tears stung her eyes.

"Look, it takes a team to make things work around here. Just because he's going to take the lead for the new campaign doesn't mean you won't have a part." Maureen's voice was patronizing. "When you get back you can work your way up to where you were before you left. When is your return date?"

"I'm finishing things up and I hope to be back when my paid time off runs out, next Friday."

"That means you'll be starting back the first Monday in November." Maureen sighed as if that wasn't good enough. "Well, you know we need your talents, Kate. Of course, you're entitled to use your time off and please believe me, I do sympathize with your loss."

Kate held her breath waiting for her to get to the point. It didn't take long.

"However, if you can come back *before* November you may find I'd be more willing to entertain giving you more of a role in this account. I'm well aware that you and Randi seemed to strike up some kind of friendship in your time working together."

The call ended with Maureen once again telling Kate how sorry she was for her loss and that she hoped to see Kate back soon. Of course, Kate knew that the world couldn't stop spinning just because she had lost someone. Just because she didn't feel ready to go back to Boston, it didn't mean that she had the luxury of staying in Deer Creek. However, the idea of going back brought Kate more pain than she had expected.

The next two days consisted much of the same routine. Kate sat with her laptop at the dining room table, scouring over apartment listings as well as job openings – just in case something more appealing had opened up. When she wasn't searching the internet, she took walks to and from her old home. It was Wednesday when Colleen approached her, concern all over her face.

"Mind if I walk with you?" Colleen asked Kate.

Kate nodded and the two started down the trail through the woods.

"I thought that after I asked Christ into my life, everything would fall into place. I thought everything would change for the better." Kate blurted out moments after they started down a trail. "But ... I feel so torn up. Why isn't He helping me like He did when I first got saved? Why didn't the feeling last?"

"Oh, Kate. What you're feeling is normal, Sweetheart. God never promises that everything will be roses and rainbows after we choose to follow Him. He promises to guide us, strengthen us, and be with us no matter what as we go through those tough times. But it doesn't do away with those times altogether."

"But *is* He guiding me? I feel confused and miserable. Work wants me back as soon as possible and I don't even know if I want to go back to this job. I feel like my world was turned upside down. I thought I had everything I wanted in Boston before I came back to Deer Creek. Now it's as if none of that ever mattered at all."

"I'm not going to pretend to know what God is telling you to do, Kate, but I do know from experience that He often uses circumstances to change our plans into something *He* designed for us... sometimes something completely different."

"Do you think He's telling me *not* to go back?"

Colleen chuckled. "The selfish in me wants to tell you to stay, but ultimately only you will be able to know what God wants you to do."

"How will I know?"

"Have you been keeping up with your Bible reading?"

Kate nodded.

"Good. Keep that up and pray specifically that God will show you what He wants you to do." Colleen squeezed

Kate's arm gently. "If it's God's will, it will be whatever will help you to grow more in Him."

Kate thought about Colleen's words as they walked in silence. Would she grow in her newfound faith in Boston? She'd have to look for a church now in addition to everything else she'd been researching.

"I don't want to say anything to confuse you, Kate," Colleen spoke up and caught her attention. They paused on the path and Kate looked at Colleen quizzically. "John and I have been talking a lot about the ideas you gave us regarding the direction we want to take the farm. We could really use someone like you to help us navigate some of the changes we want to make as far as opening the farm to the community. We'd be willing to offer you a job. Of course, it wouldn't pay the same as your career in Boston, but maybe it would be something to propel you into starting a business consulting firm here."

Something in Kate sparked to life, but she didn't know why.

"Like I said, I don't want to add confusion to what you are already working through. Just know that the offer stands… if you conclude God is telling you to stay around a while."

A moment later, Colleen caught sight of Dan going into his cabin and Colleen excused herself to go talk with him about some matter. Kate appreciated the time alone to try to sort through the myriad of emotions warring within her. *I know I'm new to how you work, God, but could you just make it really clear what you want me to do? And if it's going back to Boston, could you help me not to feel like I'm leaving my heart behind in Deer Creek?*

*****

Dan's busy schedule had been a blessing. He managed to keep away from Kate since the picnic and baptism. If he could keep himself distracted, he'd be better off when she left. At least that is what he kept telling himself. Then his mother stopped in to see him the day before and asked him to take Kate to the Fall Days Fair on Saturday.

"She's been so down, Dan. I'm really worried about her," Colleen had said. "I think the outing would really lift her spirits."

"Why can't she go with someone else? What about Jen?"

"Jen will be manning the photo booth with Ben on Saturday. Michael will be there, but he'll be working in the stand-by ambulance. Sean has a prior commitment."

He had told Colleen that he would think about it, but now as he was walking to the house for dinner, he was thinking of ways to tell his mother no. He rehearsed his words along the way and he thought he had it down pat until he rounded the bend and caught sight of Kate in the backyard, approaching the chicken coop. He shook his head as he heard her muttering to herself.

"Just stay where you are, you feathered freak. If you so much as point your ugly beak in my direction, I swear I'll have Colleen make chicken for dinner."

Kate disappeared into the coop and all seemed well for a few moments. Then all of a sudden, the sound of screaming and squawking filled the air as Kate came running out thrashing a wicker basket at the chicken that jumped and flew at her in a frenzy.

"Get away, you monster!" She yelled. The back door opened and Colleen and Jen came out to see what was going on and instantly started laughing.

"Again, Kate? I told you this morning. First, you have to throw the feed and lure Slayer away from the roost." Jen laughed as she pulled a feather out of Kate's hair.

Dan couldn't help but smile as well as he approached the scene and a very flustered Kate glared at him.

"Why are you attacking the chickens, Kate?" he asked, pulling yet another feather this time from her shoulder.

"*Me*? That ... that *monster* attacked me!" Kate jumped as if she thought Slayer was heading back in her direction. "Your mother thought it would be good to take on a few chores to keep my mind occupied. I don't think this is working, Colleen."

His mother stood on the top step of the porch hiding her mirth behind pursed lips, but her eyes gleamed with amusement. "Maybe gathering the eggs wasn't the best idea."

"You think?" Kate put her hands on her hips and tried to hide her own laughter at the situation.

"You really don't do chickens well, do you? I remember something like this happening when we were kids, too." Dan pointed out as he remembered a young Kate being taught by Colleen that chickens were harmless.

"Jen, could you ... please?" Colleen smiled at her daughter and went back inside to finish dinner preparations.

Jen took the basket from Kate begrudgingly and left Kate and Dan standing in the remaining twilight in the backyard.

"So mom's putting you to work, huh?"

"She told me that I need to keep busy. This morning she tried to teach me how to bake pie."

"And how did that go?"

Kate laughed. "You'll see after dinner. I hope you like darker pies."

"I'm sure it will be… delicious." He knew his smirk gave him away.

"Yeah, sure it is. The smoky flavor was *intentional*."

Kate watched Jen emerge triumphantly from the coop holding up the basket with a few remaining eggs that Kate couldn't get.

"I better see if I can help your mother with dinner. Maybe I can redeem myself."

"Kate, wait…" Dan couldn't believe he was getting ready to do this. *Stop talking now! Don't do it! You'll only regret it.* "Saturday night is the Fall Days Carnival. I was going to go and I thought maybe…"

"*You* thought? Or *Colleen* thought?" Kate smiled. "She seems pretty determined to keep me busy."

"I can tell." Dan smiled and looked down at the ground before bringing his attention back to Kate. "I think it would be a fun night… if you'd like to go."

He thought maybe she was looking for a way to let him down easily because she didn't answer right away. However, she looked genuinely pleased when she said, "Thank you. I would love to."

They were walking into the house when she turned to him and said, "Do they still do the corn maze? If I remember correctly, I beat you out last time we went together."

"I let you win."

"Oh really? Well, none of that this time. I've got skills, you know." Her face was challenging and Dan couldn't resist smiling.

"Challenge accepted, Kate Benson."

20

He held his breath and pressed his back against the wall in the upstairs hallway. The sound of his heart pounded so loudly that it seemed to keep time with the sounds of knocking on the front door below. Tony gulped and tried to listen to what the two police officers said to one another, but he couldn't hear. Their voices were no more than murmurs to his ears.

Tony moved stealthily to the bedroom window above where the men stood outside. He dared not move the curtains for fear of exposing himself. They spoke loud enough for him to make out their words.

"Police. Is anyone home?" one of them called out while continuing banging on the door.

"Did the lady even see the license plate or are we just going to hunt down all known Jeep drivers in the area," the other said.

"No license plate number. Just said it was a dark Jeep. Maybe green."

There were rustling noises and the other called, "There's a Jeep parked in this garage. I can see through the window."

"Are you all looking for the Smiths, Officers?" Another voice caught Tony's attention and he carefully pushed the side of the curtain to let him see who was outside.

Below the window, a woman got out of her car. "I'm Nancy Smith's co-worker. They are on vacation in Europe."

"Europe?"

"Yes, she told me I could come and borrow a wheelbarrow for one of the Fall Days Carnival displays this weekend. Here, I can show you our texts." The woman pulled out her cell phone and showed her phone to one of the officers. "Is everything okay?"

"How long have they been gone?"

"Several days. They won't be back until closer to Thanksgiving."

"Do you know if they've given anyone permission to drive their Jeep that is in the garage?" One of the officers asked looking back towards the house and garage and Tony slid back against the wall next to the window again.

"I don't think so, but I can call her if you'd like to ask her yourself. Is anything wrong?"

"We just had a suspicious report involving a dark-colored Jeep, so we're checking with local Jeep owners in the area to see if any were in the vicinity at the time of the incident."

"Well, I doubt it was theirs, but let me call her." The woman's tone changed as her friend picked up the other line. "Nancy, Hi. I just got to your place and there were two police officers. They have a question about your Jeep."

The woman must have handed the phone to the officer because it was his voice Tony heard next. "No, Ma'am. No need to worry. We had a recent sighting of suspicious activity in the area involving a Jeep and we are just following any leads. Have you given anyone permission to access the Jeep while you and your husband are away?"

There was a moment of quiet when Tony assumed she was answering.

"I see. Do you know whether this friend actually came and drove the Jeep? Yes, thank you. It would be helpful to have his information just to rule it out."

Tony's mind started going into high gear as the officers and the lady below spoke back and forth. He knew his luck couldn't last forever.

I told you not to be so obvious at Benson's funeral. You idiot! You better hope that they leave soon. You need to get out of here.

"Shh. I know. I messed up. I'm an idiot." Tony whispered to himself as he rubbed his head with the palms of his hands.

"She said there should be a key under the dog statue. If it's not there, their friend may have accessed the house to get the Jeep's keys inside. The guy had their permission." The one officer said to the other.

Idiot. Idiot. Idiot.

"I'm not seeing a key. Maybe their friend came by after all?"

"Likely. We'll call him. We're searching for a needle in a haystack if you ask me. It's upstate New York. There are thousands of Jeeps in this area."

Tony realized a few moments later that he no longer heard any voices or movement outside. He gently moved the curtain again to see the officers and the woman had left.

Get moving, Son. Pack food, clothes, and any money you can find in a bag.

Spurring into action, Tony grabbed a duffel bag from the master bedroom's closet and shoved jeans and clothing from the drawers into it. He then glided down the stairs, watching for any intruders as he filled the bag with food from the pantry. He opened the side door of the kitchen that led into the garage and realized he wasn't going to be able to drive the Jeep anymore. It was too risky. Then he saw what he needed.

A mountain bike hung off a mount on the wall. It wasn't his first choice as far as mode of transportation went, but desperate times called for desperate measures, he concluded. He got the bike down and tried it out for size in the garage before attempting to ride it out into the open. It would do. He spotted a few camping items on a shelf and grabbed the rolled sleeping bag, strapping it onto the back rack of the bike. He put his backpack on and threw the duffel bag over his shoulder then opened a door that led to the backyard. He'd go through the woods. It would be better to brave the brush than risk riding down the street in broad daylight after his near encounter with the police. He looked over his shoulder once more at the house as he left into the forest. It felt nice to have a home, even if it had only been for a few days. Soon he'd join his father and maybe then he'd finally be at rest.

*****

The air was electrified as young women dashed all over the room from mirror to mirror. Kate could hardly hear herself think over the incessant chattering and giggling. She used to be one of them. It felt like so long ago now Kate realized as she pinned up the last strand of hair into Jen's elaborate updo. Colleen stood next to them gushing and taking pictures every few seconds.

"Oh, Jen! Don't you look so cute?" A girl slinked her way next to Jen's side in the mirror. Kate noticed Jen's shoulders tense.

"Thanks," came Jen's less than thrilled response.

"Just remember, no matter what happens tonight the important thing is to have fun." The girl pulled out a lipstick and applied it to her own lips before winking at Jen and disappearing into the haze of hairspray and perfume.

"Who in the world was that?" Kate asked.

"That was Kristi Mason."

"Oh... *the* Kristi? The one that almost made you not do the pageant?"

Jen nodded. "Ben has had a crush on her since ninth grade."

"Oh? Does he still?" Kate glanced over her shoulder to see where Kristi flittered off to before leaning closer to Jen's ear and saying, "Because if I didn't know any better I'd say he seems to like *you* an awful lot."

Colleen smiled and nodded slightly, but Jen didn't look convinced in the least. "I think you're both seeing things."

Kristi's loud laughter floated through the air as she made her rounds to other contestants to *wish them well*. A lot of girls seemed to mirror Jen's reaction.

"Is it wrong to pray that someone stumbles on stage, Colleen? I'm new to this *love the unlovable* thing, but isn't there a verse about pride coming before a fall or something?" Kate smirked and Colleen play punched her in the shoulder.

"I believe you already know the answer to that, Katie Benson. Behave yourself."

Overhead an announcer called the girls to attention. "Ladies, this is the ten-minute warning. We'll begin with the choreography and casual interviews in ten minutes."

"Uh, I don't know if I can do this. I feel sick," Jen said grabbing Kate's arm for stability.

"Breathe through your nose and out through your mouth. You have this, Jen."

"You are by far the prettiest girl in this room, sweet girl. Dad, your brothers, and I will be cheering you on. We're so proud of you." Colleen hugged her daughter before heading out toward the exit.

"She's right. You shine differently than anyone else here. Remember what I taught you about not talking too quickly and watching your pronunciation." Kate planted a quick kiss on Jen's forehead before catching up with Colleen.

Once into the auditorium, Kate and Colleen took the seats saved for them by the Tyler gentlemen.

"Do you think she'll do okay? Was she nervous?" Kate heard John ask his wife after she sat down next to him.

"She'll do fine."

Kate sat in the only open seat, between Michael and Dan. Sean smiled at her as she scooted her way past him to the available seat and plopped down with a sigh. Jen's friend Ben sat in the empty row in front of them and turned to smile at her brothers. While Sean and Michael smiled politely back, Dan simply nodded.

"Stop it with the scary big brother scowl," she whispered.

"I don't know what you're talking about."

"Don't you?" Kate smiled as Dan smirked.

"I don't want him getting too comfortable. There needs to be a little bit of fear so he doesn't think he can just mess with her and get away with it."

She rolled her eyes. "And what makes you think he's messing with her?"

"I don't know, but he'll think better of it if he knows I'm watching him."

The music began and the stage lights started flashing in many different colors as the parade of young women all dressed in gorgeous formal gowns came out to the cheers of the audience. Dan probably whistled louder than anyone in the room and Kate laughed as she put her finger in her ear to muffle the piercing noise. She hoped Jen knew how loved and treasured she was.

The girls did a few choreographed moves to the song and took turns walking to the microphone and saying their names, the high schools they attended, and their grades. Curiously, Kate watched Ben's reaction when Kristi spoke to see if he had any response. None, just as she thought. Then when Jen approached the mic, the young man beamed and hooted and hollered just as loud as the Tyler family. Kate nudged Dan and nodded at the young man as if to prove he was legitimately smitten, but he just ignored her and continued cheering his little sister.

The girls stood in their respective poses as the announcer called each one forward to answer an interview question. Kate was definitely biased when it came to Jen Tyler but clearly, she was the most honest and real contestant by far. She was asked what her favorite quote from literature was and she recited her favorite Bible passage from memory.

After all the girls exited the stage, the talent portion began and many girls sang and danced their hearts out. Jen played a classical piece on the piano. When she finished, Ben stood and applauded her with such a sweet lovesick expression that even Dan had to smile. Everyone got to their feet to cheer on the youngest Tyler and when she rose from the piano bench she looked right at her crew of supporters and smiled as she took her bow.

Then came the moment that they had anticipated. They announced the third runner-up, a sweet bouncy redhead. The second runner-up was a quiet, well-mannered girl in a pink sequin dress. Kate held her breath.

"Our first runner-up is Jenna Tyler from Deer Creek High School." The announcer called out and the entire Tyler crew, Ben included, jumped up in raucous celebration.

In a moment of unchecked emotion, Dan lifted and spun Kate until he realized what he was doing and put her down quickly. The announcer continued announcing but Kate really didn't hear who actually won the title of *Miss Fall Days* because her heart was fluttering. When she finally realized it was Kristi who won overall she looked up at Jen but didn't see one ounce of disappointment at all. Only happiness.

As soon as people were allowed to approach the stage the Tyler brothers rushed their little sister, throwing her up onto their shoulders proudly and chanting her name. She was laughing so hard and trying to tell them to stop that she almost didn't notice a certain shy young man standing off to the side in adoration. Kate took in the sight and her heart swelled.

Colleen came and stood next to Kate and whispered, "Thank you."

"For what? I didn't do anything. Jen was just being herself up there."

"You helped her to see what we all already saw in her." Colleen wrapped Kate in her arms and the two joined in on the group's merriment. For the first time since her father passed away, Kate was truly happy and content. What was even more amazing, Kate felt like she finally belonged somewhere.

*****

Tony recognized the slight hill next to the old fields. It was harder to spot in the fading twilight, but he remembered the way there from the day of the funeral. Using his phone's flashlight he spotted the mound of fresh dirt and dying flowers from Tom's recent burial. He snarled at the sight. He didn't deserve flowers marking his grave. As far as Tony was concerned Tom Benson got off easy.

But his spawn would not. Tony was banking on the fact that sooner or later, Kate Benson would come to visit the grave of her father. If *his* father had a grave that he could visit, he would. At the time he didn't know it, but his mother never claimed his father's body. None of his living family members did either. The county morgue had him cremated or dumped into a mass grave. When Tony discovered this, it made his desire for revenge all the more heightened.

It would be made right. Soon, Kate Benson would return to visit her father's grave and he would be ready when she did.

21

This is ridiculous! I'm not a lovesick teenager!

Kate sighed and threw the shirt she had been holding against herself in the mirror onto the bed, adding to the heap of clothes that didn't meet her standards. It wasn't as if it were a *real* date. She was pretty sure Colleen had nagged Dan to ask Kate to go to the Fall Days Carnival in her attempt to pull her from her sadness. What she wore shouldn't matter. Yet, Kate wasn't content with her options. Her clothing selection grew slim. The four or five outfits that she had mixed and matched over the previous weeks were now dangerously close to being out of season.

"Kate, your ride is here," Colleen's voice came from the door.

"Already? Okay. I'll be there in a minute." Did she sound as nervous as she felt? She quickly threw her hair up into a clip, applied lip gloss, and left her room in the jeans and sweatshirt she pilfered from Jen.

She wasn't sure what she was expecting to find but when she came down the small hall to the living room she found the room empty. So much for making a stunning, heart-thumping entrance. She smirked as she spotted Dan looking over his father's shoulder at something on the dining room table. He looked up at her with an expression of admiration.

"Kate, *you* designed this?" he asked motioning to the open laptop.

Kate glanced at the mockup of a website she had created for the Tylers' farm. She had brought out her laptop earlier that day to show them some potential business ideas that went along with some of the visions they shared with her.

"We told her what we wanted to see happen someday and she came up with this in a matter of hours." Colleen beamed with pride.

"It's nothing. I like playing around with websites."

Dan laughed and mock shrugged his shoulder, "Oh it's nothing at all. I love creating entire businesses and making stunning websites out of thin air."

"You think it's stunning?" Kate's heart thudded in her ears.

"*I* want this website for my contracting business."

Her cheeks flushed and she knew she was smiling like an idiot.

"Enough business talk. You two go and have fun." Colleen nudged her son.

"Yeah, get going so I can take my bride on a date." John got to his feet and pulled Colleen into a tender embrace.

"A date? Are you lovebirds going to the carnival, too?" Kate asked as she melted at the sight of the Tylers acting like newlyweds.

"No carnivals for me. I stopped doing rides a long time ago. We're going to go out to eat and then see a movie." Mr. Tyler then looked at his son and added, "Do me a favor while you're there."

"Bring you home a funnel cake. I already know."

His father looked pleased. "Yes, that! But could you also keep an eye on your sister and that Ben kid?"

"Oh, John. Stop it. Ben is a sweet boy," Colleen laughed. "Anyway, they're working the photo booth. There's not a lot of mischief they can get into when they're working a booth at the carnival."

Kate didn't dare look at Dan but she could feel his eyes on her. She and Dan ran one of the game booths back in her junior year. Needless to say, it was the beginning of their dating relationship.

She cleared her throat. "We should probably let these two start their date."

"I agree." Dan smiled and moved to get Kate's jacket from the coat closet. "You'll want this."

He helped her into her coat and the two walked into the brisk late afternoon air.

"How long have your parents been married?" Kate asked wistfully after they had gotten on the road.

"It'll be 28 years in June."

Kate sighed. "They're amazing."

"They are. They've set a good example for us."

The two fell silent. Kate racked her brain as to what she could say to keep the conversation going. "I just wanted to say thank you... you know... for bringing me tonight. I'd say you didn't have to but I kind of suspect Colleen put you up to asking me."

Dan cast her a quick glance but returned his gaze to the road, a smile tugging at the corner of his mouth. "I'm a big boy. I asked you because I wanted to."

"I know, but I want you to know that I'm not expecting you to stay with me the whole time. I know things are... weird... with Staci and ..."

"What kind of guys have you been dating, Katie Benson? Why would you even suggest such a thing?" Dan looked genuinely indignant.

Her pulse quickened. "Is that what this is? A *date*?"

"I...I don't know." Dan shifted in his seat uneasily. "But I do know I'm not leaving you to go hang with someone else. I hope you know me better than that at least."

"So I'm stuck with you?" Kate flashed a teasing smile in hopes Dan couldn't sense her nervousness.

"For tonight you are." He smiled back in his typical Tyler smile and Kate thought her stomach was going to flip-flop out of her body.

They made it to the fairgrounds and parked the truck among the throng of other thrill seekers and fall enthusiasts. Dan opened his door but turned to Kate before getting out. With a mischievous glint in his eye, he asked, "Have you become one of those ladies that get offended by men opening doors for them or are you going to let me get your door?"

"Well, I don't want to take away your fun."

He smiled at her response before coming to her side of the truck and helping her down. Kate breathed in the scent of his aftershave and nearly melted into a puddle on the ground. If it hadn't been for the group of noisy teens moving past them, Kate may have been tempted to stay a little longer in his grasp. Dan didn't seem to be in much a of hurry to move either. Yet the sounds of laughing and frivolity seemed to break the spell and they followed the crowd to the entrance of the carnival.

To the side of the entrance, an ambulance was parked and Kate quickly recognized Michael in uniform leaning against the truck chatting with a friend. He caught sight of them and his face lit up as he waved.

"It's still weird to think he's a paramedic," Kate stated as she waved back.

Dan laughed out loud. "Yeah, it's hard to imagine the kid that used to eat glue is now able to save people's lives. Did he tell you he's going to start training to join the fire department full-time?"

"No! He didn't." Kate looked back at her friend in surprise. He was flirting with a woman who had stopped to engage him in conversation. "As if he needed another draw for the ladies."

They walked through an arch made of mums and corn stalks and Kate was instantly transported back to her childhood. The smell of sweet and salty delights filled her nostrils, a blend of popcorn, cotton candy, and funnel cakes. Ahead of them were rows of vendors selling a wide variety of homemade goodies and crafts. Beyond that was a magical world of lights and sounds including her childhood favorite, the Ferris Wheel.

She remembered tagging along with the Tylers every year. She had asked her father to come, but he always grunted an objection and shooed her away. For those few hours every fall that she attended the carnival, Kate was able to leave behind her sadness and loneliness to ride rides until her stomach, filled with hotdogs and caramel apples, felt queasy. She had played games that robbed every penny Colleen had given to her and every so often would have a small stuffed toy to take home as a memento. Some of her best memories were made right in that swath of land.

It took her a moment to realize that she was being stared at. She glanced to her side and saw Dan smiling at her quizzically.

"I thought I lost you for a minute there," he said softly.

"No, you didn't. You were with me."

He tilted his head and asked, "What do you mean?"

"I was remembering all the times we came here as kids." Kate smiled at him before asking, "Do you remember that time I made you ride the tilt-a-whirl five times in a row? The guy running the ride let us stay on because there wasn't a line."

"How could I forget? I threw up most of the night after that."

"I think that was because you and Sean were competing to see who could eat the most pizza."

Dan laughed. "Oh yeah. I forgot about that."

"Are you going to be brave and go on rides with me?" Kate flashed her best smile at him.

"Do I have a choice?" Dan sighed. "Well, I guess we'll need tickets if we're going to ride those death machines. Stay put. I'll be right back."

She had fully intended to comply, but Kate caught sight of the photo booth nearby. Jen and Ben were laughing and acting adorable. Their photo booth was set up with a shiplap backdrop, hay bales to sit on, pumpkins, and mums. For added photo-taking pleasure there were props and various masks and signs to use. Kate watched as a group of people had their picture taken and Jen printed out their picture from a wireless printer off to the side. A lot had changed in the last seven years, Kate concluded.

Jen saw Kate and waved her over. "Kate, you made it. Where's Dan?"

"He's buying tickets. How is the photo booth going?"

"It's going really well." Jen looked at Ben and the two smiled at each other much how she used to smile at Dan. Kate chuckled at the interaction, hoping Dan wouldn't make too much of it when he finally appeared.

Jen tugged Kate over to the corner and whispered excitedly. "He asked me to be his girlfriend."

"Ben? That Ben? The one you swore was madly in love with…" Kate's teasing was silenced by Jen's hand over her mouth. Kate moved back releasing Jen's hand from her face and smiled at the younger woman. "I'm happy for you. Just take things slow or your brother might have an aneurysm."

Jen laughed and nodded. "Speak of the devil. Here he comes. Please don't say anything yet. Mom knows, but…"

"My lips are sealed."

"You really can't stay still for two minutes, can you? I asked you to stay put." Dan's voice sounded from behind her.

"Look who I found, Dan." Kate turned to face him and gave him a look of warning, just in case he decided to pull the big brother routine again. He looked Ben straight in the eye for a moment, but to Kate's surprise, his face broke into a pleasant smile.

"Hey, Ben. How's it going?" he asked in a friendly tone. Kate was proud.

"It's going well, Sir. I mean … Dan… Mr. Tyler."

"Dan is fine, Ben."

Kate tried to hide her amusement at Dan's pleasure at the younger man's insecurity.

"Would you two like a picture?" Jen piped up.

"Sure. How many tickets?" Kate asked slipping a strip of tickets from Dan's grasp.

"Five."

"*Five*? That's robbery. No discount for your favorite brother?" Dan teased as he held his hand for Kate to join him in front of the pretty fall display.

"Aww. You know I love you, but it's still five." Jen held out her hand expectantly and Kate counted out the needed number of tickets.

"If we weren't in a competition we'd give you a discount, for sure," Ben said nervously... and then kept talking. "It's just that at the end of the night, whoever has the most tickets, their class gets money added to the end of the year field trip."

"It's okay, Ben. We understand. Back in our day, we ran the ring toss. Remember that?" Kate looked at Dan and blushed when a knowing smile crossed his face.

"Yeah, I remember."

Even with lines of people waiting for their turn at the game, Dan and Kate had found moments to stare moon-eyed at one another and laugh at everything the other person said. It was the night Dan got up the nerve to ask Kate to homecoming, their first date. The two were inseparable from that moment on. That is, until Kate left.

"Okay, how about a kiss or a hug?" Ben's voice snapped both Dan and Kate from their reverie and they stared dumbfounded at the young man across from them.

"I'm sorry... *what*?" Kate laughed and gasped at the same time. She felt Dan tense next to her and she bit her lip to stop her own amusement.

"Ben!" Jen hissed. "They're not... you know... together."

"What? Really? Because I thought you said..." Ben quit talking after Jen elbowed his midsection.

"Why don't you just make goofy faces or something," Jen directed from her camera.

Kate was nervous to look up at Dan, but she snort-laughed when she turned to face him and saw he sported the most ridiculous face she had ever seen. The awkwardness was broken and they both laughed openly.

"Hey, I really like these," Jen said as she watched the picture shoot out from the printer moments later.

Kate moved to the younger woman and looked at the strip of pictures. Her heart leaped at the sight. If she hadn't known any better, she too would've mistaken them as a couple... just as Ben had. Even when she and Mark posed for snapshots, there was never the same joy present. *Maybe because none of it was real. You sensed something was off before the truth came out. It's why you always second-guessed whether he was the right guy.* The realization struck her. She never really embraced the idea of Mark, or the man she knew as Mark. Dan had always been her ideal love. No one else measured up.

"If I give you five more tickets, can you print out another?" Dan asked. "That way Kate can take hers to Boston and I can have one too."

"Save your tickets." Jen smiled conspiratorially as she pushed the print button and pulled out her own tickets from her pocket to cover the expense.

Kate's heart felt heavy at the reminder of her upcoming return to Boston. The decision she faced was not *whether* she was going to return. That was a given. Even if she chose to accept the Tylers' offer, she would still need to get her belongings from Lilly's house. Rather, the decision she faced was whether or not to *stay* in Boston. She wished she knew what the best outcome was. If only God would speak with an obvious neon sign saying, *"Stay in Deer Creek, Stupid"*.

"Are you going to need a ride home, Jen? You can come home with Kate and me," Dan offered, bringing Kate from her thoughts.

"Uh, I'm okay. I'll need to help tear everything down later and I wouldn't want you to wait around."

"I can bring her home," Ben spoke up eagerly. "I'll have her back by ten."

Dan didn't look convinced and Kate tugged at his arm. "I'm sure they cleared it with your parents first. Isn't that right, Jen?"

"Yes. Mom and Dad are aware, Dan. Will you go have fun and stop worrying about me... please?" Jen laughed and pushed her brother from her booth.

"Fine. I'll go, but you know I'm always going to look out for you, right? I don't care how old you get." Dan smirked and leaned down to plant a kiss on his sister's forehead. Kate didn't miss the fact that his eyes were on Ben, however. The younger boy gulped and nodded, communicating some silent promise to behave.

Once satisfied Jen was in good hands, Dan turned to Kate and said, "Where to? I'll follow your lead."

"You may regret saying that because I really want to go on the tilt-a-whirl." She felt like a kid again. After the past weeks, it was a welcome feeling and a very happy distraction from trying to decide what she was going to do with the rest of her life.

Kate pulled Dan in the direction of the rides despite his protests and to his credit he was a good sport. The two took on the tilt-a-whirl, the swings, bumper cars, and even the merry-go-round. Soon Kate found herself standing in front of the Ferris Wheel, giving Dan a beckoning smile.

"Oh come on, Kate. You know I hate heights," he pleaded.

"Please, Dan. The view would be so beautiful from the top. Just find something to fix your eyes on and don't look down."

Dan sneered. "It's that simple, huh? And what will I fix my eyes on sixty feet in the air?"

"Me. *I'll* distract you." Dan made a face that Kate couldn't read, but she pressed the issue, nonetheless. "Remember when we rode it as kids? I told you ridiculous stories and you didn't even realize we were so high off the ground."

"I was just humoring you. I knew very well the danger I was in."

Instinctively, she took his hand and looked up into his face. "Take a risk. Come on."

To her surprise, he didn't immediately release her hand and they made their way through the line until they were finally seated on a bench with a safety bar across their laps. The wheel began lifting them from the ground allowing others below to get into the other benches and Dan groaned out loud.

"This is not a good idea. Why did I let you sweet talk me into this?" He clenched his eyes shut.

"Because you know I'm right."

Dan grunted and he gripped the bar tightly. "There should be seat belts in these things."

Kate laughed as the wheel began to spin in earnest. "Dan, you're missing it. Open your eyes. You have to see this."

The wind blew her hair and she felt like a bird flying through the sky. Just as she expected, the view from the top was worth it all. The city lights in the distance, the colorful carnival lights below them, and the stars in the night sky above created an image she never wanted to forget. She brought her eyes back to Dan, expecting him to still be clenching the seat with his eyes closed. Instead, she found him fixated on *her*, a warm smile on his lips.

"You're right. It's a beautiful view," he said.

Kate felt her face flush despite the chilly rush of wind around her.

"So, tell me a story. You promised to distract me," Dan prodded.

She smiled as she thought through what she could tell him and all she could come up with was her real-life dilemma. "It's not really a story, but you might find it interesting. Did you know that your parents offered me a job?"

He didn't answer, but his expression told her that he wasn't surprised.

"All my life I thought I wanted to be this bigshot advertising executive in the city. I got a fancy car. I was so close to getting my dream condo. It was beautiful, Dan. You could see the skyscrapers from the balcony."

"Sounds nice." His tone belied his words, but she continued.

"It was, but when I actually got the things I thought I wanted…" Kate sighed. "I discovered I didn't actually want them anymore."

"What do you want, Kate?"

"I want to help businesses make good decisions and see them flourish. I want to have people near me that care about me. I want to be where I will learn about God. What if I can't find a church like the one here?" Kate looked out the side of the ride before continuing. "I don't feel like the same person I was when I came to Deer Creek. I like who God is making me into. I think none of that would've happened if I hadn't come home."

"It kind of sounds like you made a decision." Dan leaned in and Kate nestled in closer to him.

"But it's crazy. It doesn't make sense to leave a job that pays that much money to start over someplace new, does it?" Kate turned to look Dan in the eyes and felt herself get lost in his tender gaze.

"Someone told me that sometimes you have to take a risk." His face was inches from hers and she so desperately wanted him to kiss her. It didn't take long for him to read her mind and he lowered his head until their lips brushed. He smiled at her before leaning back in and kissing her in earnest. He was so gentle and soft that Kate never wanted it to end, but the ride started slowing and came to a stop.

Kate's legs felt like Jello getting off the Ferris Wheel. She was grateful there was a railing to lean on as she walked down the exit ramp. Dan walked quietly next to her, clearly lost in his own thoughts. Was he regretting their kiss? Was he going to tell her it was a mistake and that maybe she *should* go back to Boston? She wasn't sure she could bear that.

"I think I actually like the Ferris Wheel," Dan said out of nowhere. His smile was perfect and Kate laughed in relief as he put a protective arm around her.

"Really? Maybe I can get you to like the Paratrooper then." Kate pointed at a ride that lifted and dropped its riders up and down while turning in circles.

"Don't press your luck, Kate Benson. I think we've taken enough risks for tonight."

*****

Tony grew impatient. In a bold move, he set out to explore the property surrounding the little hidden cemetery and discovered an empty house. It appeared abandoned though there was still electricity running to it as the porch light was lit. He was cold in that cemetery and sleep was not happening. He swore he saw shadows emerging around him from every corner. Tonight he would have protection against them.

He circled to the back of the house and spotted a door leading into the kitchen. He tucked his bike in some bushes and retrieved his sleeping bag and backpack. Grabbing a brick from what used to be a flower garden's edging, he smashed the door's window. Reaching his hand through, he unlocked the door and entered the echoey house.

This will do, Son.

It looked as though someone had recently been working inside as there were buckets of paint and new sheets of drywall against the one wall in the living room. Tony wandered through the house, making sure he was alone. It was a nice house, but not as luxurious as the home he had been in previously. Tony settled in a room upstairs and spread his sleeping bag out on the floor. Before allowing himself to succumb to his exhaustion he made sure his gun was loaded and ready to go… just in case he was caught off guard.

His cell phone vibrated and he saw someone had left a message. It was his mother.

What does that witch want?

"She says the police called her today asking about me. They want to know where I am. They asked what my relationship is to you." Tony read his mother's words. "She says she's worried about me."

Don't believe her. Don't answer her, Son. She's with them. Answer her and we're as good as done.

"What if they've figured it all out already? I thought I'd have more time."

We always knew we didn't have much time left. Tomorrow we'll regroup and find her. Sleep now. At least tonight you're safe.

22

Luke hated missing church. Sunday morning dawned and found him listening to the recorded phone interview with a woman who claimed to be the mother of Tony McCullough's son. The puzzle pieces started fitting together, but the picture coming to light alarmed him. After checking into the visitor logs of the prison where James McCullough had been incarcerated, one name showed up on a regular basis leading up to his release. Steven Connors. It didn't take detectives long to locate Steven Connors' last known address and his concerned mother.

According to the information gleaned from the interview, the woman reported her son missing a month prior and was greatly concerned because he was off his medications. The detective in Boston interviewing her had asked if her son was related to Tony McCullough.

"Why do you want to know that?" Cindy Connors asked nervously.

"We're investigating something that pertains to James McCullough. Steven visited James several times over the past month."

The woman sighed before admitting the truth. "James is Steven's uncle. His father... Tony... was an evil man. Did you know the night he was killed he was trying to kidnap Steven?"

"We weren't aware of that."

"My husband and I had filed for sole custody of Steven. We wanted Tony's parental rights taken away. He was dangerous and it was a blessing when that cop killed him." Her voice grew loud and bitter before she calmed down and added, "I just wish Steven hadn't seen it happen. I lost my little boy that day."

"Tony isn't mentioned on your son's birth certificate," the detective pointed out.

"Sleeping with that man was the biggest mistake of my life. I didn't want him to be a part of Steven's life. The only reason he was allowed any visitation at all was because he threatened us. We were scared of what he would do if we fought him."

There was silence before the detective asked, "Mrs. Connors, before your son went missing, did he say anything to you that may have caused you concern? Anything that stands out to you?"

"Why? Is Steve in trouble? What aren't you telling me?"

"Did you know he was visiting his uncle in prison?"

"He's an adult. I can't stop him from doing what he's going to do. He stopped listening to me a long time ago." Cindy wept then. "Please, whatever he's done... he's been diagnosed with paranoid personality disorder. When he's off his meds, he... he thinks his father talks to him. He calls himself Tony Jr. Whatever is going on... please help him."

Luke turned off his car and sat in front of the next piece of the puzzle, silencing the remainder of the interview. One of the houses that the officers had visited in the search for the Jeep Kate Benson had spotted had a burglary call come in that morning. The homeowners who were away on vacation grew concerned after their conversation with the officers and they called their son to come and check out the house. When he arrived that morning, he found the house in a ransacked state. Luke didn't like coincidences and everything about this situation sent red flags up.

As he entered the house and allowed the officer to show him the multiple areas where pictures were smashed, his fears began to grow that Steven, Tony, or whatever he wanted to call himself had made himself quite at home in the house.

"The flatbed is coming for the Jeep. The homeowners said to take whatever we need to find the guy," one of the officers told Luke. "The son says it looked like maybe some clothing was taken and his father's mountain bike."

"Is there any other damage to the house other than these family pictures?" Luke looked down at the floor and saw the precious faces staring through shattered shards of glass.

"The kids' room."

"*Kids'* room?" Luke repeated and shook his head.

He followed the officer to the room as the man recounted the testimony given by the couple's son. "This is the room they designate for grandchildren when they visit. Their son noticed the broken mirror and toys."

"*Why* this room?" The officer just shrugged and let Luke go into the room to look at the damage.

A mirror was smashed and a toy truck lay dented on its side on the floor. The mother's words from the interview came to mind. They weren't dealing with someone who was thinking clearly at the moment. The destruction in the house served no purpose. It hadn't come about as a result of robbing the house of goods. It was done in rage. Luke sighed as the reality of the situation became apparent. Kate Benson was still very much in danger.

*****

Kate felt ridiculous. She had laid awake most of the night going over in her mind the events of the carnival. The

Ferris Wheel and the kiss. The corn maze and their friendly competition. The ride home sneaking glances at one another followed by shy smiles. Then he kissed her goodnight at the door before making sure she was safely inside and returning to his cabin. Her insides had been turned upside down and her mind spun with wild hopes and dreams of a possible future. Then morning came...

When she saw Dan at breakfast he looked exhausted. She spoke to him and even brushed his arm with hers to get him to look at her, but he only mumbled a brief good morning and explained that he needed to go to church early and he'd see her there. He pressed a sweet kiss to her forehead before he left, but Kate knew something was wrong. Did he think she was too forward last night? Had she misread his intentions?

At church, Dan missed Sunday school and as she walked with Tessa to the sanctuary for church, she saw him come out of the pastor's office.

"Skipping Sunday school, Mr. Tyler?" Kate came up next to him and tried to sound normal.

He smiled down at her. "Yeah, that Pastor Munson is a bad influence."

Kate was relieved to hear the humor in his voice. "Is everything okay?"

"Yes. I just needed to get some advice on something."

"Oh?"

"I'll tell you about it after church. Do you want to have lunch with me? I thought maybe we could go to the lake. It's supposed to be a nice day. It might be the last comfortable day before spring." His eyes were warm and inviting and Kate laughed at herself for the rollercoaster ride of emotions she felt since she woke up that morning.

"Lunch would be good."

He smiled at her again and she felt her face flush. She took a seat next to Tess and was surprised when Dan asked to join them. Kate worried, at first, that she wouldn't be able to concentrate on the message, but soon she was fully engrossed in the various scriptures the pastor recited. She scribbled notes and put stars next to verses she wanted to come back to later to reread. Kate had been worried about finding a new church in Boston just like the one she was sitting in, but why did she have to? *If you stay here, you can keep learning and growing. Why fix what's not broken?*

As time grew closer to leave, Kate felt more inclined to stay. Tomorrow she would rent a car, but she knew she would not stay in Boston. If there was a chance to start her own business in Deer Creek and stay at the church where she was learning so much, why would she force herself to be where she didn't feel connected anymore? The decision to stay brought her heart peace. Kate glanced at Dan wondering if he knew the way her thoughts were heading. Would he be happy to know she wanted to stay?

After church, Kate got into Dan's truck and they went to grab sub sandwiches on the way to the lake. She couldn't help but chuckle at the curious smiles on the faces of the Tylers as they drove away. The conversation remained lighthearted and casual until they made it to the picnic bench and spread out their food. Her heart flooded with warmth as Dan reached for her hand and prayed a prayer of thanks over the food. *This is what I never knew I needed or wanted. Thank you for him, Lord.*

"Kate, I want to talk about last night." His words caused the bite of food in her throat to feel like gravel and Kate swallowed, dreading where his next words would take her.

"You regret last night?"

"No! Not at all." His words were quick and reassuring, but there was still something bothering him. "But I need to apologize to you."

Whew! Kate allowed herself to breathe again. "For what? Last night was… perfect."

"You think so?" His face was adorably uncertain.

"Yes, I do. Why would you even think otherwise?"

Dan sighed and looked at Kate seriously. "Kate, I need you to hear me out. I don't want you to misunderstand me."

She nodded him on.

"The decisions you have to make are serious… life changing. You need to base your decision to stay on what you feel *God* telling you to do. Not on me. Last night, I was being selfish. I want you to stay. I have never been able to shake the idea of you and me together." Dan spoke so gently that Kate wanted to interject and assure him that she knew very well what she wanted, but he began speaking again. "My heart can't take falling in love with you again and then one day you realize you stayed here out of some emotional response. I think it might be wise if you take more time to pray before you decide what to do. Maybe go back to Boston for a little while and see if what you feel God saying still rings true."

Kate slowly blinked at the man sitting across from her. What he said made sense. There was wisdom to what he suggested. Yet, at the same time, she wondered if he had lost his mind. She slid her hand out from his.

"Can I talk now?" she asked. In her mind, she could hear her father's voice say the words he said every time she asserted her will against him. *Uh oh! There she goes. Better get out of her way. She's gonna blow!*

Kate cleared her throat. "Do you think I am stupid?"

"What? Kate, no..."

"I know I am new to studying the Bible and praying, but do you think I've *not* been praying this entire time? I literally found peace in my decision to stay ... and now you're wanting me to go *back* to Boston?"

"It's not about what *I* want. It can't be. It has to be *your* idea, not mine. I don't want you to resent me one day. You're leaving a career, Kate. A whole life."

"I can think for myself, Dan Tyler." Kate got to her feet and started wrapping her half-eaten sandwich back in its wrapping. "Can we just go back please?"

"Kate... please. All I'm asking is that you make sure this is really what you want before you decide. What would it hurt to pray a little more first?"

Tears stung her eyes. Even if he were right, she didn't want to acknowledge it. Boston was not home. She knew that already. But what if Deer Creek wasn't home either? What if she prayed more and God said not to come back? Her heart hurt at the thought.

"Hey. Shh." Kate allowed herself to be pulled into Dan's arms but stayed as rigid as a corpse in his embrace. She felt his breath on her hair as he spoke into her ear. "Kate, I'm in danger of loving you more than I ever did before. I just need to know that when you come back it's for good this time."

She pried herself free from Dan and walked towards the truck. She could hear him walking behind her on the crunchy leaves. The ride home was miserable and nothing more was said. He pulled up to the house and she left the truck without a word. She was grateful that the Tyler family were still out to lunch. She didn't want to answer questions. She wouldn't know how to answer them. Kate tried to lie down, but she couldn't get comfortable. She tried watching TV, but nothing kept her interest. Finally, Kate decided she needed fresh air. She grabbed her jacket and phone, closing the back door behind her.

Dan had driven back down the driveway towards the main road so she knew she wouldn't have an uncomfortable reunion near his cabin. In fact, as Kate approached the cabin she walked briskly by, just in case. Her mind went back to their earlier conversation. He wasn't wrong in what he suggested. He was trying to point her to God, which made him even more attractive to her. Yet, the idea of leaving brought her such pain. How could he recommend such a thing if he really wanted her to stay?

Kate grabbed a handful of colorful leaves as she walked towards her father's house. She was so confused at the gamut of emotions she had experienced over the past weeks. Hate that turned to love and forgiveness. Fear turned into peace. Anxiety turned into calmness in the middle of uncertainty. God had done that. She knew she could trust Him, but she was struggling to know what was right. Praying more about her life was not wrong. But Kate instantly recognized familiar doubt bubbling up inside of her.

She stood in front of her old home as the thought struck her. *What if God doesn't really care? What if he's going to leave me to solve this on my own?* Kate remembered scripture just then. One that spoke of God having plans for her life, plans to give her a life and not to harm her. She'd look it up when she got back to the house, she decided. Then it was as if God spoke to her deep in her soul. *I'm not like your dad was. I'm not a Father that will leave you or deny you love. Trust me. Even though you couldn't trust him when you were young, you can trust me.*

Kate sniffed away tears as she felt the warmth of God's presence. Putting her hands in her pocket she realized she still had the key to the house from her many cleaning trips. Dan wouldn't mind her going inside one last time. Tomorrow she would rent her car and head back to Boston. She would take time to pray and be sure of what God was telling her before making a permanent decision to come back to Deer Creek.

With resolve, Kate unlocked the door and breathed in the scent of fresh wood and paint. She wanted one last look at her bedroom so she crept up the stairs. The only familiar thing that remained in the room was the pink lace curtain on the window. *So many changes, Lord. Dad is gone. This home is not the same. I am not the same. Please promise me that you really do have a plan for me.*

A noise below caught her attention. It was the sound of an old metal door followed by the wooden door scraping against the uneven floorboards. Kate remembered that sound well. It was the back door in the kitchen. Maybe Dan had come looking for her to talk more. She needed to apologize for how she acted earlier. He was only trying to make sure she was making a lasting decision. She saw that now. Kate walked back into the hallway and caught sight of something on the floor of what used to be her father's bedroom. Fast food trash and a sleeping bag.

A footfall sounded from downstairs and her heart started racing. The smell of body odor mixed with cigarette smoke wafted up the stairs where she silently pressed herself against the wall. She eased herself down the top step and leaned down to look in the direction of the kitchen. A man stood with his back to the rest of the house. A plume of cigarette smoke rose. He put a bag of food on the counter and started digging into a burger like a ravenous animal. It was the man from the restaurant.

Silently easing down another step, Kate took her phone from her pocket. Despite quivering hands, she opened an app and shared her location to Dan in a text. Then she pressed 911 and prayed someone would come. Until then, Kate knew she had to get out of the house. She lowered her foot onto the next step and cringed at the sound of the creak. The man paused eating as if listening to the house.

"911, what's your emergency?" The voice was muffled, but the dispatcher might as well have had a megaphone. "Hello? What is your emergency?"

The man's head turned abruptly in her direction and Kate knew it was now or never as she jumped stairs two at a time to reach the landing. She'd never make it to the door before he caught up to her so Kate threw her phone at his head hitting her mark. He cursed but did not stop. She grabbed the closest thing to her, a hammer. With strength she didn't know she had, she rushed the man and swung at his head until he fell onto the floor. He was getting up when Kate took the opportunity to run through the open back door. A hand grasped her jacket and she wriggled her way free of it, running into the late afternoon sunlight.

Don't look back. Just keep running.

A single shot rang out.

Help me, Father God!

23

Dan pulled onto the street leading home, grateful his parents decided to stay out until evening church with their friends. Jen went home with friends. Sean was busy at church working on things for the youth group. Michael was called into work to cover for a friend. He'd have peace to work through his turbulent thoughts. That is, unless Kate managed to cross his path on his way to the cabin. He hoped not. Right now they needed space. She needed to cool down until they could talk reasonably again. *How dare she act like I'm the bad guy. Couldn't she see I just want her to be 100% sure, Lord?*

As he turned onto the long driveway, Dan saw the police cars, lights flashing. Luke Martin waved him down and Dan wasted no time getting out of the truck.

"Where's Kate?" Luke yelled.

"Inside the house? I don't know. I'm just getting back." Dan felt his blood grow cold. "What's wrong?"

"She's not in there. We've been through the whole house."

"Luke, will you tell me what's going on?"

Luke didn't answer he turned to shout orders at the officers fanning out through the property. He finally turned back to Dan. "She's in danger. We need to find her *now*."

"I thought everyone was captured. Who is left?"

"Son, I don't have time to talk. If you hear from her, call me."

Dan pulled out his phone and checked it just in case she had tried to call while he was driving. A text from Kate came up and he opened it.

"Luke. She's at her old house."

"Send me the address." Luke began running to his car, but Dan stopped him.

"I can do better. I'll show you." Dan jumped through Luke's passenger side door. "It's just next door. You could take the trail but cutting across that field is faster."

"Get out, Son."

"Not on your life. If you don't drive, I will."

Luke huffed but complied and followed Dan's directions, cutting through a harvested cornfield until trees blocked the rest of the way. The house is right down that path."

"You stay back and let us go in. Understand?"

Dan nodded tersely, though he fully intended to be front and center if Kate needed him, whether he was armed or not. He led them down the small path right up to the house and the officers once again formed a formation as they entered, calling to one another as each room was found empty.

Luke came out holstering his weapon. "She's not here, but she was. Someone was here with her. There's blood on the floor near the fireplace along with a hammer."

"Maybe she'll text again." Dan swallowed against the growing terror as he prayed the blood wasn't hers.

Luke shook his head in defeat. "Not if that cell phone on the floor is hers."

Dan was about to run past his friend into the house when his eyes caught sight of something near the back of the house. Some mound of fabric in the tall grass. He ran before Luke could tell him otherwise. Kate's jacket.

"Luke! It's Kate's!" Dan's eyes scanned the wooded barrier to the Benson property hoping Kate was taking cover somewhere safe.

"Get more men out here. I want this area canvassed. No leaf unturned, understand me?"

Dan grabbed Luke's arm. "Who is this? What's going on?"

"We found out the man Tom killed had a son. He came with McCullough and Barrows to get to Tom. We found out his identity this morning and ran a check on his accounts. This afternoon he made a purchase not far from here at a fast food joint." Luke shook his head and dropped his hands. "I hoped we would get to her first."

Just then a loud shot rang out like a thunderclap and both men looked at each other as the source of the noise registered in their minds.

"That was close," Dan assessed and Luke nodded.

"What's nearby?"

Dan heaved out a long breath as he tried to think. Then a thought so terrifying hit him that he almost couldn't utter the words. "The cemetery."

*****

Her ragged breathing sounded loud to her own ears as she covered her mouth with her hands. She had slid under the low lying branches of an evergreen tree, ignoring the needles stabbing her body and scraping her back through her shirt. She had to stay still. If she moved even an inch, he'd be back. Every so often she could hear him talking to someone. *There's more? Lord, how will I get out of this? I can't fend off more than one.*

A twig snapped and Kate almost passed out from holding her breath as long as she had. A pair of jean-clad legs stood only feet from her hiding spot.

"Come out, Katie. We've been desperate to meet you in person. Haven't we, Dad?"

She hoped she had curled around the tree enough so that her feet were well concealed below the branches. She clenched her eyes shut. Tears spilled down over the hand still clasped against her face. Now was *not* the time to cry. *Hold it together, Kate.*

"Did you know I met your dad? My father was going to take me away so we could finally be together and we stopped for dinner at that stupid diner."

Kate dipped her head enough to look up at the man. He was rubbing his head and rocking back and forth, unsteady on his feet. If she could position herself just right, she might just be able to swing her leg out and knock him to the ground. *No, it's too risky. Just stay still. Wait for help.*

"I was looking out the back window when your … your… father shot him. Do you know what it's like to stare into the eyes of your dead father?"

He started laughing.

"I guess maybe you do. Eddie said you were staying close to your dad. Were you there when he died?"

Kate's stomach twisted and she fought the urge to attack the man.

"Your father was lucky. If Eddie hadn't been so slow and we had gotten to do what we planned... You would've gotten to see the blood coming from your father's body. Just like I had to watch my dad bleed out."

The man sat down on the ground and started sobbing. If he turned around, he might be able to see her. She backed in closer to the trunk of the tree.

"We have to find her, Dad. We have to end this," the man cried. "I know. I won't fail you again. I promise. Yes... Of course, I know that! That's why I'm here."

Kate's eyes moved though her head stayed still as she scanned the area looking for who he was talking to. He appeared to be alone. A moment of compassion hit her. What if she could talk him down from whatever mental break he was having? What if she could reason with him?

Then the man got to his feet and moved away. His voice grew distant as he continued talking to his invisible father. Kate waited until she felt sure he had put enough distance between them. Her legs were cramping. If she didn't straighten them soon, she'd be stuck there indefinitely. She freed her first leg from its weird position, biting her lip to keep from groaning in pain. After the first leg was straightened, she tried to free the other.

All of a sudden something clamped onto her ankle and pulled her out from under the tree. Pain seared as her face and body were dragged along the forest floor into the open. She tried kicking her legs as hard as she could, hoping her feet would land someplace sensitive enough to get him to release his grasp. The man held tight, laughing as if enjoying himself immensely.

He continued to drag her through the forest, every branch and stone ripping into her flesh. Kate reached out for a long branch as they passed and twisted herself enough into a position to stab the man in his leg.

With a shout, he let go of her legs to grab his thigh. Kate overestimated her strength and could barely get to her feet. She pulled herself up on a small tree and as soon as she was upright she tried to run.

"Now why would you have to do that?" She heard him yell. "We're not far away from where we're going. It'll be done soon if you'd just stop fighting me. You can be with your dad and I'll be with mine."

"Why ... are you doing... this?" Kate stumbled along the path clumsily, running from tree to tree.

"Justice," he hissed through his teeth.

Kate broke free from the security of the trees and found herself out in an open space. In her haze, she tried to figure out if she was on Tyler or Benson land. Then in the distance, she recognized the small hill that led to the cemetery. She gasped and realized she was going in the direction he wanted her to. She shifted course and tried to run to the edge of the field, but another shot rang. A weird buzzing noise clipped by her ear and Kate felt a burn on her temple. It took a moment to realize there was warm liquid falling from her head. Then came the hard blow across the back of her head. Kate felt herself go to her knees before everything faded to black.

*****

Dan didn't even wait for Luke to put the car in park as they landed at the base of the hill that housed the cemetery. "Hold it, Tyler!" Luke called out.

"Whether you like it or not, I'm here and I'm not letting that monster hurt her."

"If you rush up there yelling, you'll give us away," Luke said through clenched teeth and thrust a bulletproof vest at the younger man. "Now put this on, Hercules, before you get yourself killed. Stay behind us."

Dan complied, watching the men ease up the hill quietly, flanking either side of Luke using the cover of the trees. He could hear a voice speaking shakily in the air.

"It's almost done. I promise. The pain will stop soon. Just let your blood drain down on your father so he feels it."

Then he heard a whimper. *Kate!* Dan felt his chest constrict and just when he was about to defy orders and run to Kate's side, he saw a van pulling up alongside the road. Its lights were off, but Dan recognized the outline and low rumble of the engine as an ambulance. He surmised they were given the orders to approach without any lights on so as not to give themselves away. In the waning light, he saw his brother and another EMT ease from their doors and look anxiously up to the trees hiding the events occurring inside the cemetery.

Michael slid quietly to his brother's side and Dan felt his arm around his shoulder as they both helplessly waited.

"Steven Connors, drop your weapon." Luke's voice boomed through the twilight. "This can't end well for you, Son. You have a mother that is worried sick about you. You want to see her again, don't you?"

"It's done. It's too late. She's dead."

"Let the girl down to the ground… easy now."

The sound of a thud made Dan's stomach revolt and Michael now held his brother back from running onto the scene. "Wait until the all clear."

"I don't want to kill you, Son. Put your weapon down and get on your knees," Luke attempted to reason with the man.

"I'm coming, Dad," a voice shouted.

There was a rustling sound followed by a round of shots.

"Get a medic up here quick," Luke called and Dan didn't wait for the all clear.

As he got to the top of the hill and passed the gate into the cemetery he saw two figures on the ground. One off to the side and one lying across the mound of freshly packed dirt on Tom's grave.

"Kate." He ran to her and cradled her in his lap, crying out loud as he saw the blood on her face and coming from a gaping cut on her wrist. "Help her. Please."

Officers moved in and checked for life signs on the body off to the side and a call for a coroner's van was issued.

"Don't take her, Lord. Please don't." Dan prayed over Kate's limp body.

"Dan, you have to let me in," Michael spoke loudly to pierce through his distraught brother's tortured thoughts. "If you want to help, let me see her."

Dan watched helplessly as his brother applied pressure to the cut and wrapped her wrist tightly after packing it with gauze.

"Dan, hold her arm up. Hold it above her heart. It'll stop the bleeding." Michael then turned to his partner, "Let Memorial know we're en route with a severe wrist laceration and concussion. Patient non-responsive."

He turned back to his old friend, lifting her eyelids and shining a light into her pupils. "Kate, can you hear me? We need you to wake up. Kate. Get that gurney up here now! I'm starting a line."

Michael and two other EMTs lifted Kate onto the gurney and strapped her in.

"Dan, you coming? Hurry up."

Dan looked to Luke and as soon as the older man nodded him on, Dan wasted no time climbing in the ambulance alongside his brother. It was then the lights were turned back on in the van and Dan saw the true state of Kate Benson. Scrapes and cuts on her face. Some type of open wound on her temple. Her clothes were covered in blood and dirt. He prayed silently as his brother worked on Kate.

"She has a pulse. It's weak, but it's there."

Dan nodded numbly. He barely noticed the bumping of the ambulance and the sound of sirens, but before he knew it they were opening the back doors and wheeling Kate through a ramp into the emergency room. As he stayed to the side of the room listening to Michael spout out the grim reality of her wounds, Dan yelled at himself for ever suggesting Kate take time away from Deer Creek. If she lived, he'd never let her out of his sight again. Even if it meant following her all the way to Boston.

24

Was it a dream? Am I dead? Kate didn't dare move. Was she safe? The last thing she remembered was running away from the man trying to kill her. Was this heaven? It couldn't be heaven. There wasn't supposed to be pain in heaven and she felt *a lot* of pain. She opened one eye in a squint. She was in some type of cold, dimly lit room. She took a deep breath and recognized the scent of antiseptic sprays and a hint of coffee. There was a rhythmic beeping close by. It reminded her an awful lot of her father's hospital room.

Kate's eyes sprung open and she tried to sit up as if realizing for the first time where she was. Her head throbbed and her wrist was wrapped. It hurt to move it. What had happened? Wires of some dark substance pumped into her veins. Was that blood? She turned her head slightly to see the outline of someone sitting in a chair near her bed covered in a blanket.

"Hey.." Kate tried to speak, but it came out weakly. She tried a little louder. "Hello..."

The person lifted their head from the nodding off position their head had been in.

"You're awake! Oh my word, we were so scared."

"Tess?"

Kate felt a warm hand on her arm. "Yes, it's me. Let me go tell everyone you're awake. They're going to be so happy."

"No... wait." Kate tried to sit up. She leaned her weight on her bandaged wrist and fell back instantly in searing pain. "What happened to me? Why is my arm bandaged?"

"Do you remember anything that happened?" Tessa's voice was gentle and low.

"I was running away." Kate put her hand to her head and felt a bandage of some type on her temple. She remembered the pain she felt before it all went blank. Terror struck her. "Did he *shoot* me?"

"Michael said it was a bullet graze. If it had been even an inch closer ..."

"Michael?"

"He was working tonight. His team got the call that responded." Tessa leaned in closer. "It was so smart to text Dan your location. If you hadn't... well, let's not think about that."

"Why don't I remember? What happened?" Kate started crying.

"Oh, Kate." Tessa hugged her friend. "Let me get everyone from the waiting room. We've been taking shifts waiting for you to wake up. Luke is there too. He'll tell you what you need to know."

Kate nodded and then reached out to stop Tess from leaving just yet. "Just Luke. I'm not ready to see... everyone."

As the door shut, Kate tried to control the trembling that had started in her hands. It wasn't but a few moments before a soft knock sounded on the door. Luke entered along with a doctor.

"You have no idea how happy I am to see those eyes!"

"Miss Benson, I'm Dr. Preston. I need to turn on these lights and see how you're doing, okay?"

The lights came on above her and Kate winced. The doctor proceeded to shine a penlight in her eyes and test her strength by making her squeeze his hand.

"You'll have a nasty bump on your head and some scarring from your wounds, but your vitals look good. You are a lucky woman."

Luke snorted. "Luck had nothing to do with it. God had His angels protecting this girl."

"We'll probably keep you for a while longer and check your blood levels after this bag is done. Maybe later in the morning we'll get you up on your feet and see how you do. Are you hungry?"

Kate shook her head no and the doctor left Luke and Kate.

"What happened? Was anyone else hurt? Where is the man who did this?"

"Take a deep breath, Kate. I'll tell you everything, but I need to know some things too. Are you up to questions?" Luke waited for Kate's nod and pulled the chair Tessa had vacated close to Kate's bedside.

Kate answered what she could remember of her harrowing encounter and anxiously waited for the detective to fill in the missing details during the time she was incapacitated. After both had recounted their respective experiences, they sat in silence for several moments as the reality of what had happened – or almost happened – sunk in.

"He truly thought he'd be reunited with his dad. He was just a man that missed having a father... even if he wasn't the best father," Kate pondered out loud and a tear trickled down her face. "I understand that. It's why I came to Deer Creek, too."

Luke sighed sadly and nodded. "Kate Benson, your father would be so proud of how you fought. He may have been a tough dad to grow up with, but I see some of his better characteristics in you. That stubbornness and determination saved your life. In the end, isn't that all we can do? We take the good parts we want to keep of our parents and ask the Lord to purge the not so great parts."

Kate felt tears sting her eyes. Keeping the good parts of her father… yes. There were things she wanted to adopt from Tom Benson. His protectiveness. His willingness to change and admit he was wrong. Those other things – his sinful side – didn't have to be a part of her life. Kate would celebrate the good things and learn from his life what not to do.

"I also want to say, that you resemble your heavenly Father, too. Your compassion and empathy in recognizing what drove Steven Connors to act the way he did is the beginning of forgiveness."

Another tear slid down her face. Luke's heartfelt tone and his words meant more than he could ever know. He cleared his throat and tried to push his own emotions to the side. "I know for a fact there is someone out in that waiting room desperate to see you. I was close to kicking his rear end a few times when he tried to act bulletproof."

"Dan?" Kate tried to hide her amazement.

"Who else would be so foolish and stubborn?" Luke smirked. "In all honesty, he was by your side as soon as it was safe to let him up there. Can I go get him and put him out of his misery?"

"What do I look like?" Kate asked and started looking around the room for a mirror. Luke's grim expression was her answer. "Am I that bad?"

"It will heal." He reached down for his phone and turned the camera to front facing so Kate could use it as a mirror.

She gasped. The stark white bandage covered a large portion of her temple and forehead. Her hair was matted with dried blood. The scrapes on her face were scabbing over. Her eyes went down to the bandage on her wrist. "Do you think that will scar?"

"That I don't know. He cut you deep." Luke put his hand over her wrist and Kate's eyes went to his kind face. "If it *does* scar, let it be a reminder of how God protected you in the middle of the worst circumstances."

Kate nodded and tried to muster a smile. Luke left her then. She leaned back against the pillows in her bed, feeling more tired than she had ever felt in her life. Movement caught her attention and a ragged Dan stepped through the door. Was he crying? No, he wasn't the crying type. As he got closer, however, Kate could see the tears gleaming in his eyes.

Kate tried to reassure him. "I'm okay. I look like I went five rounds in a ring, but I'm okay."

"You're the most beautiful woman in the world to me." He strode to her bedside, leaned down, and gently pressed a kiss to her bandaged forehead. "I'm so sorry, Kate."

"For what?" Kate put her unwired hand on his cheek. "This wasn't your fault."

"I was so scared. I have never prayed that hard in my life."

"And God heard you. I'll be okay." It was as much of a reminder for herself as it was for Dan.

He still lingered close to her face and she could feel his warm breath on her skin. "Can I take back what I said at the park? Don't go back. Just stay here forever where I can protect and love you."

"You weren't wrong, Dan. I was." Kate paused and looked into his face. "Did you just say... *love*?"

"Did I?" He smiled and brushed her cheek with his lips.

Kate's heart started beating wildly and she wondered if the machines that she was connected to gave her secret away. Just then, the sound of someone clearing their throat at the doorway caused him to back away. A nurse entered with a medication.

"I'm sorry to interrupt. How's your pain level? Dr. Preston prescribed something to help you sleep as well if you want it."

"Can't I go home?"

The nurse looked at the amount left in the bag of blood dangling from the IV pole. "I think you will probably be here a bit longer, Miss Benson. You should probably rest because once this is finished we'll see how you do on your feet."

Kate looked over at Dan as she felt the medicine take effect. "I don't want to be alone."

"Don't worry, Kate. I'm not going anywhere."

*****

After a week of healing and keeping a low profile, Kate stood in front of the Tyler house taking in the view and wishing time would slow down. A flood of emotions threatened to undo her. The time spent convalescing under Colleen's and Dan's watchful eyes had been a sweet time that she would forever treasure, but the day she had dreaded had finally come. A rented Honda was packed with her things, a much less luxurious car than the one she had arrived in.

The family gathered around her, no one wanting to start the inevitable goodbyes.

"I don't get why this is so sad. We all know you're coming back. Right?" Jen broke the silence.

"Jen." Colleen's tone held a hint of warning. "She's going to take time to pray. It's a wise thing to do."

"It's a no-brainer though." Kate smiled gently at the younger woman but didn't attempt to explain the complexities of the trip ahead of her.

Kate's condition kept her from making the deadline her boss had set for her and she had exceeded her vacation time. When she called in to explain the situation, it was made clear she had been terminated. It stung, but God had also answered her prayer by removing a deciding factor. Deep in her heart, Kate knew very well she was coming back again. First, she needed to do a few things. Pete and Hannah's children were going to have a memorial for their parents and they invited Kate to attend. Lilly deserved an explanation of what had happened and Kate wanted to share her faith with her aunt.

Dan wrapped her in his arms and pulled her close, something she had gotten used to and would miss during her time away.

"Whose stupid idea was this?" he whispered in her ear.

Kate chuckled as she rested her head on his chest.

"I should be going with you. You're still recovering."

"I'll be fine, Dan. It's not like I'll be alone." Kate smiled as she looked over at Tess, who was laughing with Sean and Michael.

"As soon as you're ready to come back, call me. I'll drive up to help you load and bring your stuff back from your aunt's house."

"What? You don't think Tess and I can manage a few boxes?" Kate feigned indignation.

"You still need to be careful with this." Dan held Kate's wrist rubbing the area around her bandage with his thumb gently.

"Kate, if you want to get there before dark, we better head out now." Tessa approached softly, clearly not wanting to intrude.

Kate nodded reluctantly and squeezed Dan's hand before moving to the car. She pulled out a pair of sunglasses to help with the on and off again headache that seemed to be a side effect of her concussion.

"Call when you get there." Colleen hugged Kate tightly.

"I will, Mama T."

John Tyler was the next one to wrap her in his arms and then he prayed for the long drive ahead of Tess and Kate.

"Am I driving first or you?" Tess asked.

"I will." Kate smiled and jingled the keys in her hand.

Michael laughed. "Uh oh. We'd better say another prayer really quick for Tess."

Kate punched him in the arm as hard as she could before she hugged him and Sean goodbye. Then she got in the driver's seat. If Kate didn't hurry, she'd change her mind.

A moment later she couldn't help but look in the rearview mirror as she reached the end of the driveway. Dan still stood watching, much as he had the last time she had left. This time would be different, Kate determined. She'd do what she needed to do and get home quickly.

Home. Yes, Deer Creek truly had become home again. It was something Kate never imagined possible. Then again, God had done the impossible many times over right before her eyes. Her heart swelled at the remembrance of it all. She had come back to ease her father's death, but instead, Kate Benson found life.

One week later...

Her pulse quickened. It felt like the drive would never end, despite the wonderful companion she had in Tess. Kate didn't know what she would've done without her. The week had been productive, sad, and reaffirming all at once. The two ladies cheered as soon as they crossed the rushing Black River.

"Slow down, Kate. I don't want a repeat of the last time you came back to Deer Creek."

Kate chuckled. "Dial Dan's number on my phone for me, please."

"How about you just let me drive?"

"Would you?" Kate flashed Tessa a brilliant smile and pulled over to switch seats so she could get Dan on the phone.

"When I fall in love will I act this weird?" Tessa laughed.

"Oh please. I think we both know very well..."

"Stop, Kate." Tessa shushed her friend. "Just make your call."

Kate decided to let the subject of Tess's crush on Sean drop… for now. It had been a main part of their conversation the week prior. Truly, the only thing Kate wanted to think about at that moment was Dan Tyler. She dialed and waited with excitement to hear his voice.

"Kate?" He answered.

"What are you doing right now?" she asked.

He chuckled, a sound that thrilled her heart. "I'm just helping Dad in the barn. Why? What are you doing?"

"Nothing special. I just wanted to let you know that there is a delivery coming to your house shortly. I think you should be at the top of your driveway in about …"

Kate looked to Tess for a guestimate.

"Ten minutes?" Tess suggested with a shrug.

"Ten minutes."

"What type of delivery? What did you do?" Dan asked skeptically.

"Can you promise me you'll just meet the delivery person, please?"

He agreed and Kate smiled contentedly as she hung up the phone. Tess turned the car towards the familiar road that led home. "Can you drive faster, Tess?"

"You told him ten minutes, not five. Relax."

It felt like forever but they finally turned onto the Tyler's street and Kate's heart leaped at the sight of Dan leaning against the sign, arms crossed and a smile growing on his face as they approached.

"Stop the van here, Tess."

Her friend complied and Kate jumped from her side of the vehicle. All of a sudden she felt shy as she drew closer, but Dan wasn't having any of that. He scooped her in his arms and swung her.

"You were supposed to call me so I could come help you." He looked down at her.

"Turns out I didn't have that much to bring home."

He looked over at the van the rental company had let her upgrade to in order to bring home her things. "That looks like a decent amount of stuff."

"Don't worry, we had the neighbors help us."

His expression looked hopeful. "Is this everything? You don't have to go back?"

"I have everything I need right here," she said taking Dan's hand in hers.

Dan hugged her tightly again and kissed her as if he never intended to let her go.

It became obvious to everyone inside the house that Kate was back. Sean and Michael joined Tess standing next to the van and Colleen, John, and Jen came up the driveway. Kate was engulfed in hugs. It was a true homecoming.

"You girls are just in time for dinner!" Colleen beamed and linked arms with Tess walking her to the house.

"Oh no, Mrs. Tyler. I can't. I don't want to intrude on your family time."

Sean smiled at Tess and shook his head. "I wouldn't even try to get out of it, Tess. One thing you should know about Mom is that she doesn't take no for an answer."

"But I should really get home."

"How exactly?" Sean's smile grew even wider. "In the van loaded with Kate's whole life?"

"Oh, yeah." Tess grinned. "I see your point."

"Have dinner, play a board game, and I'll take you home later. Okay?"

"Board game?"

"Mom's feeling celebratory. I think she'll be busting out the games."

Kate heard Tessa laugh and glanced over to see her beaming under Sean's attention as she took a seat at the table. Michael and Jen bickered and joked. Colleen and John just shared contented smiles, beaming over their full house. Then there was Dan. He only had eyes for her. Could her heart get any fuller? Kate held tightly to Dan's hand as John quieted the group to bless the meal. Kate echoed her thanksgiving to God for all He had done in her life. While everyone prayed with eyes closed, she couldn't help but peek at the people around her. These were the people God had given to her. They were her family. The lonely little girl turned into an adopted daughter. Kate Benson was home.

Want more Deer Creek in your life? Coming soon….

Let Me Call You Sweetheart

Deer Creek Chronicles Book 2

By D. Emily Smith

Tessa Grayson was no longer that scared little girl cowering in the corner of her room as her abuser hummed over her a tune that sent fear into her soul. After she moved to Deer Creek, NY she never imagined that the secrets she buried long ago would come back to haunt her... until her phone rang. *Let Me Call You Sweetheart* began to play. Only one man knew the impact that tune had on her... and he was dead.

When Tessa became a Christian she believed that she had been healed and had moved forward from her past. Now she found herself confused and terrified all over again. Where was God? She needed a hero, someone to save her from a threat masquerading as a monster from her past. The future Tessa dreamed about faded right before her eyes. Her desire to become a counselor. Sean's Tyler's affections. All that she had worked so hard to accomplish. Would it all disappear when everyone realized how damaged she really was?

Made in the USA
Middletown, DE
28 March 2024